Naughty,
Naughty

Books by P.J. Mellor

PLEASURE BEACH

GIVE ME MORE

THE COWBOY
(with Vonna Harper, Nelissa Donovan and Nikki Alton)

THE FIREFIGHTER
(with Susan Lyons and Alyssa Brooks)

Books by Melissa MacNeal

ALL NIGHT LONG

HOT FOR IT

THE HAREM
(with Celia May Hart, Emma Leigh and Noelle Mack)

Books by Valerie Martinez

SKIN ON SKIN
(with Jami Alden and Sunny)

Published by Kensington Publishing Corporation

Naughty, Naughty

P.J. MELLOR
MELISSA MacNEAL
VALERIE MARTINEZ

APHRODISIA

KENSINGTION PUBLISHING CORP.
http://www.kensingtonbooks.com

APHRODISIA BOOKS are published by

Kensington Publishing Corp.
850 Third Avenue
New York, NY 10022

All Kensington Titles, Imprints, and Distributed Lines are available at special quantity discounts for bulk purchases for sales promotions, premiums, fund-raising, and educational or institutional use.

Special book excerpts or customized printings can also be created to fit specific needs. For details, write or phone the office of the Kensington special sales manager: Kensington Publishing Corp., 850 Third Avenue, New York, NY 10022, attn: Special Sales Department, Phone: 1-800-221-2647.

Aphrodisia and the A logo Reg. U.S. Pat. & TM Off

ISBN-13: 978-0-7582-2025-7
ISBN-10: 0-7582-2025-1

First Trade Paperback Printing: October 2007

10 9 8 7 6 5 4 3 2 1

Printed in the United States of America

Contents

Hot for Christmas

P.J. MELLOR

Special thanks to Jerry Hixson for his intimate knowledge of deer stands.

1
_____

Chris MacNeil smacked the steering wheel with the palm of his hand and let loose a string of expletives as he turned the corner of the town square.

Downshifting, he wheeled his truck into a vacant parking spot by the Roadkill Café and sat with his engine running while he willed the nausea away.

Directly in front of his Dodge Ram 4x4 was a sight that filled him with horror and revulsion: a new Christmas store.

Behind all the froufrou decorating practically obscuring the front window, several Christmas trees twinkled merrily. Combined with the other flashing lights, their manic movement and brilliance formed an electronic fist to punch him right between the eyes and bring on an instant headache.

It was not that he truly hated Christmas. At least, he didn't think he did. But nothing good, beginning with his birth twenty-seven years ago, had ever happened to him at Christmas.

Novelty stores had come and gone around the square in Flintlock, Texas, faster than the surrounding wildlife population. Chris tried to comfort himself with that thought, but there was something nagging about the store before him. Something different that scared the crap out of him.

Bile rose in his throat at the thought. Damn. The store was cute. More than cute. Classy and pretty. Successful looking.

Ignoring the sudden ringing in his ears, he hopped out of his truck and hit the alarm as he strode into the Roadkill.

Typical of a small rural town, all conversation ceased when the bell over the door of the café jingled.

"Hey, y'all," Chris said, hanging his straw Stetson on the hook by the door.

Several patrons greeted him on his way to a booth toward the back of the room.

He slid onto the worn red vinyl seat and nodded at the waitress when she tossed a menu on the table and set a small glass of water in front of him.

"Hey, Chris," Sheila, the waitress, cooed, "Whittbeck delivered my new big screen today. You wanna come over after closing and watch dirty movies on cable?" She licked her high-glossed lips and leaned a little closer, no doubt in case he'd failed to notice her cleavage. "Thought maybe we could see what comes up." She glanced meaningfully at his crotch and winked.

Maybe if he threw up on her she would leave him alone. Good grief. What had gotten into him lately? There was a time, not so long ago, when he'd have jumped at the invitation Sheila shot his way. Restless and edgy, he licked his suddenly dry lips. "Ah, not tonight, Sheila. I'm plumb tuckered out from hunting all day."

All around him, snickers sounded.

"Yeah, boy," Mr. Rogers called out, "I heard about your hunting today. What was it you shot again?"

"I heard it was Foster's scarecrow!" someone shouted. Laughter erupted as usual when Chris's hunting skills were discussed.

Chris chuckled and shrugged. He mustered what he hoped

was a credible sexy wink for the waitress. "Right now, Sheila, I need a Coke. Please."

She nodded at the menu. "Decided yet?"

"Bacon cheeseburger, I guess." It was one of the few things he found he could gag down of late. If the Roadkill wasn't so familiar and handy, he'd look for another place to eat. No doubt about it, he was in a rut.

"Regular, curly or spicy fries? Bo made a fresh pot of chili, if you want 'em smothered."

His stomach clenched in response. "No, thanks. Sounds real tasty, though," he offered at her obvious disappointment.

She gave him a peculiar look and nodded as she picked up the menu and walked toward the kitchen pass-through.

"Hey, Deadeye!" His best friend since kindergarten, Ray, slid onto the seat across from Chris. "I hear you saved the town from another killer scarecrow and made the world safer for pheasants." Ray's teeth flashed white in his tanned face. "Good job."

"Shut up. I was thinking of giving up bird hunting, anyway. I tripped over Star, the ornery mutt. I thought I saw her running across the field, but she was locked on point right in front of me. I swear, sometimes I think she does stuff like that just to make me look bad." He ignored Ray's guffaws and shrugged. "'Course, the gun went off when I fell, and that's how the scarecrow met its end." Chris nodded at Sheila when she set his Coke on the scarred gray Formica table.

"Hey, sweet thing," Ray said, once he'd stopped laughing, eyeing Sheila's ample bust when the waitress leaned close to him. "How're my girls tonight?"

"Lonely," Sheila said, flashing a pouting look Chris's way. After taking Ray's order, she strode away.

"Lovers' spat?" Ray twirled the salt and pepper shakers around on the smooth tabletop.

In response, Chris grunted and took a long draw of his Coke. "You know better than that."

His friend raised an eyebrow. "I also know you've had a long dry spell. 'Course, living with your mother doesn't help that situation. What's it been? Three years now?"

"Two. Not that it's any of your business. Mom still needs me around."

"She has Sam. He really runs the place anyway."

"Well, maybe I need to stay there. For peace of mind."

Ray slouched back in the booth. "Still carrying a torch for Kari, huh?"

"Hell, no!" Chris forced the Coke down his suddenly constricted throat. Kari had actually done him a favor by leaving him at the altar two years ago on Christmas Eve. It brought him to his senses. He should have known any wedding planned for Christmas had disaster written all over it.

Ray leaned close, hunched over the table. "Then what's eating you, man? You get to be more of a loner by the day. When was the last time we hit Freddy's?"

The mention of the town's honky-tonk tightened the fist in Chris's belly. Last time he'd been there, the music was too strong and the beer too weak.

"The smoke gets to me lately." He leaned back to avoid contact with Sheila's assets when she placed his plate on the table.

"Bullshit." Ray nodded at the waitress as she slid a plate of onion rings, smothered in milk gravy, in front of him and walked away.

"That your supper?"

"Nah." Ray popped a huge ring in his mouth and chewed appreciatively and then swiped a dribble of gravy from his chin. "Mandy's cooking for me tonight. This," he said, holding up another onion ring dripping with gravy, "is just to hold me over."

Chris took a big bite of his cheeseburger. After swallowing, he said, "Things are looking pretty serious with you and Mandy. Best watch it, buddy."

Ray grinned and took a gulp of his cherry Coke. "Under control, my man, under control. Mandy feeds me my supper . . . and I go by Sheila's for my dessert." He waggled his eyebrows. "If you get my drift."

"What if Mandy finds out?"

"We never said we wouldn't see other people."

Chris swallowed another bite. "I'm sure you didn't. Does Mandy know about your arrangement?"

Ray finished his Coke and belched loud enough to rattle the windows then grinned. "As long as I keep flipping her skirt up, she's got no complaints." He threw some bills on the table and stood. "See you around. I—hey, who's that by your truck?"

Chris craned his neck and looked out the front window of the café. Ray was right; someone was fooling with his truck. A female someone.

That could only mean trouble.

Taking a fast gulp of his soda, he stood and yelled in Sheila's general direction. "I'll be right back, don't throw away my food," then closed the distance between the booth and the front door.

By the time he got to his truck, whoever had been there was gone. A glance up and down the street then across the square failed to detect anyone.

Turning to go back to his burger, something beneath his wiper blade snagged his attention. A paper fluttered in the cool night breeze. Damn, he hated it when people stuck things on his truck.

He grabbed at the offending paper. Another damn flyer. And . . . a note of some kind. Trepidation growing, he unfolded the note. A faint scent of cinnamon and some kind of flower wafted to greet him. He leaned closer to the light from the café to read the flowery script, written on a thick piece of white stationery edged with what looked suspiciously like a row of holly leaves.

Dear Neighbor, it read, *I'm sure you did not see the new sign stating this parking space is reserved, allocated for the customers of Happy Holidays Boutique. As a welcome to our store, I am attaching a twenty-percent-off coupon for your next visit. I look forward to meeting you and serving your holiday needs for many years to come.*

Sincerely, Allison Conroe, owner,
Happy Holidays Boutique

"I'll tell you what you can do with your coupon, Miss Allison Conroe." He ground the words through his teeth while he tore the note and coupon into tiny pieces as he stomped toward the door of the Christmas shop.

Blinking at all the blinding lights, he stepped through the door. Instead of a dinging bell or even a buzzer like any normal store, the Happy Holidays Boutique played a version of "White Christmas"—with bells.

It was enough to make his ears bleed. The strong scent of cinnamon burned his eyes.

It took a second to locate the petite woman decorating a tree toward the back of the selling floor. At the sound of the door, she turned, a welcoming smile on her lips.

Had she been in any other place and been any other woman, he might have taken a moment to assess the goods. As it was, he refused to notice her pretty mouth—not too big, not too small, with soft, kissable-looking lips. Blondes appealed to him much more than women with dark, lustrous curls like the one before him. He didn't care how tall she was. Too short for his taste, anyway, he was sure. And even if she had the body of a goddess, he didn't care. Besides, it was hard to tell what she looked like under that ugly-as-sin baggy jumper and long apron covered in an eye-popping collage of Christmas scenes. It was like Currier and Ives threw up on her.

"Happy holidays," she said in a husky little voice, smiling a little brighter, if that was possible. She placed the ornament she was holding back in its box. "You're my first customer! Would you like some wassail or a Christmas cookie? I baked them fresh this afternoon. I—oh!"

Jaw clamped, he showered the coupon and note confetti over her head. It was the only thing he could do. Danger signs flashed in bright neon just looking at her. He didn't want or need the stirrings he felt just from being around her. Maybe it was just hunger. He hoped.

Turning on his heel, his booted feet ate up the distance to the front door. Not taking a breath until the door closed behind him, he sucked in a great lungful of air and headed back to the Roadkill.

Christmas. It was enough to give a man indigestion.

2

Allison Conroe gaped at the broad back of the man striding out of her newly opened store. A piece of paper fluttered on her eyelashes. She reached up to pull it away, not taking her eyes off the backside of her first customer.

Wow. Even a nun could appreciate the play of worn denim over the masculine buns of steel. Double wow.

The door clanged shut, breaking her stupor. Stepping over the box of imported ornaments, she ran after him. What she would say when she caught him, she didn't know. She just knew she had to find him. For some reason, she felt he needed her.

The air had cooled considerably since the sun set. She rubbed her arms with her hands and glanced up and down the street and then across the square of her new hometown. Empty.

His truck was still there. Since all the other businesses on the square were closed for the day except hers and the café next door, it didn't take a rocket scientist to figure out where the angry stranger went. The question was, did she dare follow?

His scowl flashed through her mind; the subtle scent of him lingered in her nose. Even if she found him, what would she say? And given his attitude, why bother? The guy could use an attitude adjustment. She glanced at the mud-encrusted truck on her way back to her store and remembered his muddy boots tromping over her freshly refinished wood floor. A makeover wouldn't hurt him either.

The inviting scent of cinnamon wrapped around her, making her smile when she stepped through the door of her very own place of business. Hers. No one to tell her what she should and shouldn't do. No one to disapprove of her spontaneity.

The frowning face of her first guest—customer—floated through her mind again. The man was rude and definitely needed an in-your-face challenge to set him straight. Her smile widened. How fortunate for him. She loved a challenge.

Chris gagged down the rest of his burger in record time. Thanks to the woman next door, the burger was now tasteless.

Throwing a fistful of money down, he grabbed his hat on the way out the door.

But once he gained the solitude of his truck, instead of starting the engine and pointing the nose toward home, he sat and waited for a glimpse of the proprietress of the Happy Holidays Boutique. Stupid name for a store. How did she think she could possibly make any kind of living with it?

He squinted in an effort to detect movement in the store. Not that he was even remotely interested in someone like her. But she was new in town, and he'd been, admittedly, less than hospitable. He was brought up better. Maybe he'd just wait to make sure she hadn't fallen off a stool or ladder or something.

While he waited, he thought of the plump sheen of her glossy lips, the soft curve of them when she'd turned to him in surprise. It was just curiosity, nothing more. He was in his sexual prime. Any female would have tempted him. Ray was right: it had been a long, dry spell—other than a fast slap and tickle with Sheila a few times, which hardly counted. He did a mental calculation. No wonder the Christmas lady had gotten to him the way she did. He hadn't had good, mind-blowing sex since before Kari left him.

A movement in the store caught his eye. His breath hitched. The woman was taking off her Christmas apron, doing a slow striptease. Well, okay, she didn't know he was there, and she still wore the butt-ugly jumper. But, damn. What he'd give to know what she wore under that thing.

With a growl, he adjusted himself and jammed down the clutch while he turned the key. Tires squealed as he backed out of the parking space.

The sound of tires caught Allison's attention just in time to see her cranky customer peel out along the square. He turned by the pharmacy, and his taillights disappeared.

Tired and more disappointed than she cared to admit, she put away the ornaments and turned off the lights. Maybe a long hot soak in the big tub in her new house would take away the sudden bout of self-pity.

Allison sank lower in the bubbles and sighed in an attempt to clear her mind. The store was progressing nicely. Check. All of the inventory was accounted for and stored. Check. Everything sparkled in anticipation of her Grand Opening Celebration. Check.

Then why did she feel so restless, so edgy?

Unbidden, the Cranky Customer sprang to mind in breathtaking detail. Instant recall dredged up his scent, the masculinity he exuded, the swagger of his lean hips as he tromped out the door.

She needed to remember his bad manners, his animosity. So why, instead, was she remembering the way the twinkling light played on the soft shine of his sun-streaked hair, the faint lines at the edge of his eyes and bracketing his mouth, the slight red-gold stubble on his firm jaw. Not to mention the flicker of interest she'd seen in his deep blue eyes just before he'd turned to walk away.

She'd come to Flintlock to make a new start, not to repeat her mistakes. Granted, Cranky wasn't as polished, as metrosexual, as Bruce. Her ex-husband had exuded urbane suaveness. But the danger was the same because it brought with it the familiar tingle of awareness, the breathless anticipation. She didn't need the complication in her life right now. Maybe never again.

It was time to turn over a new leaf. She had a business to run, a new life to build. And that life did not, could not, include a sexy, cranky stranger who made her breathless and tingly in places that had no business tingling.

Decision made, she picked up the apple-scented soap and stroked it down her arm and over and under her right breast. The soap slipped over her skin like the caress of a lover. Eyes closed, she enjoyed the tactile pleasure. The thought of Cranky being the person holding the soap made her frown. Too late. The image was firmly in her mind.

Her nipples tingled and hardened to sharp points. Round and round the soap went, teasing the tips, changing her breathing.

Would *he* like her breasts? The bane of her adolescence, they had always fascinated members of the opposite sex. Which was why she always wore baggy clothing these days. But suddenly she wondered if Cranky would appreciate them. Would he enjoy stroking them like this, testing their weight? Would he salivate to taste them, to draw them deep into his mouth? What about sex? Would he continue playing with them while he was buried deep inside her?

The thought made her shift in the slippery tub. One hand left her breast to renew her balance. The action grazed the sensitized skin of her abdomen, sending sparks of arousal shooting to her extremities. Did she dare?

She inched her hand, ever so slowly, over her hip and down.

Down to the center that ached for a lover's touch. The part of her that, even now, even knowing it was her own hand, quickened with anticipation.

Her breathing became shallow, her heartbeat echoing in her ears. She parted her folds, absorbing the feel of the warm water on her already swollen sex and aching clitoris.

Her thumb rubbed the sensitive nub, feeling it harden and swell. Her legs moved restlessly against the slick ceramic surface. The hand holding the soap traveled downward to stroke between her spread legs. Her hips thrust, moving her hands against her aching flesh, faster and faster.

Her hard nipples broke the surface of the water, puckering tighter in the cooler air of the bathroom.

More. She needed more.

Eyes shut tight, every thought, every nerve ending centered on the needy spot between her legs, she increased the tempo.

Water sloshed over the edge of the old tub. Faster. Harder.

In her mind, she rode her Cranky Customer. His head was arched back into the soft pillows on her bed, his breath coming in agonizing gasps. Close, she was so close. She pumped faster, chasing the elusive release she knew was just beyond her grasp.

Her heart thundered, her breath lodged. Her spine locked into a rigid arch. Behind her eyelids, a myriad of multicolor fireworks exploded as suddenly, everything relaxed and warmth enveloped her.

3

Chris threw back the covers and stared at the ceiling, watching the play of light from the barn reflect through his partially drawn curtains.

Damn Christmas woman. She was so totally not his type, it was ridiculous. Why was she stuck in his mind?

He thought of her stupid Christmas store and ugly jumper. Damn. Shouldn't have thought of her clothing. Clothing made him wonder what she wore under it. What if the answer was nothing?

He closed his eyes and pictured her standing on her little stepladder, him seated directly under it, looking up her long skirt. No panties. Would her pussy be shaved? Would it be shiny and slick with her excitement? His cock twitched at the thought. Maybe, if she leaned way over, he could see far enough up to watch the wiggle and bob of her boobs as she worked. Would they be large, small, just big enough to fit his palms? Would her nipples be dark or light, large or small? And did it really matter?

He flopped over on his tent-pole erection and groaned into

his pillow. He hadn't jacked off since before Kari left. He'd be damned if he'd do it over someone who ran a Christmas shop.

He could control his baser instincts. He was better than that.

Allison regarded the vibrator in her hand, torn between completing her satisfaction and being strong enough to resist temptation. Her high sex drive had already cost her a marriage and one business. Moving to Flintlock, Texas, was an opportunity for a second chance. A chance to kick her old libidinous self to the curb and reinvent herself.

She looked down at the shiny bulbous tip and swallowed. Beneath her prim cotton nightgown, her breasts formed aching peaks. The crotch of her plain white cotton panties felt heavy, drenched in her arousal.

A glance confirmed that the house was locked up tight, the windows closed off from prying eyes by the drawn draperies.

Maybe one last time would help her get a good night's sleep.

In the kitchen, she filled a small glass bowl with ice, a necessary item to prolong the pleasure. May as well grab a bowl of peach ice cream while she was there. Sex always made her hungry.

Back in her bedroom, her hands shook in eager anticipation while she stripped.

Next came the scented oil. A groan of ecstasy escaped her lips as she slicked her body in slow sensual strokes, leaving no spot unlubricated. The scent of almonds filled the air. No time to stop and enjoy the feel of the oil or the luscious scent filling the room. She was too needy. Again.

A flick of her hand plunged her into darkness. She smiled at the purple glow of the vibrator, absently wondering about its durability. It was her third in less than a year. This time, she'd sprung for the deluxe model with a stronger motor and longer warranty.

Lying on the bed now, she fumbled in the drawer of her

nightstand for her magic butterfly. It, too, glowed purple and emitted a low buzz when she flipped the switch to flutter the wings.

She squirmed, already impossibly wet with anticipation. It had been so long, but she needed to pace herself. She wanted, needed, to feel everything. Prolong her release.

Her gasp filled the air as soon as the fluttering wings pattered against the stiff peaks of her oiled nipples. Her other hand shook while petting her labia.

Not enough. No surprise there.

She moved the butterfly to her labia, only slightly surprised to find her folds eagerly swollen beyond the exfoliated lips.

Gel wings fluttered against the oiled, sensitized tissue, sending shock waves of pleasure to wash over her. In the cool air, her nipples puckered tighter, aching for release. Her sex wept.

The vibrator flicked on with the touch of her thumb. She turned on her side, still pleasuring herself with the butterfly, to dip the vibrating shaft into the ice cream.

The cool phallus soothed her heated tongue, the ice cream melting sweetly to dribble down her throat.

She squirmed against the sheet, burning up with desire. With a shaking hand she scooped ice from the other bowl and ran it impatiently down her naked, sweating torso. Down lower until it melted against her hot center. She wouldn't have been surprised to see steam rising in the darkness.

But it didn't help. The ache was still there, growing ever stronger. The sex play would have to wait for another time. She had to have it, and she had to have it now.

The ice rattled when she plunged the vibrator into the remaining cubes. With a cry of desperation, she shoved the glowing phallus to the hilt into her aching core, all but dousing its purple glow.

Buried deep within her, the coolness quickly dissipated, the vibration setting off ripple after ripple of a deep, rich orgasm.

So great was her need, so strong her climax, she screamed her release, shuddering with the violence of it.

Stupid. It was a stupid idea to drive to her house. What was he thinking?

After laying in bed, thinking about the Christmas Lady, Allison Conroe, he'd taken it into his head to drive out to the little house he'd heard she'd rented on the outskirts of town.

Torn between hightailing it home or knocking, he'd sat in his truck looking at the lights in the windows until they'd all gone out.

Too late.

Had he really thought he could come out there—and do what? Scratch his itch with someone he barely knew. True, balling her brains out would have served two purposes: relieved pressure and helped get her out of his mind.

Not that he really wanted to fuck her.

He banged his head against the steering wheel. Who was he kidding? He wanted to fuck her until they both couldn't walk straight.

Maybe it was just because it had been so long. Maybe any willing pussy would do. Hell, he was so horny now he could even get into jacking off while he watched her with someone else.

Maybe.

No, he couldn't. If he ever came while in the same room with Allison Conroe, it had to be with his penis buried so deep in her that her sweet cum washed his balls. And, the way he felt right now, even that wouldn't be enough.

Damn. What was happening to him? She obviously had a thing for Christmas. Add to that, she wasn't his type. The woman had *hands off* written all over her.

He revved his powerful engine a few times, defiantly looking back at the darkened house, dropped the truck into gear and headed for home.

Allison lay spread-eagle on her damp sheets, willing her racing heart to return to its normal rhythm, her breathing to stop coming in gasping pants.

Wow. The second climax had been even more powerful than the first. The roaring rumble in her head seemed so real. For a few seconds she thought the bed had actually vibrated.

She should probably get up and change the sheets so they could wash while she got some sleep.

Maybe later. She rolled over. Nothing like a screaming release to relax a person.

Her last thought before exhaustion claimed her was that it would have been even better if she'd had someone to hold her in her sated sleep.

4

Pink sunrise rimmed the edge of the courthouse on the town square the next morning. From her vantage point in an over-stuffed chair by the faux fireplace, Allison watched the morning glory while she sipped her almond cappuccino and nibbled on a pumpkin muffin. It was going to be a good day. She just knew it.

She glanced across the square to the pharmacy, waiting. Stupid. It was so stupid to watch for Cranky. Just because he left in that direction meant nothing. The man was probably at work. She wondered what he did.

A glance at the grandfather clock by the cash register changed her thoughts. Cranky was probably just getting up.

Her mind's eye pictured him in the shower, hot, soapy water sluicing over his broad shoulders and tight butt.

She blinked, suddenly hot, willing the mental image from her mind.

Maybe Cranky was eating breakfast. Would his wife have fixed it? Did they have children?

The thought brought a wave of sadness.

"Don't be ridiculous," she muttered. "Who would want to be married to such a foul-tempered man?" Instant recall of his more-than-interested once-over confirmed his single status. No man looked at her the way he did if he was taken.

Bruce had looked at her like that when they were first together. Before she'd alienated him with her sexual neediness.

The realization that she'd driven him away turned the pumpkin muffin dry and bitter in her mouth. Even a sip of her sweet cappuccino didn't help. Giving up, she spit the bite into the holly-trimmed paper napkin and left her chair to brush her teeth and begin the second day of her new life.

Chris threw hay out of the back of his truck with a vengeance. The cows stared at him.

"What are you looking at?" He jumped from the bed and stomped the pieces of hay from his boots and jean legs. "Get out of here!" He stomped again.

The cows blinked.

"Stupid bovines." He climbed into the cab and threw the truck into gear. Damn, he hated chores as much now as he did as a kid.

Back at the house, he strode through the back door. Grabbing a mug from the cupboard, he sloshed hot coffee on his hand in his haste to pour.

Cussing, he shoved his hand under the faucet and turned on the cold water.

"Good morning to you, too, sunshine," his mother drawled from her usual place at the oak kitchen table.

He closed his eyes and counted to ten. Twice. Finally he turned to glare at his mother.

"Morning," he ground out.

"Sleep well?"

"Yep."

"No offense, honey, but I don't believe that." She took a sip from her mug and looked over the reading glasses perched on her nose.

Did the woman never sleep? He looked her over, from the top of her perfectly styled blonde hair, past her immaculately dressed, still slim figure—today clad in tailored black slacks, a bright red silky-looking shirt and a black blazer—to her perfectly polished black dress boots.

"How long have you been up?"

She smiled and set her newspaper aside. "A while. You know I don't sleep well anymore. Not since your daddy's been gone."

"Daddy" walked out on them Christmas Day, Chris's eighth birthday, almost twenty years ago. Yet Pauline, his mother, insisted on keeping his clothing on the other side of her walk-in closet and his name on her bank accounts and the deed to the farm.

"What's that, sweetie? You're mumbling again." His mother smiled over the rim of her cup and waited.

"I said you need to get over it." There, he'd said what he'd been thinking for years. He shrugged. "He's not coming back. We both know it. I'm just saying maybe it's time for you to get on with your life."

Pauline regarded him for a moment, then set her cup aside. "I have gotten on with my life, Chris. I raised you. I've kept the farm going. I'm still an active member of the United Methodist in town. I—"

"Damnit! That's not what I mean, and you know it." He raked a hand through his hair and resettled his hat. "What are you now? Fifty? Fifty-five?"

"Very funny. You know perfectly well I'm forty-eight."

"Right." He nodded. "You were my age when Daddy left." He leaned close to her, his hands braced on the cool, smooth top of the table. "Mom, didn't you ever wonder what kind of life you could have had if you'd just been able to cut him out of your life as easily as he cut us out of his? You could have remarried, maybe even had more kids."

"Stop." His mother stood and walked to the counter, not speaking again until she'd placed her cup in the dishwasher. "I had no interest in those things. I had a son to raise, a farm to run." She turned to him, the morning sun slanting through the window above the sink to make her light blue eyes take on a glow. "Your needs and the needs of the farm always came before mine."

"Well, that's not necessary now. Maybe it never was. I'm all grown up, Mom," he said. "And Sam does a damn fine job on the farm, just like he always did." He walked to clasp her hands in his. "All I'm saying is think about it. You're still young enough to make a new life for yourself."

"And what about you?"

"Don't worry about me."

"But I do. Chris, how long has it been since you've even had a date?"

Allison's smiling face flashed through his mind. It might be fun to torment her, maybe even force her to leave town. He smiled. "I'm working on it, ma'am." He tugged his brim lower and walked toward the back door. "I'm definitely working on it," he assured her and then stepped into the morning sunshine.

"Miz Mac! You here?" The sound of Sam's deep, booming voice, a few minutes after Chris left, brought a smile to Pauline's face.

"Be right there!" She checked her recently reapplied red lip gloss then hurried to the kitchen.

Her steps faltered at the kitchen door. Sam, the man who kept the farm in the black, the man she'd known for most of her adult life, stood with his back to her, looking out the window above the sink while he drank his first cup of coffee.

It was a scene she'd witnessed countless times over the last twenty years. Why, of late, did it have the power to take her breath away?

Her greedy gaze drank in the sight of hard, lean hips and long legs encased in worn denim. Beneath the plaid Western shirt, the muscles in his back rippled with each movement. Sun shone through the silky-looking strands of his salt and pepper hair.

He turned, his brilliant blue eyes taking her in from head to toe until she could barely draw a breath. His graying mustache twitched with his ever-present smile.

"Mornin', Miz Mac," he said in his familiar deep, rumbling voice.

Sometimes she had dreams about that voice. She glanced at the work-roughened hands cupping his coffee mug and wondered—not for the first time—what it would feel like to have those hands on her body.

"You used to call me Pauline," she said, surprising them both. But it was true, she realized. Before Bill left, Sam never addressed her formally. "Don't you think we've known each other too long not to use first names?"

He cocked his head and regarded her until she struggled not to squirm. Finally he nodded. "I reckon so. *Pauline.*"

Her name sounded rusty coming from his mouth. Foreign. What must he think of her; what made her allow the formality to go on for so long?

"May I ask you a question, Sam?"

He nodded and refilled his mug.

"Would you like a bear claw to go with that? I picked some up at the bakery yesterday."

He shook his head, blue eyes twinkling over the rim of his mug. "That what you wanted to ask me?"

"Um, no." She straightened up, ignoring the way her pulse sped up when his narrowed gaze dropped to her breasts. "Do you think I'm attractive?" At his silence, she stammered on, "I mean, oh, shoot, I don't know what I mean," she finished miserably as she sank into a kitchen chair.

Sam set his mug on the table and squatted by her chair. With a rough forefinger, he tilted her chin up until their eyes met. "Yes," he said, his deep voice setting off heat to streak through her. "I've always thought you were just about the prettiest thing in these parts. Ever since high school. And Bill was a damn fool for walking away."

Tears blurred her vision. "But you didn't walk away. I'll always appreciate that, Sam. I don't know what I'd have done without you all these years."

He dropped his hand and stood. "I didn't stay for your gratitude, Pauline."

She thought about that for a minute. "Then why did you stay?" She was afraid to look at him for fear he'd see the longing she'd only recently acknowledged.

When he didn't answer, she looked up. He was gone.

5

Allison gasped and watched the melted ice dribble down her nipple, leaving a wet trail to the underside of her breast. What was wrong with her? She was so horny she could barely concentrate. Every time a truck passed her store or she saw a man across the square, her panties grew damp, her nipples hardening into stiff, aching peaks.

It was all Cranky's fault. Her male centerfold curmudgeon not only kept her awake at night—now he'd invaded her days.

She tucked her breasts back into her shirt and shifted on the hard stool in the stockroom and willed her thoughts to something, anything, else. Maybe unpacking the new order of custom-made candles would take her mind off sex. And, thereby, Cranky.

She frowned at the distinctive smell of wax when she slit open the box.

"Oh, no." The first few candles were fused together, obviously melted in shipping. A hard yank revealed the misshapen blob of wax that once was at least three candles.

A giggle erupted. Just her luck. The resultant candle eerily resembled a super-sized wax phallus.

A feminine bark of laughter sounded from the doorway of the stockroom.

"Oh, my," the elegant woman standing in the doorway said on another laugh. "I didn't realize you stocked those kinds of items."

Allison huffed out a laugh. "I don't. Well, at least I didn't." She grinned at the woman. "Think I could sell them?"

The woman's smile faltered. "I'm beginning to think I might need one. I could be your first customer."

Allison placed the misshapen candle on the stock table and wiped her hands on her apron. "Why don't you take a break with me and have some cinnamon tea and Christmas cookies instead?"

Allison picked up the cups and dessert plates and stood. "Well, what about it, Mrs. MacNeil? Sounds like you could use something to do, and I could use an assistant. But I have to warn you, I can't pay much. At least not right now."

The woman smiled and stood, towering several inches above Allison's whopping five-foot-nothing. "I'd love to work part time. But only on one condition." At Allison's raised eyebrow, she continued, "You have to call me Pauline. Mrs. MacNeil sounds like my mother-in-law." She winked. "Not to mention a little stuffy."

"Great! When can you start?"

"Well, I don't have anything else to do in town today. How about now?" Her blonde brows drew together. "I'm sorry. I didn't mean to put you on the spot like that."

"Don't be sorry! Today would be perfect. I have some errands to run." She touched her cap of shaggy curls. "And I really do need a haircut. Can you recommend a place?"

"Nancy's Swirl and Curl is where I get mine done, but she had a death in the family and is closed for the next two weeks." Pauline shrugged and inclined her head toward the left side of the store. "There's always Earl's Barber Shop, next door, if you just need a trim."

"Great! Let me show you around and how to run the register, and I'll be out of here."

Chris raked his hand through his hair before resetting his hat. Past time for a haircut. Maybe he'd just swing by Earl's on his way to the Roadkill.

Downshifting, he slowed as he approached the barbershop, scanning the area for a parking spot.

Luck was with him—he didn't have to park illegally in front of the Happy Holidays Boutique. There was a vacant spot directly in front of Earl's shop door.

Eyes trained on the barbershop to avoid accidentally seeing the Christmas Lady, he hopped from the truck and strode through the door of the barbershop.

The old brass bell jingled merrily when Chris stepped across the threshold. He inhaled the familiar smell of Barbicide. His muscles relaxed for the first time since the opening of the Happy Holidays Boutique. It was nice to know some things remained the same.

He remembered coming to Earl for his first haircut, sitting on a pile of girlie magazines in the big barber chair, sharing the sacred bond only men can share with other men.

A female laugh slashed through his veil of calm.

His steps faltered. He blinked. Unfortunately, she was still there. There *she* sat, in the middle chair, the one he'd occupied since the age of two, laughing and smiling at Earl in the mirror.

And Earl, the old reprobate, was grinning like a fat cat, doing his damnedest to make her laugh again. The barber was obviously getting senile.

Earl spotted him and turned. "Somebody's beat your time,

Chris," Earl said with a broad wink. "Now you're gonna have to wait your turn."

Christmas Lady laughed as though Earl had said something witty. The tinkling sound skipped up his spine and danced around in his head, setting his molars to aching.

She hopped down from the chair and dug in the pocket of her baggy jumper.

"Ah-ah-ah," Earl admonished, holding up a beefy hand. "None of that. I told you, the first one is on the house, from one square shop owner to another."

"You're so sweet!" she said in her husky little voice, rising on tiptoe to plant a smacking kiss on his flushed cheek.

It was enough to make Chris gag, had he had a weaker constitution. Earl, the old fart, actually blushed.

Chris rolled his eyes and sat down in the vacated chair.

"When you get finished flirting, Earl, I need a trim."

"I need to get going anyway," she said from somewhere near the door. "Thanks again! And, please, feel free to stop by anytime for cookies and spiced cider."

The dinging of the bell above the door coincided with the sharp pain on the top of his head from Earl's comb.

"Ow!" Chris rubbed his head. "What'd you do that for?"

"I'm the closest thing you got to a daddy, and you needed smacking for your surly attitude. You were raised better than to be rude, boy."

Chris munched the last of his salad, his eyes trained on the plate-glass window of the Roadkill, and wondered when Christmas Lady had time to hire help. Not that it mattered. It wasn't any of his business. It just galled him to think how fast she was ingratiating herself into the town. What did any of them really know about her anyway? For all they knew, she could be wanted or something.

He thought of his trip to her house the night before and shifted on the vinyl seat.

He snorted. Hell, yes, she was wanted. But he'd bite his tongue in two before he'd admit it to anyone. Least of all her.

As though he'd conjured her up, his latest nightmare strolled into the café. Today, he'd noticed earlier, she wore a voluminous black jumper with a black and red candy-cane print shirt. When she walked, tiny jingle bells around the bottom tinkled.

Chris doggedly stared out onto the square. In the background he heard her giving a take-out order to Louise, the waitress who shared the shifts with Sheila.

"May I?" Her voice cut through his concentration to make his resolve bleed.

He looked up at her with what he hoped to be bored indifference. "Suit yourself. I'm about to leave."

Her hand appeared in his field of vision. "Let's start over. Hi, I'm Allison Conroe."

He let her stand there for a second, hand extended, before he reached up to envelop it in his own. "Chris MacNeil."

Her eyes widened. "Are you related to someone named Pauline?"

"My mother," he said, taking a deep drink of iced tea. How would she know his mother?

"Talk about a small world!" She slid into the other side of the booth, uninvited, her smile so bright his salad threatened to make a return appearance. "I just met her this morning. We hit it off right away."

"I'll just bet," he mumbled.

"What? We did! That's why I hired her on the spot. As my assistant."

Chris's eyes narrowed. "Your assistant."

She got the distinct impression he was less than pleased with her news.

"Yes," she replied, determined more than ever to be cheerful and upbeat if it killed her. "I had just been thinking I could use some part-time help, and there she was." She spread her hands, palms up. "It was fate."

"Fate."

"Yes. Are you going to keep repeating everything I say? Because I have to tell you, it's getting old fast."

"Do you plan to keep getting you hair cut at Earl's?"

"Earl's?" She frowned. "Oh, the barbershop." She shrugged and touched her curls. "Sure, why not?"

"Because it's a *barbershop*. Not a beauty shop."

"I think he did a fine job, and he's convenient." She narrowed her eyes and leaned closer, lowering her voice. "Get used to it."

He narrowed his eyes right back and leaned closer, too. "And I suppose now you're going to start taking your meals at the Roadkill because it's 'convenient', too."

"That's right." She placed her hands over Chris's, on the table, just to irritate him. From the set of his firm jaw, she guessed it worked. "So why don't you and I play nice and be friends? C'mon. Everybody needs friends."

"I've got all the friends I need, thanks anyway." He threw money on the table and got up to leave, then turned back to her. "Is that why you hired my mother? To get to me?"

She laughed. "Don't flatter yourself. How was I to know she was your mother? Until a few minutes ago I didn't even know your name."

He grunted in response and pulled his hat lower over his eyes. "Likely story." He walked out of the café, nodding to the waitress as he left.

Allison took a sip of her Coke and wondered why their conversation had deteriorated. Was it just her, or was Chris Mac-Neil surly to everyone? He certainly was nothing like his mother.

Allison nodded slowly while sipping her soda. Chris Mac-Neil would make the perfect first Christmas project for her first holiday season in her new hometown.

A thought struck. Maybe he was just lonely and needed a friend. Like her.

6

Chris sat in his truck and fumed. Allison had the ability to tick him off without saying a word. Why did she get to him like that?

His cell phone filled the truck with the wail of an ambulance, the sharp tone piercing his brain. He glanced at the readout and flipped it open.

"Hey, Ray."

"Did I interrupt something?"

Chris held the phone away and took a deep breath. "No," he said when the phone was back on his ear. "Why?"

"I just heard you were sitting with the Christmas Lady at the Roadkill, holding hands." The sheep-killing grin in Ray's voice was unmistakable.

Chris unclenched his molars. "We weren't holding hands. I was there, she sat down. I got up and left. End of story." He glanced back as he eased his truck out of the parking place.

"Chris, my man! You're losing your touch. She sat down with you." Ray lowered his voice to an insinuating growl. "She wants you. She wants you bad!"

"Shut up, idiot."

Ray just laughed. "Now the question is, what do you intend to do about it?"

"Whatever I do is none of your damned business." He flipped the phone closed and turned toward home.

Maybe he'd take a quick shower and shave and mosey into town. Maybe he should just act on all his lustful thoughts. It might serve two purposes: slake his obsessive thoughts about the shop owner and drive her out of town. A win-win proposition.

If Allison wanted to go out to eat after closing, he wouldn't object. And if she wanted to get down and dirty with him, hell, he wouldn't object to that either. But supper was a good start.

After all, a man had to eat.

Pauline swerved to avoid a head-on collision with Chris as he came down the long drive. She smiled. Maybe he had a hot date. After the perfect day she had, it would be icing on the cake.

She'd just locked the garage and began walking to the back door when she noticed Sam sitting on the patio.

He stood as she approached, hat in his hand.

"Hey, Sam," she said with a smile, ignoring the increased tempo of her heart and the heated flush washing over her.

"Hey, Miz—I mean, Pauline." He shifted from one dusty booted foot to the other. "I was just wondering if you'd care to go for a ride before supper? Won't take but a minute to saddle up Buttercup."

"I'd love it, Sam, but you know I haven't ridden in years." She shrugged. "I'm not sure my old bones could take it."

"Your bones aren't old," he shot back, then flushed and muttered, "and neither is the rest of you."

Her hand tingled when she touched the heated flesh of his

forearm, exposed by the rolled-up sleeves of his chambray shirt.

It was past time to see where her attraction to Sam would lead.

Shoring up her confidence, she asked, "Would you like to stay for supper? I'm sure I could scrape up something for us."

Sam nodded, his dimples flashing, and held the back door open for her.

The old kitchen had never looked lovelier. The kitchen table held a bouquet of daisies and two place settings of her Sunday china. When she looked back at Sam, he shrugged.

"I was kind of hoping you'd ask," he said, his voice setting off vibrations of need deep within her. "I picked up supper from the Roadkill while I was in town."

Chris winced at the sappy door chimes of the Happy Holidays Boutique and did a quick glance around the store. Good. No one was there to witness what he was about to do.

Christmas carols played quietly in the background. The overpowering smell of cinnamon made his nose water. He wiped his nose on the clean handkerchief he always carried in his hip pocket. Where the devil was she? Now that he'd made up his mind to scare her off, he was ready to get on with it.

"Hey!" His voice sounded unnaturally loud in the little store. "Allison?" he called in a lower voice. "You here?"

"Just a sec!" Her voice sounded muffled. "Chris? Is that you?"

Tramping down his absurd pleasure at her identifying his voice, he called back, "Yeah."

"If you're looking for your mother, she already left."

He frowned. Was his Christmas Lady being deliberately rude? Or playing hard to get?

"I know," he decided to answer, "I saw her on my way into

town. I know it's kinda early, but I came to see if you wanted to grab something to eat. Or something. Together." Where in the hell was she?

Allison frowned at the side of the big box that currently held her prisoner. All it would take was to tell Chris she needed his help and she'd be free. Yet, somehow, the idea grated on her.

Maybe if she could reach the stool with her foot she would gain the leverage she needed to get out of her current klutzy predicament.

She swung her foot, stretching her toe, hoping to connect with something. Nothing.

She pushed harder. Maybe . . .

Instead of the desired result, she nudged the stool with her toe, sending it crashing to the floor. With a shriek she toppled deeper into the box, headfirst into a batch of Christmas quilts.

Chris heard something fall, followed by her muffled scream, and stiffened. Was she okay? Hurt? Unconscious? Did he care?

His shoulders slumped. Of course he cared. He was raised better than that.

"Allison? You all right?" Silence greeted his question. Damn. He was going to have to go back there and find out.

The first thing he saw as he pushed aside the curtain of Christmas fabric was a pair of shapely legs sticking out of about a five-foot-tall cardboard box. Biting his lip to keep from laughing, he asked, "Allison? You okay?"

"Do I look okay?" Her voice was muffled but definitely feisty.

He grinned and perused her lower anatomy. Ankle-high Christmas socks, with tiny jingle bells at the back of the heels, adorned her feet. Her bare legs looked smooth and shapely, making his palms itch to run his hands up and down their silky length.

"Chris?" Her voice was still muffled. "Are you still there?"

He stuck his hands in his pockets and rocked back on his boot heels. "Yes, ma'am."

"Could you help me out of here? Please? The blood is rushing to my head." After a moment she said, "Chris?"

"I'm thinking."

"What's to think about?" She wiggled, causing her already bunched-up jumper to fall farther down toward her head.

He peeked over the edge of the box and felt his jeans tighten. *Day-um.* Miss Allison surely had a fine ass, showcased perfectly by her green thong panties.

"Stop looking at my butt," she ground out through whatever it was she had her head in.

"I'm not," he lied. "I'm just trying to figure out the best way to do this." The idea he liked best was to drop his drawers and climb in with her. Somehow, though, he doubted she'd approve of that plan.

"Chris, seriously, my head is beginning to throb."

So was his little one.

"Why can't we just tip the whole thing over and you crawl out?"

"Because I think there may be some breakable stuff toward the bottom. I've already broken more than I can afford to lose."

"Okay," he finally said, taking hold of her ankles. "How about I lift you by your feet until you can reach the side of the box to pull yourself the rest of the way out?"

"I don't think that will work. Neither of us are tall enough for me to get that high."

"Okay. Plan B. I reach as far down as I can and lift you out." He stretched over the side of the box, sliding his hands down her legs in the process.

"Chris!"

"What? I'm just following your legs down so I don't grab

something breakable." He glanced at her smooth butt and barely resisted the temptation to run his hands over and around the firm globes.

And speaking of firm . . . his palms cupped her breasts through the knit fabric of her jumper and shirt. Was she wearing a bra?

"Chris . . ." Her warning voice brought him to his senses.

He lifted, bracing his feet wide and using the side of the box for leverage. All went well until he got her to about his waist. That's when the center of gravity shifted, taking them both backward.

He clutched her to him and curled to take the brunt of the fall.

His head bounced on the cement floor, bringing tears to his eyes. The scrape of fabric against skin registered a unique kind of burn as she skidded up his chest, over his shoulders and up his neck.

She came to rest on his face. Everything went black.

Against his hot breath, her skin gave off a perfume that made his mouth water. She shifted, pushing something soft and silk-covered against his mouth.

As soon as he realized what was so close to him, he closed his mouth over her soft mound and breathed her essence. Half expecting her to scream and smack him, he was surprised when she responded with a moan and ground against his open mouth.

He reached up to grasp her breasts to make sure she knew exactly what he was doing. She arched into his palms and dragged her sweet silk-covered pussy across his lips. He'd have to be a fool not to know what she was offering.

His mama didn't raise no fool.

Allison closed her eyes. Her breath hitched at the glorious sensations blasting through her nerve endings from the warm breath between her legs. It had been so long. She squirmed when Chris licked along the edge of her damp thong, his talented tongue gently nudging aside the scrap of fabric to stroke her aching folds, bathing them in hot, seductive warmth.

She wanted, she needed, more. Even if it was only for a little while, even if it was with Cranky.

She bit back a moan and moved her hips, allowing his tongue deeper access. Wow. Had she ever felt anything so wonderful? Warmth slicked between her legs, inching into a full-body flush. His fingers tweaked her hard nipples through the fabric of her jumper and shirt. She closed her eyes, savoring the sensation, thoroughly enjoying the soft, smooth lap of his hot tongue against her weeping sex, the pleasure/pain at her breasts, combined with the soft background of Christmas music . . . Christmas music?

Shit! She was sitting on a customer's face, allowing him to go down on her, right smack in the middle of her new business. The door was unlocked. Anyone could walk in and catch them. What was she thinking?

With a cry of equal parts panic and loss, she jumped and rolled from him. Her back hit the fallen stool, shoving the legs against her ribs in a painful jolt back to reality.

Stumbling back in an awkward crab walk, she tugged her jumper down as she went, cheeks burning with humiliation.

Chris lay there for a few seconds, his lips glistening—no doubt from her neediness—and then he rolled to his feet.

He reached into his back pocket, brought out a white handkerchief, wiped his mouth and then repocketed it. He leaned and offered her a hand up.

"I don't know what just happened here." He held up one hand. "Mind you, I'm not complaining. I'm just confused. I didn't mean to embarrass you. I'm sorry. I don't know what got into me."

Despite her baser inclinations, she pulled her hand from his as soon as she had her feet under her.

"Would you still like to grab some food? I promise to keep my distance."

I'm not sure I can keep mine, she thought. Instead she said, "Sure. It's not like I'm overrun with customers. Just give me a minute to change and freshen up and close the store."

What harm would there be in sharing a meal? She argued with her internal voice of reason while doing a quick change in the restroom. It wasn't like they were going to a motel for a quickie or anything. Just a shared meal. After all, they had to eat, didn't they?

7

"Have you ever been to a deer lease?" Chris asked above the rumble of the truck.

Despite her mouth watering from the smell of the burgers in the bag on her lap, she managed to answer, "No. I didn't know you could lease deer." At his quick look, she grinned and winked. "Kidding. I lived in Houston, not New York. I know what a deer lease is. But I've never been to one."

She gripped the bag tighter when he turned onto a gravel road that was really just two muddy ruts through the weeds and trees.

He turned under a big tree and cut the engine. "There it is."

She stared at the square building sitting high on stilts. "I didn't realize a deer lease was so big."

"Darlin', we're *at* the deer lease; what you're looking at is the deer stand." He opened his door and hopped out, reaching in to help her out through the driver side of the cab.

There was something intimate in feeling his lingering warmth on the leather seat as she slid across and into his waiting arms.

"I wouldn't have asked you out if I'd realized you were so short," he said, his teeth flashing in the darkness.

"I'm the same height I've been ever since we met." Reaching into the warm bag, she snagged a fry and popped it into her mouth, chewing appreciatively.

"True." He reached into the bed of the truck and grabbed a cooler, then touched her back, guiding her toward the—she now saw—dark green, squat building. Roughly ten by eight feet, it stood an easy six feet off the ground with little sideways rectangular windows cut into every side. Closer now, she could see a small door on one side with a rough wood ladder.

She'd never been fond of heights. Not to mention small enclosed places.

"Maybe we should just eat in the car." She glanced back. "Or maybe even take the food back to my house, where we'd be more comfortable."

"Aw, don't be a party pooper. There's nothing to hurt you out here." He stepped up on the ladder high enough to toss the cooler through the door and then got down and walked back to her. "It's perfectly safe."

"Safe? It's deer season! I heard some men talking about it today at the Roadkill. It's almost dark. What if someone shoots us by mistake?"

"Darlin', they don't hunt at night. It's against the law." He reached into his truck and brought out a sleeping bag and the biggest black flashlight she'd ever seen.

Was he planning to seduce her or bludgeon her if she resisted?

He grinned and bent to kiss the tip of her nose, and she melted. Probably, someone who kissed your nose wasn't a psycho.

And who said she planned to resist any seduction that came her way?

* * *

Allison wrinkled her nose as she entered the enclosure. "What's that smell?"

Chris took a big whiff and shrugged. "I don't smell anything unusual. 'Course, I'm used to the way it smells." He flipped his wrist to unfurl the sleeping bag, setting the flashlight down. He did a quick scan of the rough-hewn ceiling, checking for varmints. "Might be owl poop you're smelling. We have a devil of a time keeping them out of here."

She glanced around, hoping they were the only form of wildlife in the little building. In one corner was an office chair that had definitely seen better days, along with what looked to be a folding camp stool like her grandfather used to take fishing.

"Kind of sparse, isn't it?" She clutched the bag of food closer to her chest and hoped she didn't have a close encounter with an owl.

"My granddaddy built it way back before my dad was born. Been in our family ever since."

A metallic whirring sound filled the air. Allison shrieked and practically hopped into Chris's arms, smushing their food against his chest.

"Hey, take it easy." He gripped her arms and peeled her away. "Our food won't be fit to eat."

"But that noise—"

"Shhh," he said, tugging her toward one of the windows. "It was the feeder. It's on a timer." He pulled her closer and pointed. "Look."

By the waning light, they watched three adult deer and two younger ones approach what looked like a little water tower. After a cautious glance around, the deer lowered their heads and began eating the corn strewn in a wide radius around the little metal structure.

"If it's illegal to hunt at night," she whispered, "why is the timer set to feed now?" Maybe she'd misunderstood and the hunters were giving the deer more of a sporting chance.

He chuckled, setting off warm vibrations deep within her. "To get them used to eating here. It goes off at dawn and again around four. That's when they get shot."

"But that's not fair!" Jerking her arm from his grasp, she stepped away from the sight. "Where's the sport in getting them in the habit of coming here to eat and then killing them?"

A muscle ticked in his jaw. "No sport. It's just the way it is. The way it's always been."

"Oh, don't give me that 'always' crap. Hunters have just become lazy . . . and started killing Bambi!"

Chris bit his lip to keep from laughing. She was so cute. She had no idea. She also hadn't been in town long enough to know he had never shot a thing in his life. And only partly because he had the worst aim in the universe.

"Why don't you just put it out of your mind for now, and let's eat before our food gets cold? Since we're the only ones here and we're unarmed, Bambi is safe tonight." He flipped the light on and tugged her to sit on the sleeping bag, ignoring the tingle when her hip brushed his leg.

He reached into the cooler and pulled out two longnecks. "Beer?"

"Thanks." She surprised him again by leaning over to whack the top off her beer on the ledge of the window.

Maybe Miz Conroe wasn't as prim as he'd assumed.

He thought about that for a minute while he took his first swig of beer. "So why did you hire my mother?" He handed her a burger and a carton of fries.

She paused in unwrapping her burger. "I told you, we hit it off. When I mentioned needing to hire an assistant, she volunteered."

"Did she say she needed money?" Maybe things hadn't been running as smoothly as his mother had always let on.

"No! Nothing like that. I got the impression she was lonely and just wanted something to do." She took a quick bite of her burger and swallowed. "Is there a problem with her working with me?"

He shrugged and looked out at the deer. "You have no idea," he said in a low voice. In a stronger tone, he said, "I'm just surprised she'd want anything to do with a Christmas store, that's all. We share the same feeling about the holidays."

"Oh?"

He finished his burger and tossed the wrapper in the bag. What the hell. "My dad took off on Christmas. I was eight. I don't think she ever got over it."

"Eight? That was a long time ago. Why do you think that?"

"She never went out on a date, for one thing. Devoted her life to me and the ranch."

Her lips curled, and for a second he lost his train of thought.

"Chris, you talk as if she's ancient instead of just middle-aged."

"Yeah, well, I know her a lot better than you do. That's why I moved back a few years ago when—" He clamped his lips together and then took another swig of his beer. "That's why I moved back. That's all." No way was he going to tell her about his wedding that wasn't. Not now. Not ever. Some things were best forgotten.

She shivered slightly, and he held open his jean jacket. "Here. Scoot on over here and let me share some body heat with you."

Fighting down his grin, he watched her hesitance on her expressive face. Good. She should be scared. She didn't know him, and they were out in the country. All alone.

Time to implement his plan. Of course, a fringe benefit was getting to kiss her. Possibly even more, depending on how long it took to scare her.

She snuggled against his side, setting off sparks along his rib cage. Her hair smelled like lemons, and he resisted the urge to bury his face in it.

Finished with her food, she stretched to place her trash in the bag, her hand brushing against the hard ridge of his fly.

Her gasp filled the quiet.

Turning to hide his smile, he flipped open two of the side windows, attaching them to the hooks to prop them open.

"Fresh air," he said after he hung his keys on one of the hooks, turning back to her.

"But I'm already cold." She rubbed her hands up and down her arms.

"Here. Let's crawl into the sleeping bag and warm up a little before we head back to town."

"I'm not sure that's a good idea," she said even as she allowed him to pull her into the flannel softness.

"Sure it is. Sharing body heat is always a good thing." He pulled her close, stretching out in the sleeping bag, resting his head on one arm. She snuggled closer, not complaining when his hand "accidentally" brushed the outer edge of her breast.

That was a good sign, wasn't it?

"You're shivering," he said, pulling her closer, nuzzling her neck. "Let me warm you up."

His mouth found hers, settling in for the kiss he'd waited too long to experience. She tasted faintly of salt and grilled beef with a beer chaser. Easily the best-tasting kiss he'd ever experienced.

He paused, momentarily stunned by the realization, but she drew him back to her, drowning him in sensation.

His last coherent thought was that this was a dangerous thing to do, kissing Allison Conroe. His plan was not going as he anticipated. Not only did she taste like temptation itself . . . she also tasted like home.

8

Allison knew she should break the kiss and run for her life. And she would. In a minute or two. Or three. It'd been so long since she'd been kissed, especially by someone who obviously knew what he was doing. She wanted to wallow in it, drink in the sensation, savor it.

His hand crept around to cup her breast. When did he unbutton her sweater? For that matter, when had he unhooked the front closure of her bra?

Dampness surged, and her flesh trembled, aching for more.

His hair tickled her chest a nanosecond before he latched on to her breast, his hot suction pulling her nipple deep within his mouth, the wet velvet of his tongue doing magical things.

She squirmed, twisting to allow him greater access while he finished removing her sweater.

While he feasted on her breasts, his hand delved into her jeans, which she'd just noticed were unzipped.

A roughened finger dragged a trail of need along her engorged sex. Her hips bucked. More. She needed more.

He left her breasts, cold and aching, to trail wet kisses up to her mouth. As soon as their lips met, his tongue plunged in to perform a wicked dance of desire with hers, leaving no doubt of his intentions.

While ravaging her mouth, he continued playing with her dripping folds, close but not close enough to the spot that wept for his attention.

His talented fingers left her sex but only long enough to pull her hand to his exposed erection. As soon as she clamped her eager fingers around him, his hand was in her pants again, doing things she hadn't experienced in a long, long time.

Her climax almost roared down on her, threatening to consume her. She whimpered, every cell on alert.

He stopped and withdrew his hand, caressing her exposed abdomen along the way.

She lay there, looking at him, the cold air puckering her wet, exposed nipples to the point of pain, feeling unbearably exposed.

He sat up, raking a hand through his hair. "I'm sorry. I guess I got carried away."

He's sorry? He didn't sound all that sorry. As for being carried away . . . she was right there with him, every step of the way.

How dare he call a halt? It was Bruce all over again, wanting what he wanted, when he wanted it, and she was dang sick of it.

No more. No one was out here to know if she was the aggressor or not. No one would know how needy she was, how much she craved what Chris could give her. By golly, she was going to go for it.

She was woman, hear her roar.

"I don't think so, mister." She pushed him back onto the sleeping bag and grabbed his still-open fly and yanked, stripping his jeans and boxers down to his ankles where they stuck on his boots. No problem. She wasn't interested in his feet right now.

"What are you doing?" He looked so horrified she might have laughed had she not been so horny and so enthralled with the shining head of his penis, winking at her in the moonlight.

Shimmying out of her jeans and panties, she kicked aside her loafers and stripped her socks. It took considerable effort, but eventually she did the same to him. She wanted absolutely nothing to be between her and the hunk of burning love stretched out for her personal satisfaction.

"Allison, what are you doing?" he asked again, but she noted the interested twitch of his fully erect penis.

"My," she said in a soft voice, "I guess it's really been a long time if you can't figure that one out, Chrissy-baby." She licked her lips and straddled his lean hips, the skin searing hers where they met. "I'm finishing what we started." She lowered until she felt his bulbous head kissing her opening, making her impossibly wetter.

He bucked his hips, but when he would have buried himself in her, she drew back, deciding to play with him a little longer. Until he was as wild for her as she was for him.

Crab-walking up his torso, her nipples tingled from the feel of cool air between her legs, the soft abrasion of his skin against her sensitized, engorged folds. And, finally, his hot breath, coming in harsh pants, against her nipples.

"Suck me," she demanding in a breathless whisper, her heart pounding in her ears.

In response, he flicked the hard tip of her nipples with the point of his tongue, once, twice, three times.

She wanted to scream her frustration. "Now! Suck me now! Hard!"

He smiled against her breast, teeth flashing in the semidarkness, his breath hot and taunting. But instead of complying, he brushed a light kiss across the tips of each nipple.

She growled.

He laughed and said, "Yes, ma'am."

Before she could take a breath or think of anything to say or do, his big hands gripped her buttocks, squeezing in a not unpleasant way. He pulled her upward, his mouth opening wide to take in as much of her breast as he could manage. At the same time, his thumbs found her core, massaging her clitoris and weeping flesh, dipping occasionally, and for far too short a time, into her aching core.

Her orgasm snuck up on her, slamming into her, eliciting a scream she'd never heard before, arching her back, gripping her muscles with its intensity.

When she could take a deep breath without shuddering, she gasped, "I'm sorry. I probably scared the deer."

"Let's give them something to talk about," he said, lifting her higher and then settling her astride his open mouth.

His teeth nipped, his tongue soothed and tormented. Within seconds, her second orgasm washed over her, more intense than the first.

She was horrified to hear her guttural scream, but before she could rally, he shoved her down to impale her on his hot sex.

His equally hot hands cupped her breasts. He bucked his hips in encouragement. "Ride me, baby."

He didn't need to tell her twice.

Unfortunately it was over almost before it began. All it took was one good, deep thrust to push them both over the edge.

Gasping and panting for air, Chris finally said, "I'm s— sorry. I—"

"Don't be sorry," Allison said, pushing him back onto the sleeping bag. "Now, where were we?"

Why wasn't she running screaming into the night? He'd practically attacked her.

She chose that moment to grasp his hands and pull them up to cover her breasts, short-circuiting his thought process.

His renewed erection twitched, eager for an instant replay,

against the moist heat poised above him. It was so tempting to take what she so plainly was offering. He needed to stop analyzing and just go for it.

With a sigh, she lowered her hips until the head of his cock kissed her wet rim. In the next instant, she'd taken his full length.

Her hips performed a lazy circle, causing his back to bow off the flannel lining of the sleeping bag in a quest for deeper penetration.

On autopilot, he gripped the flare of her hips and set the pace.

It wasn't enough.

"Harder," she called over the roar of blood in his ears. "Faster!" She made a mewling sound. "Deeper." Her voice vibrated with need.

Whatever the lady wanted . . .

"Hold on, darlin'," he ground out, flipping their position.

"Yes," she huffed into his ear. "Harder!"

He put his back into it, pounding into her more than receptive body. Damn! Nothing had ever felt that good, that right. His skin tingled with the increased blood flow. Man, she was cleaning his clock and rocking his world.

He'd never had such a strong physical reaction to sex. It was like the earth moved with each thrust.

Allison didn't know if she was just so needy or if Chris was just that good, but with his every powerful thrust an old saying popped into her mind: the earth moved. Bliss. It was sheer bliss, and she never wanted it to end.

Too soon, she felt her climax building. She tried to stem the tide ripping through her, but it felt so good and had been so long since someone filled her so completely and efficiently. It had been hard to hold back when he'd first entered her; now it was impossible.

Her heart hitched, breath lodging in her throat, while her uterus clamped its excitement until the pleasure/pain was almost unbearable.

Tiny multicolored lights exploded behind her closed eyelids as she screamed her pleasure.

At the same moment, Chris reached his pinnacle. His back arched, and he roared his completion.

He collapsed on top of her, his warm weight a welcome aftermath to their coupling.

She sighed, feeling her body drift back down.

Except, it wasn't the slow kind of drift as she'd expected, and the landing was less than gentle.

With a crash that jarred her teeth, they plunged to earth.

Pain seared the top of her head where Chris's chin struck.

He curled around Allison as much as possible as soon as he realized the rocking of his world wasn't entirely sexual and that the old deer stand was literally on its last leg.

With a jarring thud, they landed. Miraculously the roof remained intact, the walls somewhat upright.

They lay, still joined, listening to the old building creak ominously as it swayed in the gentle evening breeze.

"You all right?" He moved his shoulder experimentally and winced when the pain increased. His effort to keep his weight off Allison had really taken a toll on his shoulder and elbow joints.

She moved a little beneath him and coughed. "I think so," she said but didn't sound like she meant it.

"We need to get out of here!" He jumped up, ignoring the loss of warmth and pulled her to her feet. "This old thing is coming down, and we don't want to be caught inside when it does."

He grabbed his keys from the window hook and tugged her toward the door.

"But what about the cooler and—"

"No time! I'll come back during the day and fish everything out. C'mon!"

"But my clothes—"

"I'll get those tomorrow, too, now get!" He pushed her toward the opening that had once been the door. "Watch your step. The ladder probably splintered in the fall."

The deer stand chose that moment to let loose a low, ominous groan.

Chris grabbed Allison around her waist, hefting her to his hip, and jumped as far from the structure as he could, then ran for his truck.

His hand was on the driver's door of the cab when the stand gave up and collapsed in a heap of dry wood, permeating the air with the distinctive smell of dust and owl droppings.

Allison squeaked and hid her face in his shoulder, the softness of her bare breasts against his equally bare skin setting off thoughts he had no business thinking after their close escape. He could only hope his cock didn't embarrass him.

Through the haze of decades of accumulation, the faint light of his flashlight shone. Seeing Allison looking at it, he said, "I'll have to get the flashlight tomorrow, too."

"We're naked," she pointed out needlessly. "Maybe you could use the flashlight to locate our clothes."

"Not tonight."

"But I'm cold," she complained and shivered.

Funny, he felt kind of hot.

He rummaged behind the seat and found an old blanket to cover the temptation of all her naked skin as well as a few rags to protect his modesty and then lifted her into the truck.

Cold fingers flying, he tied together the least soiled of his rag stash to fashion a makeshift loincloth.

He hopped in, noting the coldness of the leather on his bare butt.

"Don't you have another blanket?" Her voice sounded odd. Huskier than usual.

Good lord, after what they'd just done, she was modest? His next thought was he should be happy—he'd apparently scared her. Mission accomplished. So why did he feel just the opposite?

"These rags are the best I could do."

She grinned at him in the darkness. "Very inventive."

"Darlin', you have no idea." He dropped the truck in gear and headed for town.

They sat outside Allison's rental house. Damn. He didn't want to leave her.

"Would you like to come in?" She reached for the door handle.

"No, thanks. I'd better get on home."

Silence.

"I'd walk you to your door, but . . ." He gestured to the scant piece of fabric covering his lap.

She gave a little laugh. "I understand." She looked back.

"I'm sorry," they said in unison.

"What are you sorry about?" they said again.

Chris held up his hand. "I'm sorry I had to bring you home like this, naked and all. I just wanted you to know I didn't plan it." Not like this anyway.

"Of course you didn't plan it! How could you plan for the deer stand to collapse?"

"True. But I meant the naked part."

"Oh." She opened her door and hopped down, dragging the blanket with her. "I'm sorry, too. I'll wash the blanket and give it to your mother to—"

"Ah, no, I don't think that would be a very good idea." He shrugged. "After all, she is my mother. Know what I mean?"

Not really, since her own mother had witnessed naked pictures of Allison spread all over the tabloids. No doubt about it, Mom knew her daughter had sex. Lots of it, according to "sources." And, thanks to the publicity of the demise of her career and marriage, so did most of Houston.

But it was sweet of Chris to want to protect Pauline. In all likelihood, probably not necessary, but sweet.

"Thanks for dinner," she said instead and closed the truck door.

He immediately buzzed down the passenger window. "Can you get into the house?"

She nodded. "Yeah, good thing I thought to hide a spare key under the flowerpot on the front porch."

"Okay, then. See you."

"Bye," she said to his taillights.

The house was dark when Chris pulled into the drive. With any luck, his mother was sound asleep with her door shut.

Luck was not with him.

Easing the back door shut, he saw immediately that his mother's bedroom door was wide open, the bed neatly made.

Beyond the kitchen, the warm glow of the fireplace flickered on the polished built-in bookcases of the family room.

His mother must have fallen asleep on the couch. If he was very careful, he could slip past her and up to his room unnoticed.

He slid one bare foot onto the warm heart-pine plank floor of the family room and then stepped in to begin his escape.

What he saw halted him midstride.

Burnished in the glow of the fire, Sam lay stretched out on the sofa, naked as a jaybird, Pauline astride him. The sight of Sam's darkly tanned hands gripping her pale hips was forever burned into Chris's mind.

His next step slammed his bare toes into the immovable maple leg of the couch. Pain shot up his shin, ran around his knee and back down to make his big toe throb.

"Shit!" He hopped, trying to simultaneously sooth his toe and keep his loincloth in place.

Sam's eyes widened. He clutched Pauline to his chest and rolled to the side to shield her.

"What the hell are you doing to my mother?" Now, that was a stupid thing to say. He knew the facts of life; he knew damned well what Sam was doing. And, from the heavy breathing his mother was doing, Sam was doing it damn fine. But . . . shit! That was his mother.

His mom glanced over Sam's shoulder. "Hello, dear," she said as if this sort of thing happened every day. "Did you have a nice time?"

He gaped at the woman who gave him life. "Well, obviously not as good a time as you and Sam!"

She leaned a bit and glanced meaningfully at him, or, more specifically, his crotch and raised her eyebrow.

Damn. Forgot about the loincloth.

"I was in the deer stand, and it fell." It was the truth.

Sam's chuckle rumbled through the silence. "And it knocked your clothes plumb off you, right?"

"Right," he returned with as much dignity as he could muster before hobbling to his room.

A soft knock sounded on his door a few minutes later as he came out of the bathroom in a pair of sweatpants. The door immediately opened. His mother stood in the halo of light, her red velour robe wrapped tightly around her. He wondered if she was still naked under the robe and then wondered if he'd have to poke his eyes out. Or at least undergo intensive therapy. Did anyone still practice brainwashing?

"Chris?" His mother took a tentative step into his room. "I asked if you were all right."

"You mean healthwise or in the grand scheme of life or am I all right because I just walked in on my mother balling the ranch foreman's brains out?"

His mother flinched as if he'd physically hit her.

"I'm sorry, Mom." He ran his hands through his hair. "I guess I was just . . . surprised."

"So was I," she said in a quiet voice. "But I won't deny I've been thinking about it for quite some time." She walked to him and placed her warm hand on his bare chest.

He tried not to think about where else her hand had been.

"Chris, I've also been thinking about our conversation in the kitchen." She patted him just like she had when he was a little boy and needed comforting. "We were both blindsided when your daddy left us. But you're right. It's past time for us both to move on. I hid behind my pain and, later, my self-righteous anger. That wasn't good for me, and it certainly wasn't good for you."

"And Sam is part of that?"

She dropped her hand and sighed as she stepped back toward the door. "I suspect he's always been. I was just too stubborn to admit it." She raised her chin. "But I'm not going to waste any more time." She walked to the door and looked back. "Sam will be spending the night with me tonight. I trust you to be courteous to him if you run into him tomorrow morning."

"Mom?"

She paused on her way out the door and looked back.

"Do you love him?"

After a while, she said, "I don't know. But I intend to find out."

The door closed quietly, the noise echoing in his head, telling him things would never be the same.

9

For once, Allison's stash of sex toys did not call to her. After a quick shower, she slapped on baby lotion and baby powder and slipped into her oldest, softest flannel gown. Tonight was about comfort. It was a time to sleep, regenerate her career plans and decide what she really wanted to do when she grew up.

Boffing Chris MacNeil in a broken-down deer lease—make that deer *stand*—certainly had not been on her to-do list. Her cheeks heated at the thought, and then she smiled at the way the rags had looked against his tanned legs on the drive home. It was definitely a fashion statement few men could pull off. Instant recall of the flex of his bare hip when he had shifted had heat rushing through her.

Sleep eluded her. She turned on one side and then another. She'd just flopped over to her stomach and felt herself finally drifting off when she thought she heard something.

Eyes now wide open, she paused, not breathing, straining to hear anything out of the ordinary.

Like a figment of her imagination, the shadow of a man appeared at her bedroom door.

She was too afraid to scream. Scooting back until she felt her spine against the headboard, she blindly dug in the drawer of the nightstand for her Mace.

The man said something, but it was drowned out by the pounding of her heart.

Her intruder slowly walked into the room. When he was just on the edge of the light from the window, she took aim and blasted him.

"Shit!" Chris's voice broke through the terrified roaring in her ears. "Why the hell'd you do that?" He dropped to sit on the edge of her mattress, gripping his eyes. "It stings like a son of a bitch!"

"I thought you were a burglar! It's Mace—" She sniffed. Minty fresh. She flipped on the bedside lamp. A glance at the can still gripped in her hand confirmed it: she'd Binaca-ed him. "Oops. Good news; it wasn't Mace." She held out the little canister. "It was breath spray."

Chris stopped furiously scrubbing his eyes and stared at her through a very bloodshot one. "Is that supposed to make it all right?"

"Well, no, it's just that I—wait! What are you doing sneaking into my house in the middle of the night?" Maybe she should make another effort to find her Mace.

"I couldn't stay at my house. I drove by a couple of friends' houses, but they weren't home. This was the only place left." He scrubbed at his still tearing eyes again. "Could I get a wet rag or something to try to wash this crap out?"

"Um, sure." She hopped off the bed and strode into the bathroom. A minute later she was handing him a warm wet washcloth. "That still doesn't explain why you felt you had the right to come in here and scare me half to death."

"I knocked," he grumbled against the washcloth. "When you didn't answer, I remembered the key and let myself in." He folded the cloth and looked at her. "I even called your name when I first came in 'cause I didn't want to scare you."

Was that what had jerked her back from the brink of sleep?

She sat next to him, gripping the edge of the mattress to keep a distance between them. "Why couldn't you stay at home?"

"My mother was *entertaining*."

She grinned. "Pauline had a date?" She pumped her fist in the air. "Yes!"

"Wait. Don't tell me this was all your idea." He laid the damp cloth on his knee and fixed his watery blue gaze on her.

He probably wouldn't appreciate being told he was going to get his jeans wet.

She fiddled with the placket on her flannel gown and swallowed. "Well, I wouldn't say it was exactly my idea, but we had a long talk today." She shrugged. "I may have told her I thought she should start dating again."

Chris made a kind of growling sound—and not in a good way.

Allison jumped up. "Why don't we have some hot cider or hot chocolate? It would help us relax. I'll be right back!"

He watched her leave and cursed his weakness. Even the lingering scent of baby powder turned him on. Despite what Allison may have done to bring about his mother's moral decline, despite the fact she loved the holidays almost as much as he did not, despite the fact that she was probably the last person on earth he needed in his life, he didn't care.

The flannel job she slept in fit her like a tent; it was covered in little pink girlie-type flowers and buttoned tight around her neck. It covered her to her wrists and ankles in a cloud of useless fabric Yet, it was just about the sexiest thing he'd ever laid eyes on.

No doubt about it, he wanted her. Bad.

Question was, what was he going to do about it?

Allison knew Chris was there. She'd felt his presence even before her peripheral vision caught sight of him leaning against the doorjamb of her little kitchen.

She finished stirring the hot-cocoa mix into the steaming mugs of water before she spoke. "Marshmallows?"

"Are they the little kind?" he asked, the eagerness in his voice bringing a smile to her lips.

"Of course." At his nod, she dumped a generous handful into each mug. "Let's drink this in the living room, okay?"

He nodded and followed her.

Settled on the couch, he frowned when she reached out and turned on the lights of her Christmas tree. "You don't have to do that."

"Sure I do." She settled next to him and took a sip of her cocoa. "I love sitting in here in the quiet and looking at the lights. It's so peaceful."

Beside her, he made a noncommittal-sounding grunt and sipped his drink. "Good. I like it with lots of marshmallows."

"So do I." She turned and looked at him. Maybe they weren't so different after all. "So, Chris, want to tell me what you have against your mother dating?"

"Nope." He took another sip and regarded his mug. "Aw, man! Don't you own anything that's not junked up with Christmas crap?"

She stared at him for a moment, then took a sip and said, "Nope."

"You have to be the most bullheaded, stubborn woman I have ever met. Why can't you just get over the fact that not everyone loves Christmas like you do?"

"And why can't you realize you are in the minority on this topic?" She folded her arms beneath her breasts, short-circuiting his train of thought.

Instead of arguing, he did the thing he'd sworn not to do when he came to her house. He touched her.

With slow, deliberate movements he traced the outer curve of her plump breast, drawing smaller and smaller circles on the flannel until he brushed the hardened peak jutting against the soft material. "Are you as turned on as I am?" He walked the fingers of his other hand under the hem of her gown, admiring the soft smoothness of her skin.

He traced the edge of her panties and frowned. "No thong tonight?"

She shook her head and spread her legs a little wider. "No. They're not very comfortable to sleep in."

He nipped at her neck. "Who's talking about sleeping?"

She moved back and stood up. The fire she saw in Chris's eyes made her weak in the knees, but she would not give in again. She had come to Flintlock to start a new life, not repeat her mistakes. She had to be strong.

"If you want to sleep here tonight, you're welcome to the couch. There are blankets and an extra pillow in the hall closet. Good night." While she still had the strength to walk away, she did, not stopping until she'd closed her bedroom door behind her.

Heart pounding, aching with desire, she leaned against the cool wall and listened. She thought she heard some rustling of something—clothing perhaps? Then nothing.

Stupid, stupid, stupid to be disappointed when he was only doing what you'd told him you wanted.

She leaned a bit closer to the door, ears straining to hear.

"Allison?" Chris's voice whispered against the outside of the door. "I know you're there. I can feel you. Can you feel me?" Silence. "Open the door, darlin', so we can feel each other."

She closed her eyes and took a deep breath. Strong. She needed to be strong. If for nothing else but to prove to herself that she was capable of denying her baser instincts.

Pictures of Chris's lean, hard body as she rode him in the deer stand flashed across her memory, along with the ripple of his thigh as he shifted his truck, making her moist and weak in the knees.

Her breathing increased, along with her heart rate.

Cooler air bathed her face.

She opened her eyes, and he was there, standing in the open door, splendidly naked, magnificently aroused.

Her resolve melted along with most of her bones when he pulled her into his arms and took her mouth in a kiss so passionate, so carnal, it was the closest she'd come to an out-of-body orgasm.

Mind sex. If she had to put a name to it, that's what she'd call it. They were so attuned to each other a mere look or touch drove them to the brink. Well, it did that for her anyway. She was making assumptions for Chris. And, judging by the way his breath came in harsh pants and his hands shook, she'd bet money she was right.

Coolness of the wall against her back jerked her attention to the current activities.

Chris shoved her nightgown up to her armpits at the same time he plunged his heat deep within her wetness.

A guttural groan sounded, but she wasn't sure from whom. It didn't matter. All that mattered was that he keep pounding into her, slamming her back and hips into the wall with each energetic thrust.

The friction was too delicious, her need too great. All too soon, her climax rushed over her, swallowing her whole. Drowning in sensation, she clung to Chris's shoulders, riding out his passion.

Chris played with her nipple, drawing lazy circles. Somehow they'd managed to make it to her bed and were now snuggled together, naked under the soft sheets and comforter.

Her nipple puckered appreciatively, but their last bout of lovemaking had drained her. She watched his tan finger against the whiteness of her breast. Maybe she was getting old. The faint tingling between her legs told her that was probably not the case, but she was still too exhausted to do anything about it. Yet.

Chris nuzzled her hair, and she resisted the urge to purr. Barely.

"Allison?"

"Hmmm?" It was a struggle to keep her eyes open.

"You realize tonight doesn't mean anything, don't you?"

Her heart stilled. Did she? She shrugged in what she hoped was a dismissive gesture. "Sure. No problem. Just sex, right?"

"Right." He resisted the urge to clutch her to him. What did he expect her to say? He'd wanted her to know there was no possibility of a serious relationship. The sex was great, but his main goal was . . . well, hell, what really was his goal? To get her out of town? To get rid of the Happy Holidays Boutique?

And what did she mean, "just sex"? Did she do this kind of thing often? And, if so, who the hell had been her playmate since she moved to Flintlock?

10

Chris was gone when Allison woke up. It wasn't really a surprise, but she had to fight the disappointment tugging down her usually upbeat morning mood.

She should be glad. Relieved, even. After all, she was the one who wanted to make a fresh start. So what if she couldn't exactly keep her vow of celibacy. Allowing Chris to scratch her itch now and then, in the privacy of her own home, was perfectly acceptable. And it wasn't like they were some starry-eyed teenagers, thinking it was love or something.

Some of her buoyancy returned. It was the twenty-first century. Women could have sex objects, too. She'd use Chris to slake her lust whenever possible while she went on with her new life. No one would ever know.

The fact that she and Chris would know tugged at her, but she firmly pushed the gloomy thoughts away.

Would she see him today, and if so, how would they act around each other?

Less than an hour later, she had her answer when Chris strolled into the store.

She paused by the door to the stockroom and watched him glance around the store. But today he looked different. For one thing, he didn't have the look of disgust on his face he usually wore when he entered her store.

Heat streaked through her, warming her cheeks and other more private places, when their eyes met.

He flipped her window sign to the side that said she'd be back in an hour. Gaze locked with hers, he strode purposefully toward her.

"Hi," she finally managed to get out around the sudden constriction in her throat. "I—"

"Shhh." He stepped close enough for her to feel his heat through her clothing, smell the scent she'd come to think of as uniquely his, and then with a full-body nudge, he pushed her back into the stockroom.

His arms were around her, pulling her closer to his hard length before the curtains swung closed behind him. His hand cool against the heated skin of her thigh, he shoved the skirt of her jumper up around her waist, not stopping until he cupped her mound through her moist cotton panties.

Before she could form or voice a protest—yeah, like that was going to happen—his mouth closed over hers, sucking away any thought other than immediate gratification.

She fumbled with the button fly of his jeans and then shoved, groaning when she heard the satisfying thunk of his belt buckle and the chink of change as his pants hit the hardwood floor.

Her hand shook, but she managed to free his erection from his blackjack-print boxers and guide him toward her aching heat.

Instead of ridding her of her panties, he simply pushed aside the leg opening and flexed his hips, burying his hardness in her wet, needy body.

She groaned and shuddered, wrapping her legs around his

lean hips, barely registering the feel of his cotton boxers against the backs of her calves.

Her bottom perched on the unpacking counter, she leaned back on her elbows and aligned herself for deeper access while tightening her legs to pull him closer for maximum friction.

Her toes curled. Electric current shot up her legs to center on her rigid nipples, taking her breath away. A hard contraction seized her uterus when the first wave of her climax hit her, dragging her under in its sensual undertow.

With a guttural cry, she clamped Chris to her while she rode wave after wave of ecstasy.

Through the blood rushing in her ears, she thought she heard a woman's voice, but that couldn't be right.

Chris closed his eyes and gritted his teeth in his effort to hang on while Allison's climax threatened to milk him of his own.

Perspiration beaded his forehead and upper lip. His legs began to vibrate with the effort to remain upright. Sweat trickled down his back. He locked his knees, tightening his buttocks to stave off the almost overwhelming urge to pound into her.

A distant voice broke his concentration. Through a haze of passion he turned and saw . . . his mother?

Pauline stood in the doorway of the stockroom, one hand holding the curtain open, the other splayed over her chest. Her red glossed lips formed a soft O while her eyes widened.

With a gasp, his mother dropped the curtain, shielding them from her view. He thought he heard her exclaim, "My eyes!" but he wasn't certain.

"I'm so sorry!" his mother's voice came through the fabric barrier. "I saw the be-back-soon sign and wondered why Allison didn't call me to fill in while she was gone." She was talking so fast she sounded close to babbling. "Then I realized the door was unlocked and worried maybe there was a problem or possibly something had happened to Allison, which of course it had—not to say it's something wrong or terrible! Anyway, I heard a noise and decided I should make sure we weren't being robbed or anything, and I—"

"It's okay, Pauline." Allison's voice shook. Flushed, she pulled away from him, pushing down her jumper as she scrambled from the counter.

She would have tumbled onto the tiled floor had he not grasped her elbow to steady her.

"But—" Pauline continued, obviously flustered.

"Don't worry about it," she assured his mom again, smoothing her jumper with shaking hands, and then cast a meaningful glance at his glistening wanger, which was still obviously in the mood. "Would you cover yourself?" she whispered.

All the blood was still in the southernmost area, so all he did was stand and stare at her. In a minute, he was sure he would come up with a zinger. A good one. But for right now, he was just kind of . . . bereft.

Allison peeped through the curtain and then glanced back at him and rolled her eyes. Two brisk strides brought her to him. Before he knew her intentions, she grabbed the elastic on his boxers, stuffed his recovering cock inside, and released the waistband with a stinging *snap*.

"Ow!" He rubbed his belly button and tried to remain upright while she tugged his jeans up to his hips. "I can dress myself."

She huffed out a breath. "Well, you couldn't prove it by me." Her hands covered her pink cheeks. "I'm so embarrassed! What am I going to say to Pauline?"

He grinned. "How about 'Your son's a stud'?"

That earned him a punch in the arm.

"I'm serious!" she whispered, pacing to the curtain and back. "I have to work with her every day. I—"

"So fire her." Another punch. "Ow! Cut that out! Anybody

ever tell you that you have a violent streak?" He rubbed his stinging bicep. "You're apt to leave a mark if you keep that up."

"And did anyone ever tell you to keep your mouth shut if you can't say something good or constructive?" she shot back. Her shoulders slumped. "I'm sorry. I shouldn't have said that. I'm just panicked, I guess."

She placed her hand on his forearm, sending sparks zinging to places that had no business zinging, given the circumstance. "I'm going to go do some damage control," she said. "See if I can get her to run some errands for me or something so you can get out of here while she's gone."

She was trying to protect him? Why?

Allison Conroe was something he hadn't encountered in a while: a truly sweet, nice person.

And it irritated the hell out of him.

How was he going to run her off without feeling lower than a snake's armpits?

11

Allison watched Pauline leave to go get lunch and then took a deep breath and pushed aside the curtain to the stockroom.

Chris leaned against the counter, looking so sexy it made her knees weak.

Darn it all, why did she have to be so needy? Of all the men in town, why did she have to hook up with the sexiest, most addictive one? The one who made her semiorgasmic with just a glance, whose kisses she craved, whose touch she needed as much as her next breath? There was only one thing to do.

Dump him.

She didn't need or want a complication like Chris MacNeil in her life . . . did she? Of course not.

"I sent your mother to pick up lunch," she said, immediately wishing she hadn't stepped back into the stockroom. The smell of hot, greedy sex still clung to the air, along with Chris's unique scent, threatening to suffocate her with longing. Firming her resolve, she continued, "I think you should be gone by the time she gets back." Another deep breath. "And I think it's probably for the best if we don't see each other. For a while, anyway."

He cocked his eyebrow, never blinking his clear blue eyes.

"I'm trying to make a fresh start in Flintlock," she explained, "and I don't need to get a reputation before I can even get established."

"You honestly think Mom would tell tales about us?" He crossed his arms over his chest, distracting her for a moment.

The firmness of that chest was forever etched in her mind, in the tactile memory of her hands. "Ah, um, no! Not really. But if she walked in and caught us, how long would it be before others did the same thing?"

"We could always lock the door next time."

"Yeah, right, like that wouldn't cause suspicion or speculation. Especially with your truck parked right outside." She heaved a sigh. "Chris, it's just better this way. For now, anyway. Please."

Allison's softly spoken *please* was what did it. Hell, it wasn't like he was falling in love with her or anything. But now that he'd gotten to know her better, the idea of running her out of business and eventually out of town wasn't sitting as well with his conscience as it once did.

The Happy Holidays Boutique wasn't all that bad. And she seemed to generate a fair amount of business, which was always a good thing for a small town like Flintlock. Who was he to tinker with the town's economic status just because he didn't like Christmas?

And it was probably a good thing to call it quits before things got too much more out of hand and everyone thought of them as a couple. No harm, no foul.

Reluctantly, he nodded, more to himself than in answer to her question.

He shouldn't be irritated by the look of relief on her face.

But he was.

Pauline dunked her doughnut in the cup of hot cider and took an appreciative bite. "Oh, Allison, this has to be the best batch you've made yet!" she said then swallowed. "The spices are blended perfectly. Of course, the fresh doughnuts from Patti's Bakeshop aren't too slouchy either." Her grin faltered. "Allison? Please don't worry about what happened earlier. I've already put it out of my mind." She leaned closer. "And I swear I won't tell a soul!"

Allison stopped chewing on her thumbnail and took a sip of her now lukewarm cider. "I'm sorry, Pauline. I keep replaying it over and over in my head. The look on your face . . ."

Pauline grinned. "I'm sure it was nothing compared to the look on my son's face." She laughed. "Honestly, I wish you could've seen him!"

A little of her gloom slipped away as she joined Pauline in a laugh. "I know he was pretty dazed after you left."

Her employee wiped the mirth from her eyes and leaned back in the wing back chair, holding her cup in her lap. "Truth be told, I was relieved to see it." She glanced around the empty store and lowered her voice. "I've been so worried about him ever finding anyone again."

Alert, Allison set her cup on the side table. "Again?"

"He didn't tell you about Kari?"

"Obviously not. Who is Kari?"

"Oh, dear." Pauline fussed with the Christmas napkin on her lap, not making eye contact. "I think you should let Chris tell you."

There was no way she'd let Pauline out of the store without knowing. "I'm asking you. Please." She touched the older woman's fidgeting hands. "I knew there had to be something or someone in his past that caused him to be so down on the holidays and relationships in general. I had a feeling. Kari was an old girlfriend?"

Pauline nodded. "Actually, more than a girlfriend. He almost married the little witch."

She released her hand and leaned back in her chair. "They were engaged?"

Pauline looked around with an expression of discomfort. "Well, Chris was, at least. As for her, I don't think it even slowed down her dating." She leaned forward and lowered her voice. "I never liked her. Shifty eyes. Then when she insisted on a Christmas wedding, knowing full well of Chris's issues with Christmas . . . well, I knew she was up to no good." She sniffed and leaned back in the chair. "I wasn't the least bit surprised when she up and left."

"Poor Chris." Numb, Allison could only think about how devastated he must have been.

"Poor Chris is right! She didn't even have the decency to call it off and cancel everything."

"You mean . . . ?"

Pauline nodded vigorously. "That's right. The little tramp left him standing at the altar with more than a hundred people as witnesses."

"Oh, my." Her own marriage had ended badly, but even Bruce had the decency to show up for the beginning.

Pauline shook her head. "You have no idea. With all the other baggage that boy already had, it's a wonder he can even stomach the holidays."

"I heard about your husband leaving on Christmas."

"You did?" Pauline looked shocked. "Chris told you that?"

Allison nodded reluctantly. Maybe she shouldn't have said anything.

"Really. . . . What else did he tell you?" Pauline's eyes narrowed. Allison could practically hear the wheels turning in the older woman's head. "Chris must think pretty highly of you. He doesn't share personal information easily." A ghost of a smile lifted her lips. "'Course, after today, I know he's attracted to you."

Allison covered her face with her hands. "Oh, don't remind me! I'm not sure I'll ever get over the embarrassment."

Pauline touched her hands. "Hush. I'm not a stranger to getting carried away. In fact, I'm kind of tickled I was able to turn the tables on my son after he walked in on me and Sam."

"I heard." Allison peeked through her fingers. "The only thing more embarrassing than having your mother walk in, I think, would be having your son walk in when you were . . . you know."

The older woman winked and picked up their dirty dishes. "I'm too happy right now to worry about what Chris might think about the fact that his mother is having sex again." She paused on her way to the back and looked over her shoulder. "Or what anyone might say, for that matter."

"You mean me?" Allison squeaked. How could Pauline think she, of all people, would think badly of her?

Pauline set the dishes on the counter and hurried back to their chairs. "No! Of course not. I meant the busybodies of Flintlock. They've had Sam and me hooked up almost ever since Chris's daddy left. I wouldn't be surprised if some of them even thought that was the reason Bill left. I guess that's why I took so long to do anything about my attraction to Sam. I was afraid of what people would say." She patted Allison's shoulder. "Don't let that happen to you. If you're interested in my son, I say go for it. Even if it doesn't work out, you both will have some fun."

She blinked. "Are you telling me you're okay with Chris and me having meaningless sex?"

Pauline grinned. "Sweetie, you really are young. Don't you realize no sex is ever meaningless?"

12

Chris paused at the door of the Roadkill, debating. It had been three days since he'd left the Happy Holidays Boutique, three days—and four nights—since he'd seen Allison. Or held her. Or kissed her. Or anything else, for that matter.

When he'd gone to Earl's yesterday for a trim, he'd turned around and left when he saw her standing just inside the door. How could she stand there and talk and laugh with that old man as if nothing had happened?

Even his own mother was tight-lipped when it came to Allison Conroe. Whenever he asked about her, his mom would just smile and tell him if he wanted to know anything, he should call Allison.

Maybe he'd just go back home and make a peanut butter and jelly sandwich. With one last look at the impervious Allison, he turned and stalked back to his truck.

Sam was loading the dishwasher when Chris entered the kitchen.

They nodded a greeting.

Chris pulled a plate from the cabinet by the sink and went to the pantry to get the peanut butter.

Since seeing Sam and his mother, he'd avoided the man who'd been like a father to him.

"Chris." Sam ran a hand through his salt-and-pepper hair. "Look at me when I'm talking to you, boy."

Chris looked up. "I'm not a boy, Sam."

Sam snorted. "Well, hell, you couldn't prove it by me with the way you've been sulking around." Their eyes met. "You've been acting like a spoiled brat. Now, maybe you think I deserve it, but your mother sure as hell doesn't. If you're gonna be mad at anyone, you should be mad at me."

After carefully placing the jar on the table, he turned to look at Sam. "Now why would I be mad at you, Sam? Just because you're fucking my mother—"

Sam's fist connected with Chris's jaw, snapping his head back. He staggered against the sink and blinked away the impending stars. As he felt with his tongue to make sure his teeth were still in tact, Sam grabbed him by the front of his shirt and pulled him up on his toes.

Nose to nose, angry sparks shot from Sam's eyes.

"Don't you ever, and I mean *ever*, talk about your mother like that again, you hear?" He gave him a good shake. "I mean it."

Chris pulled away from the older man and stepped out of reach. "Yes, sir." He straightened his shirt. "For what it's worth, I just told Mom, the other day, that she needed to get on with her life." He held up his hand to stop whatever Sam was about to say. "Hear me out. I've been thinking a lot about this ever since . . . well, the night I walked in on you. I meant what I told her. And, well, I guess if she's going to be with anybody, I'd pick you." He forced a smile. "I just don't want to witness it, up close and personal."

Sam stood staring at him for so long he began to wonder if he was thinking about hitting him again. Finally his mustache lifted, followed by a toothy grin.

"Thanks," Sam said in a gruff voice. "I'll try to remember that."

Good-natured back-thumping followed, and then Sam left.

Chris ate his sandwich and thought about his mother and Sam. If his mom could move on and find someone new, why couldn't he? Immediately his time with Allison flashed through his mind. The sandwich formed a ball in the pit of his stomach. Why did she have to have a thing for Christmas?

Allison stared out at the rain steadily falling on the town square and sighed.

"Can't will people to come out in weather like this, you know." Pauline spoke from somewhere behind her.

"I know." She turned to look at Chris's mom. "It's just that I'm usually so busy and so happy with less than two weeks left before Christmas." She motioned around the still packed store displays. "And I thought I'd be just about sold out by now."

Pauline gave a gentle smile. "Business has been pretty good, if you ask me. Everyone who comes in loves what you've done. Maybe you got carried away and ordered a little too much inventory?"

"Maybe." She turned back to the window.

"Have you seen my son lately?"

"No, why?" She looked over her shoulder as Pauline walked to stand by her.

"I suspected not, since he's wearing the same expression as you these days. Trouble in paradise?" She touched Allison's shoulder. "I'm here if you want to talk. I know I'm not your mama, but—"

Allison's bark of laughter cut her off.

"Not hardly! For one thing, you still speak to me." She blinked furiously to keep at bay the tears she had sworn never to shed.

Pauline tugged her to sit by the faux fireplace. "Let me get us some cinnamon tea. I think we need to have a talk."

After they sat down, Allison took a healthy gulp of tea. "My mother and I were never what you'd call close. But she loved Bruce and seemed genuinely happy for me when we married." She heaved a sigh and dabbed at her eyes with a fresh tissue. "I think, if I was honest, I knew I'd made a terrible mistake before the ink was dry on my marriage license.

"I hope you don't think badly of me, but there was another reason I stayed." Glancing up through her lashes, she mumbled. "The sex. I knew I liked sex before we married, but afterward it was like I couldn't get enough. I was like an addict. When Bruce began ridiculing me for my neediness, it just got worse. Soon it was all I could think about.

"Desperate, I decided to get another degree, this one in interior design. I thought maybe I was oversexed because of some latent need for creative expression." She shrugged. "Maybe I was desperate for some positive attention.

"Anyway, Mr. Brighton was nice to me. Kind and funny, sort of like the father I never had."

"Did your daddy die, honey? Or were your parents divorced?"

"Hmmm? Oh, no. He was just unapproachable. All he cared about was work and my mother. I don't even know why they had me. Most of the time it was like they forgot I existed." Unless she counted when they criticized her. "So when Mr. Brighton offered to help me get established in return for being my first client, I was tempted. Looking back, I should have suspected something when Bruce was so supportive about me opening my own business and accepting Mr. Brighton's offer. Things went well for the first few months. But starting a business takes up a lot of time. When I'd get home, Bruce was agitated and picked fights and then wanted more and more aggressive sex to salve his alleged hurt after our inevitable arguments." She finished her cup of tea. "I don't know when he managed to get the pictures or exactly how he got them merged with similar photos of Mr. Brighton." She sniffed and grasped Pauline's hand. "Even I wouldn't have believed I wasn't getting down and dirty with my boss!"

"What happened? Did he use them in your divorce?"

Allison snorted. "I wish it had been that simple. He had an in with a few tabloids who had issues with Mr. Brighton. Next thing I knew, the pictures were plastered all over. There was an investigation. A trial. The Brightons got a divorce. I was named corespondent. Just about that time, Bruce filed on me, too. Mother was inconsolable. I'd brought shame on our entire family. Nothing I said could make her change her mind. When my office was chained shut, pending an investigation of improper business practices, I knew it was over. Everything was over. As soon as my divorce was final, I withdrew the little inheritance my grandmother left me and left town and never looked back."

Two cups of tea and half a box of tissues later, she wiped her eyes, blew her nose one last time and then looked over at Pauline, who had a concerned frown on her perfectly made-up face.

"No offense, honey, but you're so much better off without that slimy Bruce. As that guy who wrote the self-help book is always saying, he just wasn't that into you."

Allison sniffed and managed a weak smile. "Thanks. But the truth is I know I have a sex problem, and I think I just wore him out."

"Horse feathers! No man who loves you—or is *into* you— would get tired of making love with you. It's not in their DNA. And to take all those photos and sell them to the tabloids along with all those lies!" She made a growling sound. "I wish I could get my hands on that creep! How on earth your own mother could believe all that is beyond me."

"Well, who knows how Mom's mind works? As for Bruce, he's now happily married to the CEO's ex-wife. I sometimes wonder if it wasn't a setup from the beginning."

"There's not a doubt in my mind."

Allison sighed and briefly closed her eyes. "What's sad is that Mr. Brighton lost his job, which ultimately led to the demise of my little decorating business. Everyone assumed I got the contracts because I was sleeping with him." She shrugged and opened her eyes. "I guess they thought they'd make an example of me."

"Well," Pauline said, standing and collecting the cups, "it was fate, pure and simple."

"Excuse me?"

"You, Allison Conroe, were destined to come to Flintlock and open this store so you could start a new life. It's as plain as the nose on your face. Now, what are you going to do about my son?"

She stood and took the cups from Pauline's hands. It had been three weeks. If Chris had wanted to see her, he'd had ample opportunity. "Nothing. Chris and I have gone our separate ways. End of story. I just hope, someday, we can be friends."

"Chris doesn't need any more friends. He needs a lover, a soul mate, a partner." His mother cupped her cheek. "He needs you. You're perfect for him. Why can't either of you see that?"

"I don't mean to shock you, Pauline, but all Chris and I had was blistering-hot sex. And then we went our separate ways."

Pauline grinned. "Sex is a good place to start."

13

The rain had let up shortly after she'd sent Pauline home early, but still no customers.

Listlessly dusting a display that did not need dusting, she perked up a little when the door chimed, and she hurried to the front of the store.

Chris stood staring at her, rain dripping from the brim of his Stetson. Damp streaks striped the legs of his jeans. His shirt clung wetly to the contours of his chest.

As much as it stirred her to look at his magnificent body, the sight that clutched her heart was his face.

No smile lines bracketed his expressive mouth or fanned out from his eyes, eyes that looked sad. Lost.

He reached up and took off his hat, swiping at the moisture on his forehead with the back of his chambray-covered forearm.

She inched closer, and when he opened his arms, she ran to him.

His mouth devoured her, crushing her lips to his, his tongue sweeping through her mouth like a marauding vaquero.

Weak with need and something else she refused to name, she leaned into his welcoming warmth.

Without breaking the kiss, he swept her up into his arms and strode to the chairs. After placing her just so, her legs splayed on each arm, he ducked his head beneath her skirt and placed a hot kiss on her cotton-covered center.

She whimpered when he exited her skirt. Wild with need, she knew she'd allow—and welcome!—any and everything he wanted to do to her. Shameless in her desire, it no longer mattered who knew or who witnessed their passion. She wanted him, and she wanted him now.

"Shhh." He held his finger to his lips, kissed it, and then placed it on hers. "Let me take care of a couple of things first. I'll be right back."

Aching, she watched him make short work of turning the CLOSED sign out and pulling down the big shades all around the store. Next he turned off all the lights except the Christmas tree displays, which gave a warm glow to the store.

Finally, finally, he was back.

"I'm wet," he explained as he shucked out of his boots and then the rest of his clothing.

So am I. But she didn't voice her thought. Instead, she enjoyed the slow striptease Chris was putting on for her viewing pleasure.

But when he stood before her, naked, bronzed in the glow of a million or so twinkle lights, and she began to reach for the buttons on the bodice of her jumper, he stopped her.

"If you get naked, too, it will be over before it begins. Let me," he whispered, kneeling between her thighs.

The drag of her panties down the sensitized skin of her legs had her squirming on the padded cushion of the chair.

Torturing her, he removed her knee socks and kissed each of her toes; then he methodically worked his way up each leg, stopping just when things got extremely hot and interesting.

He kissed and licked behind each knee, causing moisture to gather, pressure to build.

Draping her legs once again over the arms of the chair, he disappeared beneath her skirt.

His hot breath fanned the flames. Close. He was so close she could feel the slight stubble of his chin against her eager folds. His tongue lapped at her moisture, his breath adding to the pleasure/torture. His teeth closed around her swollen nub a nanosecond before he sucked it into his mouth.

With a soft whimper, she bowed off the chair, seeking closer contact. Against her recently exfoliated lips, she felt him smile, her clit still firmly between his teeth. He released his hold to blow softly against her, eliciting another half whimper, half moan. His tongue darted out to swirl around her opening.

She arched her hips, hoping to drive his tongue deeper, but to no avail.

Beneath her jumper, his cool hands traveled upward until they cupped her breasts. She gave silent thanks for her decision to go braless that morning.

While he suckled her tender flesh, his hands kneaded her breasts, squeezing her beaded nipples.

The effect was so encompassing, her orgasm hit her, taking her by surprise.

Just as she floated down to earth, he hummed or said something against her opening. The effect was immediate and mind-blowing. Climax number two roared over her with the finesse of a freight train, slamming into her, leaving her breathless and more than a little disoriented.

Chris pulled her clothing over her head and tossed it aside. His mouth latched on to her breast, sucking hard, while his hands played with her still engorged folds and nubbin.

He slid a finger, and then another, into her wetness. Deeply embedded, he wiggled them until climax number three slammed into her.

His mouth covered hers, muffling her scream of release. He trailed kisses to her ear, his breath hot and panting.

"Condom." Pant, pant. "I brought some." Pant, pant. "Hang on." He took forever to extract the foil packages from his discarded jeans. Finally sheathed, his sex probed her.

After not using protection the other times, the cool dryness of the latex chafed a bit, dragging as he entered her.

Her moisture resurged, thankfully, as soon as he flexed his hips, plunging deeper with each thrust. She wrapped her legs around his torso and wiggled her bottom for closer alignment.

Emotion clogged her throat; tears stung her eyes. The enormity of the act, with this particular man, threatened to overwhelm her. Was she falling in love with him?

She squeezed her eyes shut and attempted to blank her mind to anything other than the magical sensation their bodies were creating. Sex. Mind-blowing sex, but just sex. They'd agreed. Hadn't they?

He stood, and sat in the chair, Allison astride his lap. A moan built in the back of his throat. In the current position, he could feel every internal wrinkle and fold, even through the condom.

Damn, he wished he hadn't brought the damn things with him tonight. He much preferred nothing between them. But he knew that wasn't practical. Or safe. They agreed their relationship was strictly sexual.

You don't ache for more closeness in a sexual relationship. And you sure as hell didn't wish you could impregnate your partner. That was just plain crazy.

Wasn't it?

He slowed the pumping of his hips and enjoyed the view of Allison bathed in the lights from the Christmas trees.

He swallowed past the constriction in his throat. She was just so damned beautiful it took his breath away.

Bending to trail kisses over her face, he looked past the top of her head to the Christmas tree, ablaze with decorations and twinkling lights.

Something strange happened: he didn't feel anger at the sight. Or nausea. Just warmth, a general sense of well-being, maybe even peace.

That couldn't be right.

He stood again, clutching her to him, and tossed the Christmas throw from the back of the chair onto the hardwood floor. With care, he lowered them until they lay on the blanket.

Stretched out on the floor, she smiled up at him. Deep within her heat, his dick stirred with renewed interest. This was when they connected best, when neither of them spoke and just let their bodies do the communicating.

His back to the trees, he focused on bringing Allison to another screaming climax.

Her eyelids were heavy as she cuddled up to Chris after her last orgasm. He held her so tightly she could barely breathe, but she wasn't about to complain. She was right where she needed to be.

Should she initiate a conversation? Tell him how she felt when they made love? And she didn't kid herself: what they'd just done was make love, not have sex. It may have taken her twenty-six years, but she finally knew the difference. And, knowing that, how could she ever go back to just sex?

Did she really want to?

She yawned and snuggled against Chris's warm chest. She'd think about it in a few minutes. Right now, she just needed to rest.

Allison awoke with her arm asleep and her right hip aching from being pressed against the hard floor. The coolness surrounding her told her Chris was gone. Again.

He'd covered her with her jumper and shirt, but her chill went bone deep. Nothing had changed between them.

Wrapping the throw around her, she got up and padded to the counter to check the digital clock by the cash register.

Three in the morning. She needed to go home and attempt to get some more sleep if she expected to be back by nine to open the store.

Funny, the thought of coming to work in her own place no longer thrilled her.

14

"Hey, Earl," she said several hours later as she bumped open the door of the barbershop with her hip. She handed the barber a steaming cup of cinnamon tea. "It's still chilly out so I thought I'd run a cup of tea over to you to help warm you up."

"Thank you, missy." He gestured toward the empty barber chairs. "Got time to join me for a while? Shirley finally did her Christmas baking last night, and I brought a big tin of cookies and fudge in with me this morning. It'd be a shame to let it go to waste."

"Sure, why not? Pauline is at the store in case anyone comes in." She'd heard of Earl's wife's baking and was anxious to sample some of it. "Wow!" Her hand hovered over the huge tin he held out. "So many choices! Is that really a gingerbread man? I haven't had one since I was a little girl." She picked up a cookie and took a bite, moaning at the delicious way the ginger melted against her tongue.

Earl popped a couple of Mexican Tea Cakes into his mouth and washed them down with a swig of his tea. He grinned and reached for a piece of fudge. "Yeah, my Shirl's still got the touch in the kitchen." He chewed and swallowed with a smile. "Guess I'll let her stay."

"You big phoney," she chided, picking up a pecan tart. "You wouldn't know what to do without her. How long was it, again, that you two have been married?"

"Thirty-seven years this Christmas."

"Christmas? Really?" Of course, her thoughts flew to Chris and his failed nuptials. "How did that work for you, getting married at Christmas?"

"No problem so far." He winked and then sobered. "Don't think I don't know what you're asking, missy. You heard about Chris's screwed-up wedding, didn't you? Don't deny it. Pauline never could keep her mouth shut for long. You two get along too much for her not to blab." He drained his cup and stood, handing it back to her. "You sell those Christmas cups?" At her nod, he continued, "Pack me up a set, and I'll come pay for them on my way home tonight. Shirley would like them." Apparently as an afterthought, he added, "Women like that kind of crap for some reason."

She stood on tiptoe and kissed his weathered cheek. "You're such a softy."

"Yeah, well, don't spread it around, okay?"

"'Kay." Smiling, she turned to leave.

"Ah, Allison?"

"Hmmm?" She looked over her shoulder.

"You know I've come to love you like the daughter Shirley and I never had, don't you?" When she nodded, he continued. "I'd hate to see you get hurt, so I want you to listen to what I'm about to tell you." He stuffed his hands in the pockets of his coveralls and rocked back on his heels. "Chris MacNeil is damaged. And it goes deeper than just not liking Christmas, believe me. The boy has his reasons, Lord knows, though he'd never admit it." He shuffled and looked at her with sad eyes. "But the truth is, he ain't ever gonna change. It's been too long, and the hurt was too deep. You need to walk away while you still can."

Impulsively she walked back and threw her arms around him to give a quick, hard hug. "Thanks for the warning, Earl, but it's really not necessary. Chris and I aren't together. Never were, really."

"Really?" He squinted down at her. "Then how come his truck was parked in front of your store until all hours? With the shades down? And I have it on good authority he bought a giant economy box of rubbers, too."

She gasped. "How do you know that?"

"This is a small town, missy. News of any kind travels fast. You'd do best to remember that."

"What's wrong? Are you all right?" Pauline hustled to meet Allison as she walked in the door.

No wonder, really, if she looked half as shell-shocked as she felt.

"I just had a . . . very weird conversation with Earl."

"That old fart! What's he saying now?" Pauline turned and fussed with the display of handblown glass ornaments and glanced over her shoulder. "Don't pay any mind to anything that old windbag has to say. I swear, sometimes I think he talks just to hear his head rattle." She gave a little forced-sounding laugh.

"He just reminded me of what a small town Flintlock is and how everybody knows everything."

Pauline slowly turned, a guilty-looking flush on her powdered cheeks. "He mentioned the condom purchase Chris made, did he? Or was it that Chris's truck was parked outside the store all night?"

"Both." Darn Chris MacNeil's hide! "I understand how

small towns are—I watched Andy Griffith reruns, growing up." She grabbed a dust cloth and attacked the counter. "What I don't understand is what Chris was thinking. He grew up here. He had to know people would be watching. And talking."

Pauline shrugged. "Well, in his defense, he did drive over to Purdy for the condoms."

Allison gaped. "How do you know that? Never mind. I don't think I want to know." She grabbed her purse and keys. "I'm going to run home for a while. I have stuff to do. And I should probably bake some more cookies. We may have a rush of last-minute shoppers."

"You're really not from around here, are you?" Pauline asked as Allison left the store.

Allison set the last sheet of oatmeal raisin cookies on the counter and turned off the oven. Glancing around the cramped kitchen, she was surprised to see every surface covered in cookies. Baking had always soothed and calmed her.

But not today.

Listless, she untied her apron. Maybe a shower would cheer her up before she went back to the store.

A knock rattled her front door. Through the frosted, leaded glass, she saw that her visitor was tall and wore a cowboy hat.

Chris?

Cracking the door open, she peeked through to find Chris, hands shoved in the front pockets of his jeans, hat pulled low to shadow his face in the weak illumination from her porch light.

"Chris," she said, shoring up her defenses, "this really isn't a good time. I need to take a quick shower and get back to the store. I promised your mom she could leave early."

The toe of his boot prevented her from closing the door.

"Are you a witch?"

"Excuse me?" She pulled closer around her throat the old robe she'd donned for baking.

"'Cause something's going on, and it feels odd. Weird. Spooky even." He eased his big body through the opening until he stood in the foyer, his chest brushing hers. "The only possible conclusion I can come up with is you've put some kind of spell on me." He dragged the tip of his finger along the opening of her robe, setting off goose bumps and hardening her nipples. "It's the only logical explanation of why I can't get enough of you."

He bent to kiss her gaping mouth, his tongue sweeping her mouth until she responded.

"I—" She attempted to speak against his mouth while her arms circled his neck, pulling him closer.

"Shhh, let's not talk. It's better when we let our bodies do the talking, darlin'."

He reached back and turned the lock and then swooped her up into his arms and kissed her thoroughly as he walked past the bedroom and into the bathroom. While the shower warmed up, he shucked out of his boots and clothes.

Numb, she stood watching the show. Any second now she'd tell him to get out. She'd tell him she had no intention of showering with him or having sex again. She'd let him know in no uncertain terms that she was no longer interested in being a sex object, and if that's all he could offer her, he could just pick up his clothes and move on.

In a minute.

For now, she was rooted to the spot, transfixed by the unveiling of the most perfect male body she'd ever had the privilege to see. Not to mention kiss, fondle and stroke. Not that she was going to do that now. Well, maybe just a little touch. . . .

Chris vibrated with need, just watching Allison watch him. He'd only been half joking about being under her spell. Why else would he continue to want someone who was so into Christmas?

His mother had moved on. Yet every time he'd tried to do it, fate had slapped him back down. And here he was, about to make love with a woman who made it clear she was using him for his body, about to set aside all his misgivings. Again.

15

Allison flopped over on the sheets and dragged air into her starving lungs. Their wet bodies were getting the sheets damp, but she was beyond caring. When Chris brought her to screaming release after screaming release in the shower, she may have even spoken in tongues. Was it possible to die from sheer bliss?

Beside her, Chris heaved air in and out, his efforts vibrating her mattress.

When she could finally speak, she drew a shaky breath and said, "Wow."

Chris's chuckle jiggled the mattress, causing warmth to circle her heart.

"Yep," he drawled. "I aim to please."

She rolled to her side, clutching a towel to her in a show of false modesty, and drew a light pattern on his heaving chest. "And your aim was perfect," she said with a laugh. "But now I really do have to get dressed and go back to work."

Before he could touch her again and make her forget everything but the feel of him against her, in her, she jumped up and wrapped her robe around her and then flipped on the ceiling light.

Chris groaned and covered his eyes with his arm.

Her gaze took a leisurely tour from his big feet up his strong legs to his equally impressive package. Afraid to linger on that vicinity too long, she continued up washboard abs to firm pecs, a strong throat and a mouth that made her weak in the knees.

"I mean it," she said, more to remind herself than him, and then she disappeared into the bathroom.

When she came out a few minutes later, fully dressed in her favorite Christmas sweatsuit, he was gone.

Just as she opened her mouth to call to him, she heard the rumble of his truck as he backed down her driveway.

She wasn't disappointed, she thought, stacking cookies in her carryall box. In fact, she was even sort of relieved. The town gossip mill would have made a bigger deal out of it than it really was. They'd made the right decision to cool things off.

Memories of the ecstasy Chris's tongue, hands and talented body had given her mere minutes before had a wave of heat washing over her.

Maybe it was her first hot flash.

It sure as heck wasn't love.

The evening dragged by after Pauline left. Allison washed the glass on the display case, vacuumed the area rugs and dust mopped the floors. It took twenty minutes.

Feeling sorry for herself, she sat and ate gingerbread cookies until she felt more than a little nauseous.

The door chimed, but she didn't bother looking up. Maybe whoever it was would just leave so she could make some cocoa and start closing up.

"I found peppermint flavored." Chris's excited voice broke through her melancholy. He strode over and flipped the BE BACK SOON sign and then the lock on the door.

Her pulse quickened at the thought of why he was locking the door. Maybe he'd missed her as much as she'd missed him.

"Peppermint-flavored what?"

Smiling, he crooked his finger and walked into the stockroom.

She followed and got her answer within seconds. Chris leaned against the packing table, his jeans and boxers bunched around his boots. He pointed to his erection. His *candy-cane-striped* erection.

"They had a novelty display at the gas station outside of town," he explained. "These are supposed to taste like candy canes. 'Course, I thought of you, since you like Christmas so much and all."

She regarded him through heavy-lidded eyes, her mouth already watering. And it wasn't necessarily for candy canes.

Dropping to her knees, she barely noticed the hardness of the plank floor. Her attention was focused on a hardness of another kind.

Tentatively she drew a circle with the tip of her tongue around the bulbous, striped head. Yep. Definitely peppermint. She swirled her tongue over and around again, this time taking him deeper into her mouth.

The smell of peppermint wafted to clear her sinuses and make her eyes water a little.

She glanced up at Chris's rapturous expression. It was so worth it.

While sucking greedily, she ran her hands up his inner legs to play with his testicles. He immediately rewarded her with increased pumping of his hips.

She sucked harder.

He pumped faster and deeper.

She gagged.

Before she could recover, he pulled her up, shoving her sweatpants and panties down, one of his hands wedging her legs apart.

He gave a grunt of satisfaction at her moisture, taking a second to smooth and pet her before laying her over the packing table on her stomach.

Aligning himself with her opening, he leaned over and said in her ear, "Merry Christmas, Christmas Lady!" and plunged into her to the hilt.

"Ho," he said, thrusting deep and hard, "ho," another thrust took him incredibly deeper still, the tip of him touching her uterus to set off sensations of pleasurable aches, "ho!"

The last "ho" was yelled with enough exuberance to rattle the glassware in the stockroom.

Behind her, he shuddered his release. But instead of collapsing on her back to warm her, he withdrew his heat.

Spent, she could only lay on the cold tabletop, the cooler air of the room chilling her wetness. Behind her, the unmistakable sound of jeans being tugged up and zipped sounded.

Her muscles felt like Jell-O. Maybe Chris would help her out by pulling her clothing back up her sexually induced comatose body.

Instead, he nipped each of the cheeks of her buttocks, tenderly kissed her pussy . . . and left?

She lay across the table for several beats after the chimes sounded, signaling his departure.

A tear trickled onto the table surface. Chris didn't care about her. He sure as hell didn't love her. Tonight's activities proved all she'd ever be to him was a convenient sex partner. There was a time she would have agreed to that.

But not now.

Tugging her pants up, she walked out to the front to begin closing for the night.

She'd just finished the bank deposit when the door chimed again. She frowned and looked up to tell whoever it was that she was closed.

Sheila, one of the waitresses from the Roadkill Café, stood in the middle of the store, her pink uniform looking less than fresh after a long day at the diner.

"Sorry, Sheila, I'm closed. Unless you know exactly what you want and can pay by credit card, you'll have to just come back tomorrow."

For a few minutes, the waitress didn't answer as she walked around the store, touching delicate items until it was all Allison could do to refrain from telling her not to touch the displays.

"Sheila? Were you looking for something in particular?" Uneasy, she silently closed the cash drawer and turned the key and then slid it into her pocket.

The woman regarded her, then said, "Yeah, you could say that." She strolled to the counter. "I came to give you a piece of advice."

In response, Allison raised her eyebrow.

"You need to stay clear of Chris MacNeil." She ran her hands up her torso until she cupped her gigantic breasts. She shoved them up until they threatened to escape her uniform. "Like my titties? Got 'em last year. For Christmas. They're about the only thing Chris likes about Christmas, if you know what I mean." She leaned closer and said in a conspiratorial whisper, "He just loves to play with them and, lordy, he could suck on them all night long if I'd let him."

Heat seared Allison's cheeks.

Sheila grinned and took a step back. "I bet you didn't know he's been diddling both of us, did you? No, I can tell by your face he never said a word. By the way, he really loves to have his cock sucked—oh, but I guess you already know that, don't you?" She patted Allison's hand. "That's okay, sugar. I don't mind sharing. For now."

"So that's why you're here?" Allison barely managed to speak above a horrified whisper.

"Naw, I thought we needed to have a little heart-to-heart.

What's that fancy word they always use? Teat and teat?" She giggled. "Sounds kind of kinky, doesn't it?" Her eyes widened. "Hey! Are you interested in a threesome?"

"No!" In another life, possibly, but now she found the idea of sharing Chris, even for an evening, repulsive.

Sheila nodded and popped a piece of gum in her mouth. "That's okay. I understand." She walked to the door and then turned around. "I just wanted you to know you're wasting your time on Chris if you think he'll ever make a commitment."

"What makes you think so?" She gripped the counter so hard her knuckles turned white. Blood pounded in her ears.

Sheila laughed. "'Cause he's not the commitment kind. Maybe never was. He could never trust anyone to get that close." She snapped her fingers. "Hey! How about we test that? I can see by the look on your face you want me to leave, right?"

Allison nodded, her teeth clenched.

"You really think Chris trusts you like that?"

She hoped, but again she nodded.

"Okay, answer me this. What is his full name?" She laughed at the continued silence. "That's what I thought."

The door chimed at her exit, and Allison ran to throw the bolt home.

16

Pauline raced into the store the next afternoon. "What in tarnation is wrong with you, young lady?"

Allison looked up from her paperwork.

"I heard you put the Happy Holidays Boutique on the market. Without even mentioning it to me! That true?"

"You know it is." Her shoulders slumped. "Let's face it, Pauline, the store isn't making it. And neither am I. It's time to cut my losses."

"Never figured you for a quitter."

"Stop it. You know I'm not a quitter. Well, not usually, anyway." She turned off the calculator and sighed. "I'm just tired. Tired of beating my head against the wall, hoping the town will accept an outsider. Tired of being the brunt of jokes. Tired of worrying if I will make enough money to pay my bills." Tired of loving a man who, according to popular belief, would never love her back.

"What can I do to help?" Pauline laid her hand over Allison's on the counter. "How about working for free? Would that help?"

Allison's derisive laughter sounded unnaturally loud in the empty store. "Hardly! Pauline, the amount I pay you would barely cause a ripple in the ocean of debt I'm drowning in. Besides," she said, squeezing the other woman's hand, "you're worth every penny." Her throat clogged. "I don't know what I would have done without you the last month."

Both women wiped their eyes.

"Well, there must be something," Pauline declared.

Did she dare ask? What the heck. Maybe Sheila was wrong. "What is Chris's name?"

Pauline laughed and avoided eye contact. "Why, you know his name! Chris MacNeil." She began fidgeting with the Christmas throw folded on the display case, smoothing imaginary wrinkles. "Why?"

"Someone mentioned not knowing his full name, and I realized I didn't know it either. What's his middle name?"

Pauline smiled. "Everybody knows that. It's my maiden name."

At that moment, the chimes sounded, announcing their first customer.

Possibly their last, given the way business was going.

"You think if you stare long enough, it will change?" Sam's voice rumbled behind Chris as he stood looking out at the barn.

"No." He turned to regard Sam and wondered when he had turned so gray. "I was just thinking how much I hate chores." He shook his head and laughed. "Almost as much as I did as a kid."

Sam chuckled. "That's a lot, if I recall." He narrowed his eyes. "Why do you stay?"

Chris shrugged. "At first, I was busy growing up. After college, I thought Mom would need me here. Then, after my, ah, wedding went down the way it did . . . I guess it was just easier to stay."

"And what do you want to do now?" Sam's voice was low, his eyes piercing, shoulders set.

"I want to move on. Maybe get married." He grinned. "Someday make my kids miserable by making them do chores."

Sam nodded, a slight smile curving his mustache. "Sounds like a good plan. Got anyone in particular you might want to marry?"

Allison's smiling face flashed through Chris's memory. "Yeah, you know, I think I do."

"If it's that Christmas gal you been carrying on with, I suggest you get a move on."

Had Allison been seen with someone else? "Why's that?" he asked, his breath on hold.

"Heard she's put the store up for sale and is plannin' to close by the end of the week. Fliers are already up all over the square, advertising her going-out-of-business sale."

Of course Chris wouldn't have seen them, since he'd been avoiding Allison of late.

"I'll see you later, Sam." He strode to his truck and revved the engine.

Damn her hide! How could she turn him inside out the way she did and then just up and sell out without even saying a word to him?

He took the turn into town on two wheels. Once he was face-to-face, he'd know what to say, what to do, to convince her to stay.

17

"Earl, this really isn't necessary." Allison paused with her pen poised above the document to blend her store with the barbershop. "I'll find a buyer soon."

"Missy, it is too necessary. Why, I'll have you know we're cramped up like sardines most of the time over there." He nudged her hand closer to the signature line. "It'd make my life a whole lot easier to get a little elbow room. Besides," he added in a choked-sounding voice once she'd signed, "I don't want just anybody in here. And I figure all this cinnamon smell would be a nice addition to my musty old shop."

"You want me to leave all the potpourri?"

"Why not?" he shot back.

She bussed his cheek. "Thank you, Earl."

"Now don't go getting all girlie on me, missy. This is a business deal, pure and simple. Buyin' your store is a good deal for both of us."

Behind him, Pauline sniffed, blotting her eyes with a wad of tissues.

The door chimed, drawing their attention.

Chris stood, framed by the afternoon sunlight spilling in from the square, his hair burnished gold.

He and Allison stood, looking at each other.

"C'mon, Pauline," Earl said, taking her elbow in his hand. "Let me buy you a soda."

Neither Chris nor Allison spoke until they were alone.

"Why didn't you tell me you were planning to close the store?"

"Why should I?" She made a production of straightening the stacks of tablecloths she was sending back to the vendor. "You made it perfectly clear, right from the beginning, how you felt about it."

Chris grumbled something.

"What did you say?"

"I said maybe I've changed my mind." His narrowed gaze met hers. "Maybe it's not as bad as I thought." He glanced over to the spot they'd made love. "I have some mighty fond memories of this store, in fact."

"No one is taking away your memories, Chris." She walked into the back and placed the tablecloths into a packing crate, Chris right on her heels.

"Well, what if I'm not done making memories here? You ever think about that?"

She turned, hands on hips. "Well, Earl just bought it. You can add to your memories every time you get your hair cut."

He grabbed her elbow when she began to turn away, pulling her to face him. "But you won't be here," he said in a strangled voice. "It won't be the same."

"What are you saying, Chris? That you want me to stay? That you love me? You're going to have to spell it out, because I'm not getting the message. I—"

His mouth covered hers with a kiss so deep, so carnal, it curled her toes.

Desperate for his taste, his touch, even if only for one more time, she put her arms around him, rubbing against his hard body.

Cool air brushing her legs barely registered before Chris pulled her baggy stock-shipping dress over her head and away, its jingle bells chinging all the way to the floor on the other side of the room. Her holly-sprigged panties soon followed.

He gave a low groan, looking down at her nakedness, while he jerked at his fly until he was free. He shoved his clothing down his lean hips and grabbed her waist.

The hot tip of his penis plunged into her welcoming moisture, eliciting a comingled groan. Immediately his hips began bucking.

She crossed her ankles at the small of his back, loving the skin-on-skin contact, and held on, enjoying the ride.

The sound of grunting and the distinctive slap of skin against skin filled the little stockroom.

He staggered to the wall, slamming her back against the cool plaster, his hands holding her poised above him for maximum thrust potential. And he definitely lived up to his potential.

She didn't even try to stop her scream of release. She was leaving town, anyway. Who cared if she went out with a big bang, literally?

Hard on the heels of the first release, a second thundered up her spine, gripping her in its strength, not easing until it had wrung the very breath from her lungs.

She hung, impaled on him, too weak to move or speak. She knew he'd avoided answering her questions with hot sex. She would smack him for it, but she couldn't make a fist at the moment. Besides, it felt so good, she really didn't mind.

And it was important she store up as many memories of him as she could for the bleak years that lay before her.

Tears prickled her eyelids at the thought.

Chris chose that moment to suckle her breast. Immediately her visit from Sheila came to mind, stiffening her spine.

Reaching between them, she detached his mouth from her aching breast, gently pushing him back, but careful to not sever their intimate connection. She wasn't ready yet.

"Chris." She put her finger beneath his chin. "I'm up here. Look at me. I need to ask you a question."

He made a move to withdraw from her needy body. She tightened her legs. "Don't. Not yet. Please."

He cocked his head, waiting.

"Have you been sleeping with Sheila while we've been together? Tell me the truth. I mean, it's not like we had anything exclusive, but . . . well, did you?"

"Nope." He met her gaze. "You're the only woman I've been with since way before you came to town."

Her breath caught when his sex stirred, deep within her, and he grinned down at her.

"I told you, I think you put a curse on me." He leaned to nuzzle her neck, his hips beginning a slow rotation that had her wiggling for closer contact.

She arched her back, allowing greater access to her neck and for him to massage her breasts, her head resting against the wall. "So," she said in a halting whisper, "you've never, um, had sex with her?"

He stopped. " 'Course I fucked her. Just about every guy in these parts, from eighteen to eighty, has." He frowned. "Except maybe Sam. He's always had the hots for my mom, I guess."

In direct opposition to her desire, she broke contact and let her feet slide to the ground; then she reached for her dress. "I see."

He grabbed her wrist. "No, I don't think you do." He tweaked her nipple, causing it to stiffen into an obedient peak. "Don't go."

Maybe if she told him all about her sordid past, he would come clean with whatever it was he was hiding.

"When you hear about how I came to live in Flintlock, you

may not care if I go," she said in a watery voice, clutching her dress to her chest.

He brushed a strand of hair from her eyes and stroked her cheek. "Allison, darlin', we all have a past. I already know yours. Mom told me. You lost your business in Houston because your were set up by that rat-bastard ex-husband of yours, and even your own mother didn't believe in you. That pretty much sum it up?" He bent his knees to gaze into her eyes, the tenderness there making fresh tears sting the backs of her eyelids. "Unless there's more?"

"No, I think I pretty much covered it all with Pauline."

"But you didn't do any of those things, did you?"

"No. But I told you, I suspect I have a sex addiction."

"Bullshit."

"No, I—"

"Who, besides me, have you had sex with in Flintlock?"

"No one, but—"

He pulled her into his arms, running his hands over the skin on her hips, gripping her buttocks. "Doesn't sound like much of an addiction to me. Stay."

Blinking back tears, she pulled away and slipped on her dress. "I can't. I have to go, Chris, I just have to."

Give me a reason to stay, she silently pleaded. *Tell me I mean more to you than a convenient sex partner.*

His silence spoke volumes.

18

Chris jerked his pants up and stalked from the Happy Holidays Boutique without a backward glance.

Humiliation stung his cheeks and burned his eyes. He revved his engine and popped the clutch, squealing the tires as he backed onto the square and peeled away.

He blinked in an effort to clear his blurred vision. What a fool he'd been. Needy. He'd been needy. And lonely and vulnerable. That's how he'd played right into her hands, how she'd forced him to fall in love with her.

He slammed his fist against the steering wheel. He'd sworn never to let this happen again.

He downshifted at the turn for home and squealed through the gate. He got over it once; he could do it again.

In the kitchen, he rummaged around for the bottle of Kentucky Bourbon in the back of the corner cabinet. Not bothering with a glass, he tilted it up, eyes continuing to run from the strong alcohol, nothing more.

"There're glasses, you know." Sam's voice rumbled right before the kitchen light flipped on to temporarily blind Chris.

He quickly wiped his eyes and mouth with the back of his hand. "Don't want one." Damn, what was wrong with his voice?

Sam walked closer, dressed in nothing but a pair of unbuttoned jeans as far as Chris could tell. Since the foreman had walked from the direction of Pauline's room, it didn't take a genius to figure out what had been going on before his arrival.

"Your mother was worried. You weren't answering your phone." Sam gently pried the bottle from Chris's hand and set it on the table. "That won't help, you know."

Chris shrugged. "Won't hurt. Nothing else to do, anyway."

"I'm gonna take a huge leap here and assume this is about Allison Conroe closing up shop and leaving town. Your mother's all shook up about it, too."

"Allison's a grown woman; she has the right to do whatever she wants." He reached for the whiskey again, but Sam's hand stopped him from lifting it to his lips.

"Bottom line: do you love her?"

Miserable, Chris nodded.

"Then tell her. Don't be as damn stubborn as I was and let your life slide by while you wallow in it. Tell her! Go on. Tell her now."

"But I—"

"She's leaving, you know. Tonight. If you hightail it to her house, you may have time to stop her."

Allison heard the rumble of a truck but refused to look out the window. The disappointment would be too great. It wasn't Chris, and she really didn't want to see anyone else. Mom was right. Moving to Flintlock was a mistake.

But, she reasoned, at least now she knew. She knew she could run a business on her own. Next time, she'd make sure she chose a place with more foot traffic. She knew she could make it alone. And she also now knew what true love was and would never settle for less. If that meant spending the rest of her days alone, so be it. She picked up her suitcase and took a last look around.

The rattle of the knob on her front door preceded the loud banging.

"Allison!" Chris's voice boomed with enough force to rattle the windows. "Open up."

Dropping her suitcase, she stomped to the door, throwing it open wide. "Do you mind? You're going to wake up the whole town."

He grinned and stepped into the foyer.

She stepped back, allowing him to close the door, and willed her heart to slow down while she drank in the sight of him.

His hair was messed and in need of a haircut. The guy seemed to always need a trim. Broad shoulders, clad in a soft plaid flannel, looked strong and dependable, able to carry any burden.

Only, he carried a burden he refused to share.

"You don't have to leave," he said, hands stuffed in his front pockets.

"Yes," she said around the tears choking her. "I do."

"I thought we had a good thing going on," he said in a sullen voice. "Why do you want to up and leave and ruin it?"

Dabbing at her eyes with a tissue from the end table, she busied herself with double-checking to make sure she hadn't missed anything.

"I asked you a question," he grumbled when she walked back into the room. "The least you could do is answer me."

"Okay. Here's your answer." She picked up her suitcase and opened the door. "I decided maybe I wanted, no, I *deserved* more than sex. You, obviously, have not. And you refuse to open up to me, even after I told you all about my past." She shook her head and stepped out onto the porch. "I don't blame you, Chris. Not really. I just realized everybody was right about you. You're not capable of anything more." She pulled the door shut behind him and locked it, tucking the key under the mat. "I am. And I intend to find it. Good-bye, Chris."

Praying the tears would hold off until she was safely in her car, she concentrated on placing one foot in front of the other.

"Wait! Allison, wait!" He caught up with her, grabbing her arm, and then turned her to face him. He took a deep breath. "Okay. You win."

"I win?"

He nodded and smiled.

"What did I win, Chris?"

"I love you. I swore I wouldn't say that to another woman ever again. But you won. I said it. Now will you stop all this nonsense and stay?"

In reply, she drew back and smacked him in the shoulder with her suitcase. The surprising strength of the blow knocked him to his butt on the dusty driveway.

She proceeded to hop in her little red car, started the engine and drove away.

He rubbed his shoulder and watched until her taillights disappeared; then he got to his feet and slowly walked to the car. She'd be back. He'd just wait in his truck so he'd be available for make-up sex.

Two hours later, he admitted defeat and started his engine. Allison had left in the same direction as his house. Maybe she'd be there, talking to his mom, when he got home.

Considerably brighter, he headed down the road.

At the last run before home, a taillight reflected his high beams.

Allison's little car sat by the side of the road. But where was she?

He braked and slid to a stop in the gravel behind her car. Almost before the truck rolled to a complete stop, he jumped out, looking for Allison.

He found her at the front of her car, sitting on her suitcase on the gravel shoulder. Crying.

His heart clenched with each heartbroken sob. Damn. Bad enough the love of his life ran a Christmas shop, did she have to be a crier, too?

She gave a hiccupping sob, and he realized it didn't matter. He loved her. And he didn't want to go even one more day without her. Hell, if it would make her happy and help her stop crying, she could open a hundred Christmas stores.

"Allison? Honey? Are you all right?" He squatted by her side and took her cold little hands in his, rubbing his warmth into them.

By the light of his truck, he saw the tears swimming in her pretty blue eyes.

"I—I may never be all right again." She sniffed.

"Stay," he urged in a choked whisper, "and we'll make it all right. I swear."

She shook her head, curls bobbing. "No," she whispered. "I can't."

What was that saying? If you loved someone, let them go? Damn, that was a hard one, but he'd do it.

"Sweetheart, please stop crying. Did your car run out of gas? Stall? Whatever it is, I'll take care of it. Or I'll drive you to wherever you want to go, if you'll only stop crying. Telling me you love me might be a nice touch, too."

For some reason, that made her cry all the more.

"There's n—nothing wrong with my c—car," she finally choked out. "I just realized I don't have anywhere to go, even if I wanted to leave."

"Hush, hush," he crooned, arms around her, rocking her. "I don't want you to leave either. Let me drive you home, and we can come back for your car in the morning. Things will be better in the morning."

She nodded and let him help her up and walk her to his

truck. After he'd thrown her suitcase into the back and climbed in, she sniffed and said, "Chris?"

He paused in starting the engine. "Hmmm?"

"I love you, too, you know."

He grinned, the weight in his chest easing, and pulled her to him. "'Course I knew it. What's not to love?" Before she could smack him again he gave her a quick kiss. He had never planned to say the words again, but found them falling out of his mouth. "Will you marry me?" At her shocked look, he hurried on. "You don't have to answer right away. Think about it a while. I—"

She placed her fingers on his lips, her skin cool against his heat. "Shhh. There is no way I can marry you. Not unless you're willing to tell me everything. No more secrets."

"You already know everything. Everything but . . ." Head hanging, he dug his wallet out of his back pocket, holding it just out of her reach. "If you read my driver's license, you have to marry me."

"I can live with that." She smiled up at him and snatched his wallet, holding it close to the dash to see the small print.

Her peals of laughter rang in the cab.

Jaw clenched, he tucked the wallet back in his pocket. "It's not funny. Bad enough being born on Christmas Day. My father was a cruel man with a sick sense of humor. But, in his defense, the middle name was actually my mother's maiden name."

She wiped her eyes and grinned over at him. "I think it's sweet. Christmas Snow MacNeil." She slid the rest of the way over until she was half sitting on his lap, her free hand tucked snuggly against his happy cock. "I knew there was some reason I've always been hot for Christmas."

He pulled her tight against him, kissing her until they both experienced altered breathing. "Yep," he said against her lips. "I guess it was fate after all."

Cabin Fever

MELISSA MacNEAL

1

"*Ohhhh, the weather outside is frightful!*"

"Oh, shut up!" Norah muttered at the radio, gripping the wheel harder. She squinted at the white road ahead of her between weak, squeaky swishes of wipers weighed down by eyebrows of wet snow. If she heard one more too-cheerful verse about corn for popping and the snow not stopping, she'd scream. She didn't dare look away from the road long enough to turn the damned radio off.

"*Let it snow, let it snow, let it snow!*"

"Shit! Oh, my God—"

The car swerved in a direction all its own—diagonal, mostly. Good thing no one else was on the road to run into. But then, since she'd probably already missed her turn-off, the sight of another car might be a sign she hadn't totally left civilization. It was way too late now to turn back for home. And those little kids at the homeless shelter were counting on her to bring—

Her cell phone tinkled the first notes of "Angels We Have Heard on High."

"Forget it!" she snapped. She exhaled loudly when the car finally stopped sliding, but where the hell was she? The Wyoming countryside was a deep blue void, accented with heavy white flakes that taunted her in the beam of her one remaining headlight. She tugged her beaded halo back from her forehead.

Again the phone trilled. *Angels we have heard*—

Norah grabbed it. The number on her screen made her scowl, but she might as well deal with him now, while she wasn't sliding.

"What?" she rasped. "I told you I'd be there by—"

"Are you out there in this storm?" His reptilian voice slithered into her ear. "Stupid move, Miss Dalton. If you don't make it back by—"

"I'll be there, dammit! Don't you dare touch my stuff!"

"Ah, but beggars can't be choosers, can they?" he replied in an oily tone. "I have gifts to buy. Bills to pay. You can't expect me to float you—"

Click. She tossed the phone back into the passenger seat, knowing it was her own throat she'd slit . . . knowing there was no way, come hell or hallelujah, that she'd make it back to her apartment tonight, much less to the homeless shelter for the Christmas pageant and party. The red digits on the dashboard mocked her: 8:13. Already late for her entry with Santa—if indeed the Man in Red had made it there through this storm.

Norah's throat tightened around a sob, and for the gazillionth time she straightened her homemade halo. If she sat here much longer she'd be stuck out on this godforsaken road for sure.

Cautiously she eased her foot against the gas pedal. . . . Creeping . . . creeping . . . caught sight of an intersection— maybe her turn-off?—and hope flared anew. Taking the short-cut through the countryside had been a major mistake, but up ahead she saw the lighted window of a cabin. Maybe she could ask for directions or—

The cell phone jangled again. *Angels we have heard—*

Norah clenched her jaw as she inched the car around the snow-clogged corner. Leon Scurtz could screw himself. Was no doubt fondling his crotch anyway, at the prospect of—

"No—no! Oh, *shit!*" Norah cranked the wheel frantically—did you turn into a skid or away from it?—as the old Grand Prix's back end just kept making the circle after she'd turned at the intersection. Powerless to steer it—too damn scared to watch the tilt-a-whirl of the snowy nightscape—she gave it more gas.

And for just a moment the car righted itself. She shot forward down the road toward that lone, lighted house.

Angels we have heard—

"Get out of my life!" she cried.

And when the car started to spin in another lazy, surrealistic circle, she held her breath and held on to—

Whump. Her breath left her in a gust when the car stopped. It didn't sound good.

"Let it snow! Let it snow! Let it—"

She jabbed the radio button and then sobbed with all the pent-up frustration of this past half hour. "Oh, fine! Now I'm off in the frickin' ditch, and I don't know where—"

Again the phone chimed to life. *Angels we have heard—*

"Yeah, well hear *this!*" she cried into it. "I've just gone off the road, so you're gonna have to keep your pants on, got it? I told you I'd be there, and I *will* show up—"

"Ah, but will you be able to unlock your door by then, Miss Dalton?" came Leon's edgy question. "You know our arrangement, little lady. And you've passed the eleventh hour—"

Norah yanked her keys from the ignition. Ignoring the *ding-ding-ding* warning about her lights being on, she shoved her door open, upward. Propelled by her wrath, she got out of the car, which was sitting off the edge of the snowy road at a crazy tilt. Her single headlight sent a sickly ray across the road, illuminating the flake-filled sky.

She swiped angrily at her tears. How had her entire life gone to hell so fast? Ever since Alex had disappeared with the entire inventory of their shop, she'd endured one damn thing after another: lost her income, couldn't pay her rent, and now she was stuck out in the boonies in this storm. Well, by God, it was coming to a halt!

Had come to a halt. And now she was lost on this snowy road to nowhere, getting evicted from the rat hole she'd called home. Sighing tiredly, she put her phone to her ear.

Leon cleared his throat, a sound that always promised more crap to come. "Since it's so close to Christmas, I suppose the Christian thing to do would be to come and fetch your sweet little ass in my four-wheel drive—"

"Even if I knew where I was, I wouldn't tell *you!*" she shrieked. And, so the damn thing wouldn't ring again, she threw the phone into the open car. It hit the dashboard with a satisfying *whack*. Then she slammed the driver's-side door to stop that damn *ding-ding-ding*.

Silence.

The muffled hush of a winter's night. The whisper of snow drifting across the road.

Norah shivered, scared out of her mind. Pissed at herself for thinking she could beat this storm to the homeless shelter . . . where she might be taking up residence anyway, right?

Swallowing hard, up past her ankles in wet, heavy slush that had soaked through her shoes, she focused on that single square of light across the road.

What if they didn't let her in?

And if they did, what if they, too, took advantage of her disadvantaged state? Out here in this vast pasture land, there was no telling what might happen to her . . . when she might be seen or heard from again, if some drunked-up ranch hand with a mean streak met her at that door.

The wind hissed around her, cutting through her flimsy costume like knives of ice. Sighing heavily, she straightened her halo again. Then she trotted toward that isolated house, praying for something good to come of this gawdawful night.

Danny Black grimaced with another swig of his whiskey. What the hell was that light shining in his eyes? Was the TV on the blink, or was he so fuckin' drunk he was going blind?

He focused on the porn flick again, watching two chicks in black leather outfits circle each other, sniffing like bitches in heat. The one with the spiked hair and the tattoo on her ass was making him hard, and as he tipped the bottle to his lips again he imagined ramming himself beneath those lush half moons she was wagging at him.

Whump.

He blinked into that faint beam of light, frowning. Nobody on the tube had taken a tumble, and there wasn't a fool on the face of the earth stupid enough to be out driving tonight. But curiosity got the best of him, so Danny stood up and stared out the window. Cold as it was, he should shut the drapes, but these days he didn't really give a damn about energy efficiency or—

For a second he swore he saw an angel out on the road. She was flying toward him—had a halo and wings, no less! Then the light blinked out.

Or had he died and gotten a glimpse of heaven before falling the other way?

Leaning his forehead on the cold glass, Black stared out into the storm. If that was an angel, maybe it was Mariel coming back to haunt him. Like those three spooks in the Scrooge story.

Danny's heart skittered, and he clenched his eyes against her image. Took another long chug of Gentleman Jack. He'd spent the six months since her death pretending he could run this ranch without her—had told Chico and the other hands to vamoose this week, so he could wallow in his grief, here in Chico's place, without them watching. Without turning everyone's Christmas into a pity party.

So if Mariel was out there trying to scare some sense into him tonight—telling him to get a life or to let her kids take the place—

But, no. His wife wasn't blond. Or skinny. And she wouldn't be caught, well, *dead* wearing a silly-ass halo that sparkled with sequins and beads and tipped to one side over a lopsided smile—

Nightie. Lace nightie with a string bikini under it.

Frantically he wiped the fog of his breath from the glass. Damned if she didn't wave back at him. She was shivering, pounding on his door. "Please, mister! Sorry to bother you, but—"

Danny shook himself. He wasn't hallucinating—some blonde tricked out as an angel was out there freezing her nubs off! Stumbling over the duffel he'd dropped when he got there, Danny hauled open the door. She squinted when the light hit her, skinny and shivering and, yes, that was the flimsiest nightgown he'd ever seen.

"Where the hell's your coat, little gurrrrl?" he slurred. When she winced, he was sorry he'd snapped at her, but Jesus! Anybody out in a nightie on a night like this was too stupid to live!

"It—it's in the car because—it didn't fit over my wings, and—" she wheezed, "and when my car—well, I slid off the road over there—"

She was pointing, but all he noticed was the way those boobs made that bikini sparkle when she moved. Then he saw those feathery wings quivering in the wind, and the cold sobered him up some.

"Here, come on in—"

She yelped and drew back when he grabbed her wrist.

Danny sucked air, willing himself to see just *one* of her, so he could get his head on straight. He was hot and horny, and here was this blond angel at his door, and he'd already scared her— and then scared himself at how far he'd fallen.

Moving on fumes, he stepped aside and gestured for her to enter. Where were his manners? Mariel would expect him to act like a gentleman and let this poor Christmas angel inside to warm herself by his fire while he hauled her car from the ditch.

But Mariel's not here, is she?

Danny suddenly felt like the big, bad-ass wolf greeting Goldilocks. As the blonde stepped gingerly past him, her white nightie clinging wetly to the length of her body, his grin became a leer. He was all but licking his chops.

Of *course* he'd haul her car out of the ditch, before she could even ask. And then she'd owe him a really big favor, wouldn't she?

2

Norah got caught like a deer in his headlight gaze and saw it all: lust and hunger. Desperation and despair. *Need.* The need to come out on top after a long, long struggle.

The fact that she instantly knew so much about this stranger shocked her, but it shocked her even more that his situation was the mirror image of her own. His fumes nearly knocked her over. And it took more than a high-dollar bottle to wash away his low-life intentions, didn't it?

No sense in kidding herself about why his zipper was ready to split. She looked quickly back into his eyes, hoping he hadn't noticed she'd noticed.

Those eyes . . . so devilishly dark, and so damned *familiar.* A lock of straight blue-black hair dangled down his forehead, and when his coffee-colored face tightened, the stubble along his jaw made her insides clench. He was long and lean, with a hip cocked and a thumb hooked in the loop of beltless jeans that came just below his waist. Where his black shirt gaped open, a heavy chain made a vee down his chest, and an ornate iron cross dared her to believe in his saints and angels despite his wicked gaze. He looked like the morning after a helluva drunk, yet Norah licked her lips before she could catch herself.

"Hungry?" he breathed.

She shook her head vehemently, knowing exactly what he could see through her flimsy costume. Knowing exactly what he must be thinking of her.

One brow arched like a raven's wing. "No?" he teased before tipping that whiskey to his lush . . . very kissable lips. "My mistake, maybe, but I'm sayin' you ain't no angel, honey."

"So?" she bleated. "You're not, either, or you'd be offering to . . . oh, my God. Oh, my God, you're Danny Diablo! The bull rider!"

He grimaced and then wiped it roughly away with his shirt sleeve. "Sorry, but you're mistaking me for—"

"No way! I had your posters plastered all over my room when I was—"

"—*somebody else*," he snarled, leaning closer to drive his point home. Then his lips twitched. "Don't feel bad, though. Happens all the time. Better sit over there by the fire while I pull your car out."

He shrugged into a jean jacket that had a gray sweatshirt tucked inside it and then yanked the hood over his dark, uncombed hair . . . hair she knew by heart because she'd gazed at it during countless pro rodeo performances and then again when she'd returned home, to her room, to ogle his posters.

And here she was in his home! Alone with him! After all those years of fantasizing about the hot Latino bull rider, who'd disappeared after a brutal goring ended his career, she was about to be snowed in with him.

When he stepped outside and slammed the door, she jumped.

He *was* Danny Diablo—Danny Black was his real name, but the "devil" part had made her crazy for him all during high school. So why was he denying his stellar career in the arena? And what was he doing *here*, out in the middle of nowhere?

Norah shivered, glancing around. The cabin was nothing fancy, but it was cozy . . . fire flickering in the fireplace with a bear rug in front of it . . . a smallish living room in which the dark leather furniture was set off by colorful serapes and throw pillows. It opened into a kitchen that looked dated but clean. Beyond that she spotted the door leading to his bedroom—

Don't go there! her thoughts warned.

So she turned her back on temptation. This, however, brought her face-to-face with a big-screen TV on which two very tough-looking women in black leather corsets and thigh-high boots were circling in a bedroom, like wrestlers ready to spring.

The rumble of a truck made Norah look out the window. Danny Diablo could look in and see exactly what she was doing . . . exactly what she wasn't wearing, as she stood in the light. He had good reason to ask why she'd come out in this storm dressed only in a lace nightie with a beaded bikini under it. And he'd have every reason to laugh in her face when she said she'd been headed to a Christmas pageant for homeless kids. Who would believe that?

We all have our little secrets, don't we?

Since Danny Black wasn't admitting to who he was, she saw no need to reveal her situation with the scumbag landlord who dangled her key over her head. Why dwell on how far they'd both fallen? On how their circumstances had spiraled downward into the pits of existence?

It was Christmas, after all. Fa la la la la, and all that.

Sighing forlornly, Norah gazed out toward the road. Danny's black pickup lurched in the snow, and then her little red car came up over the edge and followed it obediently across the road.

Signs of things to come, chickie. That big black, macho truck and that big fancy bottle of whiskey pretty well tell the tale about who'll lead and who'll follow, don't they?

Despite the blowing snow, she dashed outside when he pulled up alongside the cabin. He'd barely come to a stop when she popped the trunk with her key clicker and threw open her driver's-side door.

"What the—you buckin' for pneumonia, or what?" he ranted. "Trust me, honey, you don't want me for your nurse, because I ain't goin' there!"

"Well, I'm not going *anywhere*, am I?" she threw back at him, grabbing her phone. "Get those boxes out of my trunk while I—"

Norah gasped when the ring tone kicked in from a phone she thought she'd destroyed. *Angels we have heard on—*

Click. "Now what?" she rasped, turning her back to Danny. "Look, you were right! I was stupid to start out to the party with the storm blowing in—"

"Doesn't matter that I was right." His voice coiled in her ear. "Ya didn't bring me a rent check, didja? And then, after I so gallantly made an alternate arrangement for payment, ya ducked out on me. That's not smart, sweetie pie. Not—"

Shutting her eyes tightly against tears, Norah flung the phone into the car again and slammed the door. Which left her with snow clinging to the lace of her nightgown and a man in black staring at her like she'd lost her mind.

And maybe she had.

"Sorry," she muttered. Although she owed this guy no apologies, did she? "I—I really appreciate you hauling my car out of the drift, and if we carry in these boxes of goodies, I can repay you for your hospitality."

His smile turned foxlike. "Goodies? What sort of party were you headed for, sweetheart?"

"Get your mind out of the gutter!" She hefted the nearest box in the trunk. "I baked cookies and packed up cocoa and candy canes for a Christmas pageant at a homeless shelter just outside Jackson Hole."

"And you ended up *here*?" His gaze angled into a sneer.

"Probably missed a helluva turn, talking on your phone when you shoulda been watchin' the road."

Norah glared at him, holding the large box against her hip so she could open the cabin door. Didn't help that he was right—but she'd be damned if she admitted the sorry situation with her landlord. Danny Diablo, professional tough guy, would never see her side anyway: he'd say she had it coming, for selling herself out to Scurtz in the first place.

And, yeah, he'd be right about that, too.

"We all veer off the path now and then or get kicked when we're already down," she replied stiffly. "And how we respond to those circumstances tells a whole lot about what we're made of."

He snorted, bumping her butt with the box in his arms as they stepped inside. "You've got no call to get holier than thou, honey. Not when you look like a hooker come callin'."

Norah gritted her teeth against a retort, focusing on the kitchen table. Putting on the cheesy beaded bikini—even making it in the first place—hadn't been one of her better ideas. But Leon was demanding his due, and time was tight—and then she got caught out here in this snowstorm after all her instincts had warned her to stay home.

She dropped her box on the table, glancing back, hoping a partial explanation would shut him up. But those obsidian eyes stole her breath—and her words—away.

Black looked up from ogling her ass into a face poised on the verge of a crying jag. He flinched. Gentleman Jack was prodding him on, to goad her into admitting what sort of woman she really was, so they could get on with the inevitable.

But those green eyes shimmered with pain and a desperation he knew well. Her hair, wet and windblown, fell about her shoulders in shaggy layers of blond that suggested she'd applied those highlights herself. And then there was that damn halo flopping sideways on her head. She sniffled, looking like a lost puppy. A mutt, maybe, but still the most adorable thing he'd seen in years.

He gently untangled the halo from her hair. Its gold metallic pipe cleaners came unbraided, and a couple of sparkly beads bounced on the table.

"Thank you," she wheezed. She blinked rapidly, denying her tears. "That halo was really getting on my last nerve."

Something in him warmed. Maybe his heart thawing out after a winter that set in with Mariel's death last June.

He stepped away. "Look, we're gonna be here a while, so let's just keep our personal questions to ourselves, okay? Two strangers brought together by a blizzard, making the best of the situation and all that."

When she nodded, those green eyes got wider. Her face took on the dangerous delicacy of the waylaid angel she might be beneath that questionable get-up.

But he wouldn't let his thoughts stray down that nice-guy path. He was still rock hard, and it would take more than pretty, polite talk to relieve him.

He turned toward the living room. Plopped into the chair facing the big TV. Those two hard-ass hunnies were looking better by the minute: at least a guy knew what to expect from chicks like that.

He sucked down some more whiskey, trying not to listen to the sounds behind him . . . the rustling of paper and the running of water into a pan . . . the opening of a cabinet and the clink of a spoon in a mug.

She appeared beside his chair with a smile and a plate of cookies like he hadn't seen in years. Mint-scented steam rose from the mug, which had a candy cane hooked over its rim so it melted into the cocoa. She set it on the table beside him after pointedly removing his big bottle of Jack.

"Hey!" He grabbed, but she was faster.

Danny angled an eyebrow at her, not letting on that *two* lace nighties swam before his eyes. "I know your tricks, little vix," he muttered. "Try all you want to sober me up with those cookies, but I'm not fallin' for it. Not unless you lemme see that sparkly underwear without the nightie."

3

*N*ot gonna pussyfoot around, is he?

Norah swallowed. That chain around his neck rippled with each breath he took as he stared her down, daring her to accept or refuse.

No doubt Danny Black was a man of his word—at least when it came to doing what *he* wanted. So it came down to this: If she sobered him up, he stripped her down. If she didn't, well, he might strip her anyway. And who knew what came next? He was a sleek, powerful puma nursing a deep, dark wound. And she'd seen a lot more bottles in the kitchen cabinets.

Oh, who are you fooling? her thoughts taunted again. *You used to pray to be alone with Danny Diablo. Wanted to feel his hot coffee skin against yours. Wanted him to be the man who made you a woman. You've given yourself to him a hundred times . . . if only in your dreams.*

Norah shifted. Her stall was bad strategy: he could read her wayward thoughts, and he sensed she'd made her decision long ago. The two girls in the porn flick were making sex sounds that didn't help her case one bit.

She wasn't an innocent, after all. She felt wet and ready as Danny stared at her over the cookie plate. And considering the nasty man she could've been with right now . . . well, this situation was feeling sweeter by the minute.

But dammit, she didn't have to play by Danny's rules! Leon had taught her a hard lesson about letting a man get the upper hand. If she danced to this devil's tune, she'd leave here a whipped pup. It was time to take matters into her own . . . hot little hands.

Leaning over—giving him a good eyeful down the front of her see-through nightie—Norah lifted a large raspberry brownie from the plate and waved it teasingly in front of his face.

"Here's the deal, cowboy," she whispered with her best come-on smile. "For every cookie you eat—every cup of cocoa you put down—I take something off. Got it?"

When he opened his mouth to go for the chocolate, she jerked the brownie out of his reach. "But since you already took off my halo, you owe me this one. We'll see where it goes from there."

His black eyes flashed, but how could she lose? He was her life's temptation—and he had little else here to eat—so she'd make him grateful that he'd taken her in tonight. It sounded like a fine distraction from Scurtz and all the other realities that could ruin her Christmas.

"You're on," he rasped with a sexy hint of snarl. "Sugar in all my favorite forms. I *almost* wish you were wearing more clothes."

Norah snickered, a wicked sound that left no doubt about her answer. It matched the feral expression on his face as he stood up to pluck the brownie from her hand. From this close, he was so much taller than she, with a whipcord body reminiscent of his bull-riding days, yet more alluring. The past few years had done Danny Diablo some mighty fine favors—or did she just prefer a man who knew what he was doing? She stared at his lips as they closed around the large brownie.

Danny stopped midchew. Closed his eyes—partly because he was ready to devour this woman as fast as he wanted to wolf her cookies, but mostly because this was the best damn brownie he'd ever tasted. Moist and dense . . . studded with nuts. Raspberry jam oozed out from under its thick chocolate frosting.

As he tucked the rest of it into his mouth, he laughed low in his throat. How could he lose? She'd brought in *boxes* of this stuff—and she had nowhere to go but his bedroom! Or the bear rug. Or the couch. She'd be a fine way to satisfy a hunger that had gnawed on him too long—not to mention a warm, sexy distraction from the cold, hard realities of life without Mariel and the hassles her death had brought on.

He swallowed the last bite, grinning. "That makes us even. How 'bout that Christmas tree next? And how 'bout you feed it to me?"

Her eyes grew a deeper green. They never left him as he sat down in the leather chair, patting his lap. Coyly, Norah picked up the sugar cookie. She'd frosted it bright green, with a garland of sparkly yellow sanding sugar and M&M's for ornaments. She perched carefully on his knees, aiming the cookie at those lush lips, star first.

Danny moaned as he bit down. Sugar cookies had always been his favorite, and this one had a solid, moist chew to it. Those chocolate candies crunched between his teeth.

He kept gazing at her, captivated by the way she watched him chew. He was savoring the treat in his mouth almost as much as the one in his lap. She was a brazen little puss beneath that angel outfit—just as he'd figured—and he admired her for playing along, but *her* way. She kept him guessing, and he liked that. Pondered which piece of clothing she'd take off for him.

"Good boy," she murmured seductively, reaching down toward the floor. "Off comes a shoe! And as a bonus, I'll take 'em both off. They're so wet and squishy—"

She gasped when he gathered her against his chest and then wrapped his hand around her bare insole.

"Cold feet. I can fix that," he murmured, loving the weight of her, the slender, high arch he was massaging and the long toes with nails painted candy pink. "But don't think for a minute you're winning, Norah."

Her mouth clapped shut. "How'd you know my name?"

Danny smiled at how damn hot she looked when she got flustered. He could've fed her some cock-and-bull story, but a straight answer might win her trust a little faster. Why he wanted that, he wasn't sure. Gentleman Jack was still singing loudly in his head, but his heart danced to the beat of a different drummer now.

"The box I carried in had a mailing label on it." He reached for her other foot and glanced at the plate. "You made all these goodies? How 'bout that coconut one with the red and green cherries next."

"Yep, I did," she purred. "It's my passion at Christmas. A chance to let my inner kid play with the cookie cutters and decorating tools. "Most days I make jewelry, though," she added in a faraway voice. After a moment's hesitation, she fingered the cross on his chest. "What a handsome piece—lighter than it looks. Titanium, isn't it?"

He nodded, chewing the macaroon to cover a rush of emotion. He'd seen it online, and Mariel had ordered it for him when she was too ill to shop. It was the last gift she ever gave him.

"What's *your* passion, Danny?"

Her question caught him in the gut, halfway between pulling her in for a hard kiss and insisting his name wasn't Danny. But what would that accomplish? Why was it such a chore to bask in a little hero worship from days gone by? To be who he was—or who Norah wanted him to be? He saw raw desire in those green eyes and felt the heat kicking up to fever pitch as she shifted gingerly against his erection.

"When I'm not devouring hot blondes who stop by my cabin pretending to be angels," he replied slyly, "I play classical guitar. These wings gotta go, honey."

Norah followed his gaze to the corner, aware of how this lifted her breasts to within an inch of his lips. He could probably see how rigid her nipples were between the beads of the bra. "It's a beautiful instrument. I'd love to hear you play some—"

"Right now I want to play big, bad-ass wolf," he growled against her ear.

She giggled, and the childlike sound set something loose in him that hadn't roamed free for a long, long time. When she turned, he had to dodge the first wing, yet she was opening herself to him . . . letting him have his way.

"Untie my sash, and you'll see how they're hooked on. They're a nuisance, but what kind of an angel would I be without wings?"

Oh, he had an answer for that! Danny focused on the sash, though, which he suspected had belonged on a white dress at one time. A wedding gown? He blinked that thought away. Norah was holding herself rigid, holding her breath as he unsnapped the flimsy band beneath the breasts his fingers itched to squeeze. Somehow, he set the filmy wings on the floor without ripping off her entire costume.

"Good boy. Nice wolfie," she whispered.

"Show me your underwear, Norah."

When she looked over her shoulder at him, one eyebrow arched. A blatantly sexy move. "My necklace has to come off first," she challenged. She speared her fingers up under her mop of drying hair to raise it off her slender neck—a neck just begging for his kisses. "If you're steady enough to unhook it, you get—"

His hands flew to the back of her neck, and when his calloused fingertips found the clasp, Norah sucked air. God, he looked ready to swallow her whole. She could feel his hardness prodding her through their clothes. Every little fumbling on her sensitive skin sent goose bumps down her arms, and when he lifted the string of chunky crystalline beads with a victorious snicker, she got lost in his bottomless black eyes.

"—another cookie as your reward," she finished weakly.

"You know what I want, Norah. I refuse to beg."

He inhaled, catching the peppermint in that cocoa and the intimate scent of the woman who gazed at him like the girl she'd been back when he was riding high. Yet he wanted the wayward angel she'd become. She was wet and ready. It was too damn long since he'd caught a whiff of a filly in heat, but as his body remembered, his nostrils flared.

"It's only a nightgown," she murmured. "Gonna let that stand in your way, cowboy?"

4

"*Madré de Dios,*" he rasped. He hooked his hand around her neck and pulled her face to his, staring into her eyes like a man possessed. Norah opened her mouth to speak, but he was on her in a heartbeat.

His lips—oh, God, his lips were lush and urgent against hers, opening and testing and tasting. Norah surrendered too fast, but there was no sense in pretending this wasn't what she'd wanted ever since the first time she saw him in the ring.

She'd been too young to know what she was wishing for, but now, as a woman who'd been around this block a time or two, Norah understood exactly how Danny Diablo was kissing her: *it was exactly the way she'd always longed to be kissed.*

He moaned softly, easing up now that the first line had been crossed. She lay cradled in his lap, succumbing to mind-altering kisses while giving as good as she got. He angled her head into his elbow while his other hand went on its own seductive mission: those long, lean fingers brushed the lace nightie and enclosed one breast, exploring the texture of her beaded bra.

Danny's calluses rasped against the lace, massaging her flesh, avoiding her nipples . . . playing the cat-and-mouse game he seemed so good at. He breathed into her mouth as he kissed her, while drawing his very breath from her soul. His lips lit fires on hers, demanding his due for helping her on this wintry night—but because he, too, had a hunger that went beyond two strangers meeting in a storm.

Norah shifted against him, and when they finally came up for air, her lace got caught on the rough edges of his iron cross. The fabric clung to his medallion just as she wished to cling to him, and when she worked it loose she tore a hole below the shoulder seam.

Danny smoothed the rough edges, tracing her collarbone. "Didn't mean to rip your—"

"Yes, you did," she countered in a silken whisper. "You wanted to rip this thing off me from the moment you laid eyes on me."

A growl rumbled in his throat. "Better watch who you're teasing, little girl. We made a deal, and I don't intend to let you off—"

Norah grabbed the neckline of the old nightie and yanked. The fabric gave with a sigh, relieved of its duty to come between their two bodies. She felt brazen and bold, lying across his lap with the halves of the nightie in her hands, exposing her bare chest and the sparkly bra.

"That what you wanted? You've seen it now. Are we done yet?"

With another feral growl, Danny pulled her hard against himself to kiss her bare skin. His urgency warned her that this would be no ordinary coupling: Danny Diablo, bull rider, was about to harness her with all the skill and passion he'd once invested in his eight-second rides in the ring.

Except he was going to spend a lot more time riding her.

Norah moaned when his hand slipped beneath the beads to

squeeze her breast. She speared her hands into his thick black hair, marveling in its silk. Reveling in the way the soft growth along his jaw and upper lip tickled her as he kissed her long and hard.

As the lace gave way to his caress, Danny's hand traveled lower, to rub a circle just above her thong . . . teasing and testing. Making her beg for it. Her hips wiggled shamelessly, but Norah didn't care: she was too caught up in his passion, in the heat she'd never expected to find on this snowy night.

He thrust his tongue into her mouth just as his fingers found her mound. Groping, squeezing, he slipped two fingers inside her.

Norah gasped into his mouth. He kissed her harder, refusing her the chance to protest.

His fingers spread her wetness in tight circles. In and out he delved, rubbing her clit with each stroke, mercilessly pressing her with the heel of his hand until she was writhing against it, demanding more. She felt that inner straining toward release, that tightening of intimate muscles driven by nerves set a-jangle each time he touched her.

Danny pressed her mound and relentlessly pumped his two fingers against her inflamed flesh until Norah cried out, bucking against him.

On and on he stroked her. She was too far gone to open her eyes, but she felt him watching her climax. When had she ever felt so damn hot and sexy?

And when had she ever let a man pleasure her this way, withholding nothing?

When she went slack, Danny pulled her close again. "*Querida . . . chica bonita,*" he murmured against her hair. "You're an awesome woman to watch. Tell me what comes next. I want to hear you say the words."

Was this man actually giving her the options? Asking her to

call the shots for her own pleasure—again? Norah studied his face, framed by that raven hair her hands had mussed. His onyx eyes shone with a dark desire reflected in her own heart.

It was dangerous, how much she wanted this man.

"Take me," she breathed. "Years ago I dreamed of this moment—this coming together—because I was so in—in *lust* with you," she confessed. "You can't make a wrong move, Danny."

"Spell it out," he insisted, running a rough fingertip over her lips. His smile was tight with need, yet he acted like he could wait as long as she decided he would . . . and wasn't *that* a turn-on? A man apparently willing to bring her off again and again before he received his own pleasure.

Norah closed her eyes, unaccustomed to asking for what she wanted. Alex had simply expected her to hitch along on his ride.

"Take me to bed," she rasped. "Make love to me—"

"How?" he demanded. His lips remained a tantalizing inch above hers as his breath warmed her face. "What position makes you scream for it, Norah? I want to hear my name bouncing against all four walls of that bedroom when I claim you. There's no going back now. We might as well do this right."

She exhaled slowly. This guy was into the details, wasn't he? How to choose her favorite way . . .

"Take me from behind. Angle your cock inside me and then ride me hard while—"

Danny scooped her up and carried her into the bedroom.

5

This angel in her tattered costume felt as light as a child in his arms. So fragile, compared to Mariel.

But he shoved his beloved wife out of his mind: Norah was the answer to a prayer he'd been sending up for months. Running this ranch and fending off legal threats from Mariel's kids had put his more personal needs on a back burner.

But he was smoking now! Here, from out of nowhere, was this splendid young woman begging to be in bed with him. He laid her across Chico's double and then switched on the bedside lamp. He felt more alive and lucid—was seeing more clearly—than he had in months.

It felt right to be loving Norah on neutral turf, where she wouldn't intrude on Mariel's territory and memories. While this fire had blown out of control way too fast, he accepted Norah for who she was: an angel who'd maybe strayed from the path but who clearly adored him. A good girl who'd left some questionable problems behind to solve his.

He vowed to fulfill those fantasies she'd confessed, because at this moment nothing mattered except sweet release . . . making Norah writhe and cry out so he, too, could howl like the lone wolf within him yearned to do.

"Norah, I—"

Damned if she wasn't ripping the rest of that lace nightie off as she gazed at him, straight on. He sucked air at the sight of her baring herself, so blatant and beautiful in the lamp light.

"You like?" Her voice, girlish and high, made Danny wonder how much younger than he she was.

Not that it mattered. A woman who'd made that sparkly thong and bra, and then wore it to a Christmas party for all to see, was old enough to know this score. She'd matched him challenge for challenge. As he fumbled with his buttons and then his zipper, Danny felt a surge of need like he hadn't allowed himself for a long, long time.

"God, but you're gorgeous," she whispered. Norah's green eyes followed every move of his hands as he yanked off his shirt—

Danny stood absolutely still when she nipped her lip. Awaited her verdict on the long, ragged scar that snaked from his hip bone down through his pubes, where his thigh hooked on.

"God, that must've hurt."

He nodded, waiting for more. Would she turn away from him now?

"I was there when it happened. Too horrified to watch," she murmured. Her swallow clicked in her throat. "You're lucky to be alive, aren't you?"

Danny nodded again, aware now just how lucky he was. "If it makes you squeamish, honey—"

"Don't you dare back out on me, cowboy!" Her grin came out to play again, and she flashed him a twat shot. "Finish what you started!"

When he shoved his pants down his cock sprang out, eager to fill her—

His mouth went dry. He hadn't had to think about protection in years—had taken risks when he was younger, but marriage had made him much less cavalier. More aware of his responsibilities.

He jerked open the drawer of the bedside table, praying Chico was a careful man when he entertained the ladies here. Two foil squares made his insides sing.

"Thank you," Norah murmured. "I was going to fetch some from my purse, but—"

"You were a Scout, too? 'Be prepared'?" he teased as he ripped one open. Never mind that he was leading her to believe this place was his—keeping some very important secrets from her.

Right now, it was all about sex and satisfaction, and if they came to a point where they shared their lives, so be it. Norah was spreading her legs and squirming at him, her slender arms folded beneath her head. The last thing he wanted was her pity.

"Scouting wasn't my thing. Not much of a joiner," she mused aloud. "I was more into making stuff, like this awful outfit—"

"Not awful," he countered, rolling on the condom in one swift stroke. Her essence was filling the room, driving him nuts. "I love it when a woman shows herself off rather than hiding behind bulky clothing or false modesty. Nothing fake about you, honey. It's all right out there for me to see."

Her breath escaped in a hiss. She sat up to get into position, but he placed a knee on the mattress between her long legs . . . willowy legs he could already imagine wrapped around him. Had he really thought she was too skinny earlier? Thank God her cookies had soaked up his whiskey. Taking her head between his hands, he kissed her crazy, to drive himself that way, as well.

God, how she responded! Her tongue dueled with his, and her eager lips met his every dare. As he laid her back on the quilted comforter, Danny reminded himself to listen to her requests, to rein in his own desires. It was the most valuable love lesson his older wife had taught him: if he played his partner like a prized guitar, she would make the music they both danced to. Norah's beaded bikini rasped against his chest and erection, driving him on in an animal way.

"I don't want to break your beads, baby, so—"

Norah giggled. "Lobster-claw clasps," she whispered mysteriously. "Pretend you're unfastening a prized diamond necklace."

The lilt in her voice played with him, yet he couldn't argue with her imagery: she glimmered in the low light, a diamond in her own right even if her car and costume suggested less. Here again, Mariel had taught him to treat a lover like a rare jewel because she would surely shine with her gratitude and please him beyond his expectations.

Norah lifted her slender hips, and he hastily unfastened each side of the thong . . . pulled the beaded triangle away . . . let out a low moan at the sight of her pale curls, clipped close.

"Turn around now," he rasped. "Gotta have you, puss."

Norah sat up, placing her hands in his for assistance. Such small yet capable hands, he noted—no polish on the nails, which were also clipped close. The hands of a woman whose work and life made fancy manicures too high maintenance.

Danny nuzzled her knuckles. Her eyes widened. She was breathing as quickly as he. So eager. So needy.

"Unfasten my bra," she breathed. "I want you to see the girls."

He suddenly felt jittery, like a kid doing it for the first time. Plenty of female fans had propositioned him when he was a single man—and even after he married Mariel. But *this* woman! She was all vixen and all angel and all about sex in its purest, dirtiest form: a great way to let off some steam and get through a snowstorm. An extended one-night stand.

Or was it? Those green eyes glimmered at him in the lamplight, and Danny fell head over heels for this total stranger. He was already a sucker for the trust and hope that shone all over her pretty face.

"I—I would love to see the girls." He inhaled deeply to regain control. No need to rush things and ruin this fine, feisty mood. If he messed up now, it might be a long day or so, cooped up with a disappointed woman and that bikini she'd beaded . . . for another man.

He smiled slyly. "I'm not going to ask who you made this for, so—"

"And I'm not going to tell you!"

He heard an edge in her voice—a hint that Norah's little secret might be more compelling than his grief and the denial of his identity.

So he kissed her, holding her head in his hand to taste those sweet, generous lips again. She undulated when his other hand went to the center of her back . . . such soft skin . . . and the layered hair he wanted to explore more fully. This *was* like unfastening a diamond necklace: not a job for one hand in a hurry.

As Danny's fingers found the clasp, Norah's arms went around his neck, and she kicked the kissing up a notch. Finally the beaded bikini top separated for him, and his hands found their way to . . . those girls.

She released her breath into his mouth, guiding his hands over her soft, willing breasts. So damn fresh and sexy she was, he nearly threw her backward to take her right then and there. The straps slipped down her shoulders. She shrugged out of the raspy fabric, eager to be free of it. Eager to rub her bare body against his.

"Danny," she moaned. "Turn me around. Take me hard and fast. I have to have you inside me *now*."

Who could argue with a request like that? "I don't want to hurt you, entering you too—"

"You know how wet I am! Take what's been yours for a long time—if only in my dreams."

Looking at that slender, muscled ass she pointed at him—at the dusky folds of skin inviting him inside—Danny knelt behind her. She was rocking forward and back in her excitement. Lord, had he ever seen a woman so hot and eager for him?

"Humor me," he muttered, pausing with his aching cock positioned to plunge. "Have you always had a thing for cowboys, or was it—"

"Only you, Danny Diablo." Norah looked over her shoulder at him in the most provocative gaze he'd ever seen. "I knew that was your stage name, but I wanted the *real* you—without any bulls or clowns or groupies. Just you and me, making love. Just like we are right now. It's already perfect, Danny."

And when had he ever heard *that* from a woman? Her voice, subtle and sultry, teased at his cock, and he slipped quickly inside her.

Norah exhaled, throwing her head back. He felt huge and hard, yet he was hesitating—probably controlling himself for her sake. She took a moment to center herself, to grin over a dream a long time in the making.

Then she squeezed him. *Hard.*

Danny thrust, grabbing her hips. He'd been invited to dance, and he didn't need to be asked twice! He began the ride slowly, with firm strokes, gritting his teeth to maintain control. She was so warm and smooth and perfect. . . . Only once since his wife died had he ventured into sex, and it had been a disaster.

But this. This was ecstasy. This was *Norah.*

"Gimme more," she rasped. "I want to shatter with it—I want you to ride me like—"

In a heartbeat he was caught up in the mindless need to fill and spill. Danny plunged deep, entering the rhythm as old as time yet as fresh and free as this woman Fate and a storm had delivered to his door.

She clenched around him, panting. God, the ache—the need

and the hunger all centered between her legs. Danny's hands slipped around her hips until his fingertips parted her folds. He found her nub and began to strum it from both sides as though she were a fine guitar.

Her insides bunched, and she shoved back until his balls slapped her wetness. With a long, low cry she rode the madness he'd created inside her. Suddenly there was only the vibration they created between them, the feverish need for release—

And then he convulsed against her backside, letting out a raw cry and a string of rapid Spanish words that needed no translation. Norah let him slump forward and then eased herself to the mattress, still joined with him. His breath teased her shoulder. Then he was nuzzling her neck.

"Norah . . . Norah," was all he could manage. He'd shot his wad, and his brains had gone right along with it. Easing her onto her side, he pulled her close against him while he caught his breath.

"You don't have to say anything, Danny," she breathed. "Just hold me now, while I collect all my pieces. I didn't know a first time could feel so wonderful! But then, maybe I've been with the wrong guys. Right?"

6

Danny bit back an answer that sounded gushy—and where had *that* come from? Norah was a stranger, the proverbial perfect stranger come from out of nowhere, but it was too early to address real-life questions. Too scary.

"That's behind you now. Just like my past is," he hedged, nuzzling her hair. It felt downy soft, except for stiff ends where her hair spray had hardened from getting wet. Such an angel of contrasts she was. He didn't want to ruin his chances with her by saying all the wrong things.

He reached to the end of the bed for a folded quilt and drew it over them. Already Norah was breathing deeply. Danny held her bare body to his, inhaling the hint of her perfume and the tang of their sex. Too long it had been since he'd embraced a woman, and he closed his eyes to savor this peaceful moment, to see her again as they'd made love . . . as she'd caught him in her emerald gaze . . . as she'd bargained with cookies and cocoa. He smiled into her hair, incredibly happy.

Norah let out a long, low breath. Asleep. Exhausted from

her ordeal on the snowy roads, running from whoever had made her throw her cell phone.

He rose carefully, wrapping the old quilt around her. After a lingering look at her childlike face, he turned out the light.

As he dressed in the darkness, it occurred to him that he now had a guest with only a torn nightgown and a beaded bikini for clothes, in the dead of winter. He stepped into the living room to turn off that stupid DVD in which the two chicks in leather were still panting over each other. The cocoa had cooled, but it slid down his throat with a minty chocolate richness, satisfying him in ways Gentleman Jack never had.

He realized then that his head was clear.

His heart was, too.

Danny went to the window, amazed at how fast the snow was piling up: already the whistling wind had drifted the road shut. Good thing they'd moved the cattle and horses to the lot closest to the bunkhouse so Buck and his boy could tend them this week. Times like these made him glad ranch hands were a hardy, independent lot who didn't need bosses with cell phones telling them how to keep the livestock alive.

On impulse, he went outside to fetch Norah's phone from her car. Sure, he wanted the name of the jerk who'd upset her, even though he *told* himself she might have family or friends calling to see if she was okay on such a treacherous night. The snow was up to the Grand Prix's axles, and when he opened the door he sensed the vehicle needed some work. Her phone was a dinosaur, too.

Sympathy stabbed at him, but Danny slammed the door on it and dashed inside. He thumbed the POWER button. *Beep.* The screen lit up, gave him the menu for accessing her calls and directory. She had new voice mail.

Should he? He remained with his back against the door, itching to know who'd made Norah throw her phone—and who she'd beaded that bikini for. Had he thrown her out? Would she go back to him?

None of your business. Check her message, and you won't be able to break away. She'll know—and never trust you again.

Glancing toward the bedroom door, he turned off her phone. Set it on the kitchen table and reached inside her box for another brownie. The fire was burning low, so he put on more logs. Thank God he'd stacked firewood out back, because if the power went out, what the hell would they do?

Like you don't know, his inner wolf taunted.

It had been a good enough plan to feed the fire and wrap up in blankets and thaw out with the whiskey—but he wasn't by himself now. Had nothing decent to eat because food was the furthest thing from his mind when he sent Chico and the other hands away for the week.

How would Norah handle being snowbound? Maybe without electricity? Some women couldn't be cooped up for long, especially without their blow-dryers and makeup mirrors and microwaves.

Danny walked quietly to the bedroom door and peered in. She hadn't moved. Sleeping like a baby.

Stirred by the sight of such trust in him—lots of women would be on the phone, stressed about the weather or giggling with girlfriends about being here with him—Danny stripped off his cold clothes and cuddled against her under the old quilt.

As he drifted off, he couldn't recall the last time he'd felt so relaxed. So at peace and ready to face whatever daylight might bring.

Norah stirred, burrowing beneath the blanket. Had she slept a long time, or fallen into a very deep sleep only an hour ago? She recalled coming into Danny's bedroom, making wildly satisfying love and then conking out.

And before that, of course, she'd gone off the road into the snowbank—and it was surely the morning after, so she'd better collect her clothes and see about getting home!

She sat bolt upright, her heart racing. Clutching the soft old quilt around her, she worried that Danny had abandoned her here—clenched her eyes shut against images of Leon tossing her belongings out into the snow—felt so strangled by fear, her landlord might've been standing behind her, choking her with that beaded thong—

Guitar music drifted in from the other room . . . a mellow but very complicated version of "Angels We Have Heard On High." It reminded her of the ring tone on her cell, except, well, the runs and little squeaks of calluses against the frets held her spellbound. This version of "Angels" had nothing to do with threats from her landlord: the notes, plucked with precision—and more talent than Scurtz could muster in five lifetimes—sang to her of a man who'd studied his instrument for years and who turned to it like he would a trusted friend.

Norah sat motionless, wrapped to her nose. She closed her eyes to let the song ripple over her soul like a healing stream. . . . Lord, but Danny could play that thing. Kind of jazzy and free, yet hitting all those tricky harmonies and melodic strains with breathtaking clarity.

He played his guitar like she made jewelry and cookies: because it came as naturally as breathing. And because it gave her life meaning.

As he segued into another song—*Chestnuts roasting on an open fire*, she silently sang along—Norah rose from the bed. She stopped in the doorway, still wrapped in the quilt, to drink in the sight of Danny Diablo sitting on the hearth beside a crackling fire, leaning into a glossy black twelve-string trimmed in silver. His fingers found the notes unerringly as his body swayed with his playing. He had his eyes shut. Long, dark lashes accented the most gorgeous expression on his mahogany face . . .

When Norah's breath escaped in an *ohhhh*, those eyes popped open.

Danny gazed straight at her, never missing a note. The music poured from his heart through his guitar. His fingers were merely messengers of such intense love that Norah sucked in her breath.

She gripped the quilt, spellbound until the last notes lingered in the air around him. "Danny, that was the most wonderful—I've never heard anyone play that way!"

He rested his hands on the guitar's shoulder. "Sorry I woke you. Been a while since I felt like playing, so—"

"Don't stop! I'll make us some breakfast," she said as she shuffled toward the kitchen. "I'd love to bead some ornament doodads while you play. You know—something to decorate the place a little!"

He looked ready to laugh but nipped that luscious lower lip instead. His gaze said he understood her need to create, just as he had to play ... at least until the heat between them flared into wildfire again.

"I could probably find you some jeans or—"

"You don't like it that I've ripped my clothes off and have nothing to wear?" Norah grinned as she piled cookies on a plate. "I was just thinking how ... *cozy* that might be—say, if I sat in that chair by the fire so I could watch your fingers play, and you could watch mine."

"Like I'm going to watch your fingers."

She laughed. How was it they could talk so comfortably? None of the usual awkwardness that followed a first time in bed—as though they'd spent many a night snowed in together and welcomed the seclusion.

She found mugs and checked the water in the microwave. Then she spotted her cell phone on the table. He must've brought it inside after her little meltdown, to see—

Had he found Leon's number? Called him to find out what the hell was going on last night?

Behind her, Danny strummed a few stray chords that eased into "Rudolph, the Red-Nosed Reindeer." She stole a glance at him as she poured their hot water . . . hoped the phone's *beep* didn't interrupt his playing . . . saw the new voice mail, and every fiber in her body screamed *don't open it!*

Norah closed her eyes and turned off the phone. Her host hadn't been nervy enough to check it. And didn't his cheerful music tell her that? He was playing with too much happiness—having too much fun!—to be aware of her skanky situation with Leon.

Is there a lesson here?

She carried their cocoa and cookies to the hearth in three trips, because she had to hold the quilt on with one hand. Nodding to his music, Norah grabbed the box of bright, shiny beads that held her wire cutters and needle-nose pliers and settled herself in the chair across from him.

Danny finished "Rudolph" with a flourish that made her grin. As he reached for the biggest brownie on the plate, he eyed the string of bright red beads she'd threaded onto a pipe cleaner.

"You always carry a tackle box of beads and tools, right?"

Norah smiled. "I was going to make each of the kids at the shelter an ornament last night. String together the letters of their names or make a Santa like this one, or a snowman. Whatever they wanted."

He quirked an eyebrow. "And you can just *do* that? Without a pattern or instructions?"

"And you can just *play* those Christmas songs, without any music or apparent effort?" she countered.

Danny licked his fingertip and marked a point on an imaginary scorecard. Then he reached toward the plate again. "Since you decorated this cookie of a house with curtains and a wreath and a string of Christmas lights, I guess bead ornaments would be a no-brainer."

"You got it."

He licked yellow frosting from his fingers and pondered the cookie plate again. "You saved my life last night, showing up with these," he ventured.

"Had I gone off the road anyplace else, I'd be frozen stiff in my car," she replied just as emphatically. Then she held up her ornament, grinning like a kid. "Here's Santa! How 'bout if I hang him on the lamp switch, so he'll catch the light?"

She felt his gaze following her fingers . . . sensed his sincere admiration for the ornament she'd whipped together in about two minutes. How could anyone live in a house without a single Christmas decoration?

Norah watched him deciding between a cherry macaroon and a PB&J sandwich cookie—a man who satisfied specific tastes rather than just grab any ole thing. An artist in his own right. Just one more intriguing—yet sad—facet of the man determined not to admit who he was, even though he knew she knew.

And why was there no sign of a woman living here? Danny Diablo's gorgeous body oozed sex out of every pore. Even out of that scar. Norah sensed he hadn't been here long: although this cozy little cabin with its colorful serapes and fireplace made the perfect rendezvous, it didn't feel like a home.

Or at least not *his* home. The duffel she'd stumbled over last night was still by the door. And although lots of singles didn't keep a full fridge, he was right when he'd said there was nothing here to eat.

So why was he here? As Danny closed his eyes in ecstasy over that soft, chewy peanut-butter cookie, Norah went fishing. She picked up a handful of clear star-shaped beads, because she did her best thinking with her hands engaged in a repetitive task.

"So how many cookies did you bake? I haven't seen two alike." Danny picked up a mocha truffle, moaning appreciatively as its rich coffee-flavored chocolate melted over his tongue.

Was that a hook buried in his complimentary question? Was Danny fishing, too? Norah strung six of the shiny beads and gave the wire a twist, pretending to calculate her answer . . . considering the question she wanted to ask in return.

"I made a ton of sugar cookies because kids love those, and—"

"That would be me," he agreed, choosing a holly leaf with cinnamon red hots for berries.

"—they're not as expensive as the ones with nuts and chocolate."

Oops. She'd just admitted she was basically broke. Yet he was happily licking green icing from his lips as though he hadn't noticed.

"I make a mean pot of soup or chili, too," she continued quickly. "If you'd like me to stir up something besides these—"

"Wish you could," he said with a shrug, "but I don't have the makings here. And it's not like we're going anywhere soon."

While the prospect of being snowed in with him sang in her heart, Norah smiled in sly triumph. "So how'd you end up being here when the storm blew in? You strike me as a man who's always prepared—like the Scout thing we talked about."

He blinked. How *was* he going to explain the fact that he had condoms but no canned goods? Would she be disgusted if she knew he'd used Chico's stash?

"This is a line shack, Norah. A place where ranch hands stay while they're checking fence on this section of the ranch," he explained carefully. "We don't keep food here because of the spoilage issue. The hands usually bring in enough groceries to hold them for their stay."

"But you brought only booze?"

Danny took his time selecting another cookie, a smile flirting with his lips. No harm in letting her think she had the upper hand in this little chat—and he *wasn't* lying to her.

"Like I told you, honey, you saved my life last night," he murmured. He gazed at her until her green eyes connected over the top of that snowman she was making. "I was feeling low, and Jack Daniel offered to be my friend while I holed up here, licking my wounds. Knew better than to hang around after the snow started—but I'm sure glad I did."

Norah twisted another section of pipe cleaner and chose smaller beads for Frosty's arms. She knew a dodge when she heard one: he'd admitted this place wasn't his without telling her one damn thing, really. But then, Danny Diablo wasn't the only one cruising around the outskirts of the truth, was he?

Then she squealed: he was kneeling in front of her chair now, offering her a gingerbread man and a smile that glowed red like sex.

"You're not eating any of these," he murmured. His index finger went between the cookie's legs and he wiggled it at her.

Norah let out an unladylike snort, and beads pinged to the floor. The little brown boy with the oversize weenie made her giggle so hard the quilt fell away from her bare shoulders.

"You can't tell me you're not hungry, Norah," he went on in that suggestive voice. "You didn't eat any dinner last night, so you have to be—"

"Are you asking for a blow job, Danny?"

7

His dusky eyes widened, and he clenched his jaw . . . that lean, mean jaw where the short stubble of hair drove her nutty with lust. "I can't believe you just said that."

"Why not? You were talking about eating—wagging that cookie's cock at me—" Norah shrugged, feigning exasperation, letting the quilt slip past her breasts. "It seemed like a natural connection to make."

Danny smiled and set the cookie on the table—along with her unfinished ornament. "I like how your mind works, pretty lady. But you're gonna wait while I indulge myself in one more . . . treat."

He tugged the quilt to bring her butt to the edge of the chair and then peeled it away from her body so she sat before him naked. Brazen. And, yeah, she liked the idea shining in those wicked eyes. A lot.

"Put your legs up on the arms of the chair, baby. Now."

Norah's pulse shot into high gear. She heard the wind driving snow against the windowpane, yet she'd never felt hotter. He'd flipped her switch with a *cookie*, of all things, and now he was making good—and making her squirm in anticipation. She raised one leg and then the other, opening herself to his eager gaze.

"What a naughty little angel you are," he crooned. "Hold your lips open. Point to where you want me to lick you silly."

Her jaw dropped. Before she could get her fingers in place, Danny placed his warm hands on her inner thighs to spread her. He licked his lips with a pointed tongue . . . looked from her eyes down to her open puss and back again.

"Show me," he prompted.

Feeling lewd—and loving it—Norah slipped her fingertips to either side of her sex and lifted. "That little button's throbbing so hard you can probably see it move," she rasped.

"Hmmm . . . lemme look closer. Right now all I see is pearly, slick liquid. I'd better taste it."

Before his tongue even made contact, her head fell back against the chair and she moaned. He was on her then, tickling her clit with his tongue's rough tip as his breath fanned her sensitive flesh.

When had she ever had a man who challenged her this way and made *soooo* good on it? Where his fingers had blazed a trail last night, his agile tongue now followed. Her hips wiggled, beyond her mind's control now that she was completely open to him . . . open to every advance he made with that luscious mouth.

Danny drove his tongue inside her and then drew it up to tickle her clit. Then he did it again, more insistently. His dark eyes dilated as he watched her response. She was so beautiful when she moved with him—so free, to let her body go wherever he led. He moved in for the kill, sucking her hard while getting in one last tease with his tongue.

"Danny! Jesus—Danny!" Norah bucked, gripping the chair to keep a hold on reality. Now that he'd inflamed her, he paused a few seconds to let her come down—and then he attacked again, relentlessly. Until she screamed.

When he raised his head, his grin looked slick and very, very sly. "That's your favorite way, isn't it?"

Norah opened her eyes, not knowing whether to reveal that answer yet. Now that she'd met Danny in the flesh, what did she really know about favorite ways? "You took me exactly where you wanted me to go. I was merely your obedient slave."

"Yeah, we'll get into that act sometime, too," he quipped. Then he grabbed the curled pipe cleaner with the beads threaded on it. "But first, I bet you'll quiver for this."

When the textured nubs slid between her sex lips, she jumped. He was holding the pipe cleaner vertically, kneading her clit with those bigger beads. She was once again at his mercy. "Danny, you—"

"Knew you'd love this," he finished with a snicker. But when he spotted the candy cane in her cocoa cup, he decided to drive her beyond wild, into the outer galaxies. "Hope this isn't too hot to—"

Norah cried out, damn glad no one else could hear the edge of madness in her voice. He'd replaced the beads with that peppermint cane! He held its crook; maneuvered it around her clit to spread minty fire all over her sensitive flesh. Her hips and thighs couldn't hold still. No matter how hard she tried to regain some semblance of control, Danny Diablo outfoxed her.

Diablo means "devil." Remember?

The contrast between his black hair and shirt and those midnight eyes against her fair skin wasn't lost on her, either. While she was no angel, she felt like a lot of wings were flapping all around her body. She'd be airborne any minute!

"I've never tasted a mint pussy, Norah," he breathed. "I sure hope you're ready!"

Another hoarse cry escaped her as her lover—and *what* a lover!—tongued her again. He licked her slowly, lightly, purposefully. As though he had all day.

Which of course he did. They were going nowhere.

So Norah forgot about being polite and floating down from her own high to give him a turn. It was ecstasy to hang here, wide open and moaning, to see how long she could remain in this state of blissful oblivion with a man who obviously adored sending her there.

Danny sighed over her tender flesh, tasting and licking and damn near creaming his jeans—except they were cutting into a cock that ached for relief. Never had he met a woman who let him play this way.

But then, when had he ever been around someone who spiked his cocoa with a candy cane and decorated dozens of different cookies? She belonged in some lucky guy's kitchen, even though she bore *no* resemblance to Betty Crocker or Martha Stewart in this indecent . . . awfully damned exciting position.

Once more he brought her to a peak. Held her suspended so he could watch the flex of her legs and the grimace that told him he'd pushed all the right buttons. Then he tickled her thighs with butterfly kisses to bring her back to earth.

Norah went limp in the quilt-covered chair, feeling like a hot cooked noodle. Had they been in her apartment, she would have worried about wet spots on the furniture. Leon would've put his ear to the wall at her first outcry. But here, there was only the crackling of that nice fire, and those sultry eyes looking up at her, and the lingering tingle of mint in the air and on her skin.

"My God, Danny," she managed.

Those three words, uttered with the last of her strength, crowned his efforts. Made him feel like a king again. He gently lowered her legs onto the cushion, kissed her knees, and then rested his head in her lap. When her fingers found his hair, and her short, sturdy nails found his scalp, he totally fell in love.

Now don't go getting any wild-ass ideas about—

He exhaled that little voice away in utter ecstasy: Norah's

firm strokes were finding all the right spots . . . scratching his scalp, massaging his temples, as though she knew just how helpless it left him. He didn't even care who she'd practiced on. They had nowhere to go and nothing better to do in this secluded world but pleasure each other.

"Strip off your jeans," she whispered against his ear. "Lie back on that bear rug while I find a way to get my revenge, beastie boy."

"Like you hated the way I—"

"Like I can't wait to take your cock in my mouth and suck you dry."

Danny's eyes flew open. She sounded like a hard-core whore, and his body went hot with need. He'd paid for a lady's favors once, so far gone in grief he couldn't connect any other way after Mariel's death. But *this*. This was real sex, with a woman who responded because she wanted to—because she loved what he'd done to her.

So he stood on his knees to unzip, and then eased back onto the rug made from a bear he'd shot in New Mexico while with a guide. Mariel had despised its bared teeth. Claimed there wasn't a room in her house where it would look right, so he'd found a home for it here.

Good thing, too. The thick fur felt prickly, but it was great for getting laid by the fire.

Danny stretched out, feeling loose yet tingly tight as he watched Norah rifle through her box of tricks in the kitchen. What the hell would she use on him, a cookie? She was humming a catchy little tune in a voice made for a torch singer. . . .

Ohhhhhhh, the weather outside is frightful!

He snickered. Long as the power lines stayed up, yeah, let it snow! This was the finest Christmas he could recall in a long time. Danny licked his lips, trying to figure out those dark red squares in her hand, watching her sway like some exotic goddess come to anoint him.

"Whatcha got?"

"You'll find out. Patience is a virtue." She placed the red squares on the hearth, very close to the fire.

"Virtue has never been my forte, Norah."

"Mine, either. Good thing, huh?"

She grinned like a kid, her face devoid of makeup. Freckles on the bridge of her nose suddenly fascinated him; he noticed the natural arch of those brows a few shades darker than the fly-away waves framing her face. She wasn't the drop-dead-gorgeous type who stopped traffic when she was all tricked out, but then, how many of those women would look this good—*love* this good—after getting waylaid by the weather? They'd be drumming their fake nails, watching the snow pile up or calling on their cells, expecting some poor fool to risk life and limb to fetch them.

But here was Norah, kneeling beside the hearth wearing only the smile of a very naughty angel. Her breasts bobbed above a flat stomach; his gaze followed the alluring curve down to her hips as she fiddled with those little red squares.

"Whatcha got there, Norah girl?"

"Goodies," she purred, her gaze turning feline. "Nothing compared with this goody sticking straight up in the air"—she grasped his cock then, to be sure she had his attention—"but I guess we could call this the frosting on the cake. Or whatever. I'm not all that hot with words."

Danny's laugh sounded tight. "Hot enough for me, honey. Why would I care about words, when your mouth's gonna be full of me?"

"Excellent point." She carefully peeled back the red foil on a couple of those squares, chuckling softly. "And since I just love hot fudge, you're about to become my sundae, Danny. I'll eat this big pink banana with some Dove dark chocolate, and then we'll see where you end up. Your banana in my split, maybe."

He curled inward with the first warm stroke of the melting chocolate against his skin. Norah spread the dark candy all over his cock, using the red wrapper carefully so she wouldn't nick him with the foil. It was a thought that kept him on edge, and he couldn't take his eyes off the dark goo . . . the sensation of it sliding slowly down the length of him.

She made a playful O with her mouth—wiggled the tip of her tongue at him as she dragged his jeans off his legs. Danny folded his arms beneath his head, sinking into the coarse bearskin as she knelt between his legs, brazen and hungry. The first touch of her lips made him growl.

"Mmmmm . . ." Norah closed her eyes as she went down on him. He gathered her hair in his hands—partly because he wanted to feel it, but mostly because he wanted to see every flicker that crossed her expressive face.

Those delicate lashes fluttered against her cheeks. She licked him like a lollipop, up one side and down the other. He ached to feel that full O taking him in, yet it was pleasure enough to watch this arresting woman take her sweet time lapping at that chocolate. She had to lick and suck pretty hard to clean the molten candy from his skin.

He inhaled between clenched teeth when she started at his throbbing tip . . . pushed slowly down his entire length. Her moan reverberated against his skin and into his balls, and Danny grabbed her head to set the pace he needed now. Her sucking noises were driving him nuts, and a rush of heat and need drove him toward release.

"If you don't want me to squirt in your mouth—it won't be long—"

Norah raised up, gripping the base of him. "Thanks for being so considerate," she whispered, "but gush away, big boy. You're going to erupt any second now, and I want to catch every drop."

Oh, God, when had any woman ever said that to him? While Mariel had been a responsive lover, she hadn't given him nearly as much head as he would've liked—

Get real. You had to beg her.

—and now here was Norah, poised to run that ring of her lips down him again.

He began to quiver. Before he could make an intelligible sound, she was on him, hot and hungry and going for his load. Danny grimaced when the lightning hit. With hoarse cries he shot into her mouth, spearing his fingers into her hair to hang on for the ride.

Norah rode with him, up and down that solid pole. She sucked in her cheeks, creating a vacuum around his cock. He was going nuts, writhing and thrashing to get the last of it out, straining to ride that untamed beast within him, as if he were in the arena again.

And what a sight he was, all tanned angles and black lashes and hair flying wildly as he thrashed. Never had she felt such a sense of power over a man. He'd surrendered to her, holding nothing back, and she felt more intimately connected to him than she had with any other lover.

He fell back, panting. Jumped when she flicked her tongue over his tip.

"Norah . . . Norah . . ."

Her name crackled like the fire and whispered in the wind. The sound touched her deeply. Smears of chocolate lingered in his pubic hair and the crevices of his cock, and when Danny opened his eyes, his fingertip traced some that had strayed to her cheek. His eyes beckoned, and she obeyed.

Silently she stretched over him, succumbing to lips that laved the remains of her game from her face. He kissed her endlessly, in hunger and gratitude and something else she couldn't name: a wistfulness that told her she'd given him much more than an orgasm. His thigh trapped her so he could bring her alongside him in the thick, bristly rug and kiss her senseless.

Norah lost herself in him then.

When he'd kissed himself out, Danny sighed deeply. "Shall we shower, *querida?* A lot can be said for starting fresh."

Spoken like a man with a past—who knows mine.

But she forgot about Scurtz and Alex and all she'd lost to them as she stepped into the hot spray that filled the little bathroom with steam. Danny slid the shower door closed, his face dark with mystery and promise. He pressed her against the wet wall with the length of his lean body, kissing her with an animal passion that rekindled her need to be taken.

"I want to slide you up this wall; wrap your legs around me while I shove my cock inside you," he muttered against her damp hair. "You're making me crazy, woman. We're going to rub ourselves raw by the time the plows get—"

The ceiling light died.

Danny scowled, listening. "Shit. The power went out. We'd better wash fast while we still have hot water."

8

Quickly they lathered each other's hair and then used the suds to wash their bodies. Norah moved with an urgency he admired: instead of spazzing out on him, she was making do. With her hair plastered wetly to her head, she looked like a sleek, sexy model on a girlie calendar, flirting with her eyes and her hands.

Danny kissed her nose and finished rinsing. While losing power wasn't a total inconvenience—he was rubbing against a very hot woman, after all—it posed a problem. Firewood was stacked high against the back of the house, so they could stay warm and boil water . . . except out here in the far reaches of his ranch, the pumps that got the water to the house and the cattle troughs depended on electricity. Chico moved to the bunkhouse when he needed to, so this place didn't have a backup generator.

For himself this wasn't a big deal. But now that a lady was present, the romance might disappear in a hurry if Norah got finicky about not being able to . . . flush.

Kissing her deeply, loving the slick heat of her slender body against his, Danny cranked the faucet off. The kiss continued, heating him to the bone—including that bone that rose between his legs. He framed her wet face in his hands, looking deeply into green eyes that returned his heat. His need.

"Norah, you impress me as a rational, adaptable person," he began quietly. He watched the planes of her face for a reaction.

"Will we have enough firewood? Are we able to get out in your truck, if we need to?"

"Yes. And probably."

She smiled slyly. Any man who postponed sex in this steamy shower to *talk* was concerned about something.

"Out here where we're surrounded by grazing land, we need electricity to pump our water from the wells—for the cattle when they're in these pastures, and for this little cabin," Danny explained. His low voice echoed alluringly in the shower stall. "If you'll get squeamish because we can't flush the john, we can leave our little love nest for someplace . . . cozier."

Her eyebrow rose. "You have someplace in mind?"

Hesitation flickered across his dark brow like the flutter of a raven's wing. "Yeah, I know a place. About fifteen minutes away."

"And do you think we'll be better off there? Safer?"

He smiled wryly. Her definition of "safe" wasn't the same as his, because taking her to the main house would expose a lot more than why he didn't admit to being Danny Diablo. And yet, spending even a few more hours with her would make him want her long after this snow melted—no matter where they went. So "safe" really didn't exist anymore, did it?

"We'll be warmer. And we'll have something besides cookies—not that I couldn't exist on your goodies for days on end," he added with a suggestive chuckle. "As your . . . lover, I feel responsible, Norah. We have our romantic notions about this little love nook, but it gets cold here pretty fast. And you've already put up with your share of cold. On a lot of levels."

How did he know that? Had she given too much away when she threw the phone into the car?

Norah rested against the wet, warm shower wall and wished they could just stay this way. Danny was doing the right thing, taking care of her . . . but her harsh realities might make him think again about being her knight in black denim armor. He was standing with his thigh between hers, prodding her decision with the head of his cock.

"What will I wear if we go there?" she wondered aloud. "It was really stupid to leave home with just my—"

His finger shushed her. His face was mere inches from hers, and those dark eyes promised more of the hot lovemaking they'd already shared—if she didn't freak out about clothes, that is.

"You can wear the extra jeans and shirt I brought along. At least until we're in the house," he replied. His smile turned fox-like. "Then I plan to strip you and spend a long, long time snuggling under the covers in a warmer place than this one."

He wanted to take care of her . . . felt responsible for her welfare—unlike Alex, who'd run off with her livelihood, hopes, and dreams.

Norah relaxed. She would trust Danny Diablo to be the perfect gentleman she'd concocted in her youthful fantasies. It seemed a good sign that although he'd brought only a duffel with booze—to drown out whatever demons haunted him this holiday—he'd at least planned to be clean. And he was sharing all he had with *her*.

She couldn't say that about Leon Scurtz, scumbag slumlord. She blinked away the image of the balding sleazebag who'd probably already emptied her pit of an apartment and stolen what he wanted of her stuff. She couldn't think about that yet. Not while she stood in this steamy shower with a rodeo rider, naked and eager for another go-round.

She widened her eyes at him. "Tell ya what, cowboy," she

drawled playfully. "I'd like to ride this thing out a little longer. If you get my meaning."

When her hand closed around his erection, Danny sucked air. "And your point would be—?"

"No, *your* point is making itself perfectly clear," she said, "and that idea about me wrapping myself around you while you leaned me against the wall? Well, we surely have time for that before disaster sets in, don't we? I just hate to keep such a fine, upstanding man waiting."

Her voice was a siren song, speaking directly to the nerve endings all over his body . . . all the hot spots that longed to take this woman one more time before too much truth came between them.

"Why do I get the feeling there's just no end to the ways you like to be fucked?" he murmured.

"Guess you'll just have to find that out for yourself, won'tcha?"

"Norah—"

Her kiss shut off all words and reason, and he let himself rise like a hawk on the updraft of her wanting. God, she was rubbing against him, needing it every bit as badly as he did. Had no problem dealing with the inconveniences of nature. No qualms about her hair drying funny or the lack of explanation he'd offered.

"You're somethin' else, you know it?" he muttered against her ear. His hands were caressing her wet, silky skin, and when he cupped her hips to lift her, she giggled.

"Damn straight I am! I've spent many a night longing to be alone with you, Danny Diablo," she rasped. "You're way better than those naive fantasies I had back then."

Her legs spread for him as he slid her up the wet wall, and he was desperate to be inside her again. That hero-worship thing nagged at him. Even though they'd proven themselves as wayward, willing lovers, he still had plenty of opportunity to disappoint her when they left here. And right now, that was the last thing he wanted to do.

"Who am I to poke fun at a young lady's fantasies?" he asked softly. "Since you're so willing to make mine come true, I'll bring you the pleasure you've dreamed of, too, *querida*. We both need that right now."

"What a sweet thing to say," she murmured. Again she wondered how he *knew* her circumstances—and again she shoved those circumstances far, far from her mind. "Let's don't talk about reality, okay? Let's just screw ourselves silly and then go wherever it is you're taking me."

His cock found the wet slit between those outer lips, and he rubbed her up and down, up and down to spread her silky slickness. He kissed her then, bumping her head back against the shower stall in his need to connect deeply with her, to leave his loneliness behind. He had to bury himself within her, to hide within her sweetness, her willingness to go along with what he offered. It wasn't much—and most of it had been Mariel's. But he couldn't let that sentiment stop him any longer, could he?

Danny inhaled her wet, fresh scent. "I slipped a little present behind the soap for you, Norah. My hands are full of woman right now, so if you'd do the honors—"

Norah grinned at how he'd anticipated this—how he'd surprised her with yet another considerate gesture. She grabbed the packet and ripped the crimp with her teeth.

Once again Danny could only stare at her spirited smile, and those white teeth opening the condom with that happy energy that radiated from everything she did. What a great change from being sucked dry while Mariel's leeching children closed in on him.

Deftly she slipped the rubber from the packet, her eyes never leaving his. "Step back a little, so I can reach you."

He obeyed, resting her shoulders against the stall wall . . .

watching her slender fingers, adept at crafting cookies and jewelry, pop the ring over his tip and then slowly, lovingly inch the condom down his cock. This one was as blue as the waters of an island paradise—at least the way he'd pictured one—and Norah was transporting them to places beyond their wildest imaginations.

When she'd sheathed him, she wiggled suggestively. "Do I get that thing inside me now?"

She was stroking him firmly, with the exact amount of pressure he preferred. Her pulse raced through her lovely legs, inviting him to play—and play like he meant it.

With a single lift, Danny positioned her. Then he lowered her slowly until she surrounded just the tip of his cock with her wet warmth.

He inhaled, trying to maintain control. Norah was driving him nuts with need—when had he ever done it twice in an hour? She was working herself down over him, swallowing his cock in her hot, wet cunt because she had to have this as badly as he did.

"Danny . . . Danny, shove it up inside me." Her legs went around his waist, and she squeezed his hips between her knees.

He was buried to the hilt. Trying not to shoot first and answer later. She wrapped her arms around his neck, coaxing him forward with her wrists.

Norah met his kiss head-on. Whatever came next, wherever they went from here, she wanted these memories as mementos of the biggest coincidence of her life . . . the hottest time she'd ever spent with a man. When he rubbed against the deepest parts of her, she moaned into his mouth. He was sliding up and down, thrusting into her heat, and she squeezed him hard.

"Norah, I don't want to hurt you—"

"You're not!"

"—but I want to thrust really hard against your bone . . . might mash against your clit—"

"Oh, God, I'm gonna come!" she rasped and then held on for dear life.

Just the way he talked to her, so hot and edgy and desperate, propelled her to a climax that came from out of nowhere. He was filling her, stretching her, and when the ring of his condom rubbed against her rim the fireworks burst forth. She threw her head back and bucked against his hips, meeting him thrust for thrust as she cried out wildly.

Once again Danny shot into her and wondered, with what little brains he had left, if Norah would be driving him crazy this way when the new year rolled around. Would she want to? He buried his face in her wet hair, still throbbing inside her. If that answer was no, he didn't want to hear it.

He watched her dry herself, wishing he were the towel, letting her use it first because he'd found only one. He would never forget the vision she made in this unlit bathroom, rubbing her hair into a wild halo of blond-streaked waves, totally unaware of her naked beauty. Danny dried quickly, hoping to preserve this intimate sense of connection they'd come to in such a short time.

"We've made some magic, haven't we?" she murmured.

Danny let out a long sigh. "Damn straight we have. Let's do our best to make it last, honey."

9

He dressed quickly, watching Norah's long legs disappear into his clean jeans. She zipped carefully, so her curls didn't catch, and then smoothed the old denim down over her thighs. Bent over—flashed him a playful butt shot—and rolled double cuffs.

His shirt hung like a loose dress on her, and again she made double cuffs. Red plaid flannel belonged on her. Real homey. She fluffed her hair, sighing at her image in the mirror, yet he'd never seen anyone prettier.

"I miss seeing that beaded bikini through your angel outfit," he teased. "But knowing you're naked underneath my clothes makes me want to rip them off you again. Soon."

Norah smiled at the husky edge in his voice. Alex had been more concerned about his own appearance. His own pleasure. She hoped her fluttery feeling lasted a while: this cabin had been their original nest, and when they left it the fever might break.

She was about to ask him where they were going, when the roar of heavy road equipment made them both look up.

"There's the plow! I'm going out to ask how the roads are."

Her eyes followed his sleek body, clad in black, as he shrugged into his hooded sweatshirt. She watched from the window as he dashed out into snow that came to his knees.

The sun shone brightly, as if no storm had ever passed through—except that the soft blanket of pristine white, sparkling with a gazillion diamonds, proclaimed Mother Nature's Christmas gift. This pastureland needed the winter snow to feed cattle come summer, and even though Norah knew her low-slung car was going nowhere until the roads were cleared, its brilliance dazzled her.

Danny talked above the roar of the plow, his hands animated, pointing down the road. Clearly he knew the driver . . . another sign that he belonged here, and yet he didn't. She glanced around the little cabin again, wondering what other details he was keeping from her.

He'll tell you when he's ready.

She walked to her box on the kitchen table, chose a chocolate star cookie and turned on her cell.

No more calls. Just that voice mail she knew better than to open. It amazed her the phone even worked after the way she'd abused the poor thing. She put it into the tackle box with her beads. She was fetching the Santa ornament from the lamp when Danny came in.

He stomped the snow from his feet, grinning at her. "Lyle says the snow quit around midnight, so his crews have made the main routes passable. We can close up the cabin and—don't move, Norah."

She blinked, half a star sticking out of her mouth.

Danny beelined toward her, toward that cookie in her lips. His arms went around her waist, and he bit off one of the chocolate tips.

Norah giggled. Her green eyes challenged him to take another bite before she tipped her head back to claim the rest of the cookie.

He went for it, pressing into a sweet chocolate kiss that had some chew to it. His hand found the back of her head as they slowed down together . . . to chew and swallow . . . and kiss. Such a simple game, yet he'd never played it.

"Thank you again, angel, for bringing these cookies," Danny whispered. "I was pretty far gone, to come here without any food. Maybe that's why you showed up at my doorstep."

Norah considered this. "Like my going off the road was an act of God?"

"Stranger things have happened."

Providence. Now wasn't that a fine idea? The glimmer of that cross and chain around his neck renewed her sense of Danny being a part of her life before either of them realized it . . . yet another piece to the cosmic puzzle. A piece that might or might not fit, in the end.

He grabbed a raspberry truffle, on a mission now. "I'll clean off the truck. We can probably leave in about ten minutes. Already feels chilly in here."

Norah hadn't noticed. When she gathered their mugs and plates, however, the water running into the sink barely got warm. The engine of his big pickup turned over with a surge of power, and when Danny came inside again she glanced over her shoulder at him.

He leaned against the door to close it, thinking how good she looked in the kitchen with his sleeves folded to her elbow. The halo and wings beside her box reminded him of the wicked things they'd done last night when she entered his desperate domain, proving herself so loving and generous.

Yet Norah was vulnerable, too. As fragile as that old lace nightgown. He still wondered what she'd been running from— marveled that she'd driven out into the storm to take homeless people some Christmas cheer.

Danny hoped she'd rise to the occasion when she saw the truth about *him.* And he hoped some of her bravery would rub off.

"Ready?" He doused the remaining embers with water and shut the glass fireplace doors.

She stood by the table, her arms around her box, watching him. What did she see? The bull rider he'd been in his glory days or a man running from his own shadow now that he was alone?

Danny basked in the glow of her hopeful smile, praying it would last once they walked into the other house. Mariel's house.

Norah shivered as she stepped up into his truck. The coat she'd brought along wasn't enough even over Danny's clothing. What had she been thinking when she'd started out with it? Her red Grand Prix sat beside the cabin under a thick blanket of snow, its tires barely visible. She felt funny leaving it behind: she'd be at Danny's mercy until he brought her back here to clean it off and drive away.

But at least we have to come back, she thought with a secretive smile.

"So, how long have you worked on this ranch, Danny?"

He heard the spinning of a fly line behind that blandly conversational question. And now, with the bright light of day making him squint as he steered onto the road, the truth was begging to be told. No sense in keeping up pretenses. A woman like Norah deserved a straight answer before she figured things out for herself.

"I've been here going on . . . six years," he said, keeping his voice steady. "Hope you didn't think too badly of me last night when I denied being Danny Diablo the rodeo man. Norah. I—"

"You were sloshed," she murmured. "And I came on like a clueless groupie, thinking I could fix everything with—"

"Never clueless!" He braked carefully at the intersection, turned down the blast of the fan and then looked directly into her eyes. "You saw my scar, honey. Knew I'd been gored by a bull, right?"

She nodded. "I was there when it happened."

"The press didn't make a circus of it, thank God, because it took several months to recover from those internal injuries. Took another while before I could even walk again," he went on quietly. "You can imagine how high the hospital bills climbed—and how a rodeo man, flying by the seat of his pants, didn't have any money saved up or enough insurance to weather that storm."

Norah winced. Insurance wasn't her strong suit, either—which was why her business had disappeared with Alex.

"If it hadn't been for the generosity of a . . . very well-to-do, good-hearted woman, I'd have been up shit creek without a paddle."

Something kicked around in her heart. Norah knew where this story was going—but then, Danny had belonged to her only in her fantasies. Like most people, he didn't control all the circumstances—much less that longhorn bull that had thrown him out of rodeo for good. It made perfect sense that a wealthy older woman would take a handsome man like Danny under her wing.

"I . . . I had a feeling your life took a different turn after the accident," she murmured. "Didn't see your obituary, though. I looked every day."

"Didn't see much in print at all, thanks to . . . this same woman." He eased the truck onto the snow-packed main road then, gripping the wheel to control his galloping pulse. Would she believe he'd chosen the road to survival? Or would she think he'd wussed out?

"I'm glad you had someone to look after you," she said quietly. "We could all use a guardian angel when times get tough."

There it was again, that hint of vulnerability that made him want to be her hero. But the hard part was still coming. Danny loosened his grip on the hard wheel. Shifted in his seat.

"Mariel was that," he agreed. He wasn't prepared for the pain that shot through him, just saying her name. He cleared his throat and stared carefully at the road for a little while, just driving.

"She paid my medical bills, Norah. Paid for physical therapy that kept me out of a wheelchair for the rest of my life," he murmured when he could go on. "She . . . was twenty years older than me. Widowed. Offered to marry me so she could take care of me, not knowing if I'd ever walk again. Asked only for my companionship in return. When I recovered beyond the doctors' wildest expectations, I took over as her ranch manager."

Mariel. The name shimmered in her mind—not just because Danny had been married to her, but because more pieces might be fitting into an incredible puzzle. After all, how many wealthy Mariels could there be around Jackson Hole, Wyoming?

Norah gripped his forearm. "Of course you accepted her offer, Danny. No one could blame you for not wanting to be crippled and . . . dependent . . . all your life." *But did you really love her?*

No, don't answer that!

She let her hand drop, watching the snow-filled fields roll by. It wasn't so different from her own situation, in which she'd agreed to Scurtz's proposition so she'd have a roof over her head, yet Danny's scenario sounded a lot more honorable than hers. A lot less sordid.

It struck her then, what he wasn't saying. Why he spoke in past tense. Why Mariel hadn't called a few months ago to order the unique custom-designed pieces she loved to give her man for Christmas. Why Danny went to that cabin with only Gentleman Jack for company.

"Are we possibly talking about Mariel Langston?

He fought a grimace. Nodded and kept watching the road.

"I'm so sorry you've lost her, Danny," she breathed. She rubbed the bend in his elbow, not knowing what else to do or say.

He choked. Focused on the high-piled snow along his edge of the road, hoping she wouldn't despise the tears streaming down his cheeks. "The cabin is where Chico, my herd manager, lives when the weather's fit. I gave him the week off."

Norah nodded, accepting his story without comment or any doubts on her face. The conversation had gone much better than he'd anticipated. And why had he doubted her reaction, anyway?

Because when she sees the house . . .

And there it sat, up ahead. With its bold lines of timber and stone, and the rough-hewn porch railings that accented the two wings flanking the main house, the Langston mansion had always reminded him of a fine hunting lodge where Old Money went on vacation.

Because Old Money had built the place. And Old Money's heirs were fighting him for it now.

Danny pressed the button on his visor flap. As he entered the driveway, the massive wrought-iron gates swung slowly open. Just as Lyle had told him, the driveway was dug out because the guys on the county plows had always taken good care of Mariel. She was the kind of woman who commanded such loyalty.

As he drove slowly up the snow-packed driveway that circled around the front entrance, he glanced across the seat.

Norah could only stare. While Mariel Langston had spared no expense on the jewelry she'd ordered, who could've guessed from her basic denim skirts and cotton blouses that she lived in a castle like this? Danny Diablo the bull rider could never in a million lifetimes sock away the money it took to buy this place.

He'd been a kept man. That's what he couldn't admit back at

the cabin, wasn't it? He'd become Mariel's ranch manager, but what did that really mean? Had Danny merely been his wife's stud puppy? An older woman's trophy?

Questions whizzed in her head as the truck stopped in front of the shoveled steps. Maybe he should just take her back to her car now so she could drive back to her own life—her *real* life—before she set foot on Mariel's turf. If Danny suspected her financial troubles—the dubious direction she took after Alex stole her livelihood and Leon pawned her soul—he'd toss her out like the cheap trash she was. How could he expect her to—

A sniffle made her head pivot. In a heartbeat, Norah slid across the seat to coax Danny's head to her shoulder.

"Danny, I'm so sorry, honey," she murmured into his clean black hair. "There's never a good time to lose your wife, but at Christmas it's just the shits."

He shuddered into her coat shoulder. Hid in her embrace until he could breathe again.

"She . . . she'd be disappointed that I didn't hang the greenery garlands on the porch railings," he wheezed. "Always decorated a huge live tree in the front parlor, so you could see the lights clear out on the road. I—I just couldn't get the Christmas boxes out of the storage shed."

Norah ached with his pain. "And you think Mariel could've done any better, had it been *you* who died, Danny? I seriously doubt it."

He laughed bitterly. "Her daughter and two sons have all called to tell me it's just one more sign I never loved their mother. Just married her money—which is why they're contesting her will and my right to the ranch," he explained in a heated whisper. "Never mind that I kept Mariel profitable by diversifying her herd into specialty rodeo stock. Never mind that it was my idea to irrigate—" Danny clapped his mouth shut. "Sorry. Didn't mean to download the down and dirty. You probably think—"

"You loved Mariel so much you had to get out of her house and drown the memories of your holidays with her," Norah murmured. "I *so* understand why you didn't want to admit that to a half-naked stranger who drove off the road because she was too—too stupid to stay home."

"You sound pretty damn smart to me, Norah." Danny sighed and looked toward the double front door. "If you don't want to go in, I'll understand. We can—"

Norah yanked on the door handle, challenging him with her gaze. "Let's go in where it's warm. You can tell me whatever you care to about your wife—and then I'll tell you how *I* knew her."

10

How the hell could she have known Mariel? This is too freakin' weird.

Yet the slender blonde following him to the kitchen claimed she had things to say about his wife . . . things that would dredge up his pain again. On this day before Christmas, he'd planned to be too hammered to remember.

The house felt cool, but the hum of the fridge and the furnace welcomed them into the large, open room. He set her cookie box on the island and smiled apologetically. "I'd offer you something, but I gave the cook the week off to—"

"Do you think I've had *staff* to open my cans and make my sandwiches?" she teased. "We'll be fine, Danny. It's not like I'm royalty who expects—"

"But you are, Norah. And—as you saw back at the cabin—I'm not much of a hostess," he quipped. "My wife was the one who orchestrated the huge charity receptions and bridge parties. I . . . was mostly the token male her lady friends liked to flirt with."

Norah watched the emotions flit across his face as if some-

one were surfing with a remote: resentment, resignation, re-
morse . . . tinted with a whole lot of loneliness that echoed in
this cavernous house.

She smiled, hoping she didn't sound simplistic. "Well, if the
place is yours now, you can run things any way you want to,
right? If your wife's lady friends treated you like a boy toy, you
don't have to—"

"That sounded terribly childish, didn't it? Downright un-
grateful." He gazed around the large kitchen, where copper-
bottomed pots hung from hooks in the ceiling and the latest
stainless-steel appliances gleamed around the outer walls. "Mariel
was the best. Proud to call me her man—"

"And who wouldn't be?"

"—but her kids—in their thirties now, with high-dollar
homes and stock portfolios—insist I seduced her into leaving
the entire estate to me—"

"You could do that," she said with a quiet laugh.

"—or that I hoodwinked her into believing they all had an
overgrown sense of entitlement."

"Which they probably do."

Norah pondered this a moment, searching for an affirming
response. "It's very common for the surviving spouse in a marriage to control the property because it's often in both their
names, anyway. That's how it was with my parents."

"Yeah, that's how Mariel set it up with her attorney, not long
after she married me."

Should he be airing his dirty laundry this way? Laying all
this nasty stuff out to a stranger? Danny shoved the hair back
from his face, captured by the look of empathy in those emerald eyes. He'd known Norah only a day, but she'd never really
been a stranger, had she? And if she'd known Mariel, well, what
better recommendation could anyone have? His wife had been
generous with her charity but very selective about her friends.

"At first, she wanted to be sure I had enough income if I remained unable to work after she was gone," he continued in a low voice. "Then, when I recovered and took over the herd management, she said I'd earned the house and the land because I'd upgraded everything. Including the fortune her kids are fighting for now."

"And she left her children nothing?"

Danny's laugh had a bitter edge. "I don't consider five hundred thousand apiece 'nothing,' but with these people, it's never enough. They want it all, and they want it now."

Half a million bucks. How different would her life be right now, had someone left her half a million bucks?

But that wasn't the point. Mariel's adult children felt they'd been screwed over by Mama's boy toy, and they wanted him out of the picture. Then they'd fight over the ranch and the house anyway, most likely.

"I'm sorry you have to deal with this," she murmured. She stepped over to him, placing her hands on his, hoping the words came out right. "While I never knew it was *you* she had me design those chains and chokers for, it was obvious in the way she talked about her Daniel—in her attention to the details—that she not only loved you very much, Danny, but she was flat-out *crazy* about you."

His long lashes fluttered. Mariel alone had called him by his full name, and he could hear her voice in his ear, saying it right now.

"It probably sounds like I was just latching on to—but I came to love my wife very much during our six years together, Norah," he confessed softly. "When her doctors discovered her inoperable brain tumor, I never left her. It was . . . a privilege to care for Mariel because I loved her—and to repay the way she saved *my* life. In the end, only music seemed to ease her pain. I was playing my guitar for her when she . . . stopped breathing."

Tears dribbled down her cheeks. The raw devotion in his voice was an awesome declaration of feelings so deep she envied Mariel. Would she herself ever know such wondrous love from a man?

"Well, I can tell you this," she said in hoarse whisper. "While your wife indulged herself in some fine pieces, she was truly tickled to give *you* the most unique jewelry I've ever designed. Sorta says something that she never ordered any for her kids, doesn't it?"

Danny blinked, gripping her fingers to keep his hold on sanity. Here stood Norah in his wife's home, telling him how deeply she'd loved him. Not a flicker of jealousy toward Mariel or derision for him.

And once this wave of pain passed, he realized Norah was also saying his prized chains and chokers . . . the bold, heavy pieces he couldn't bring himself to wear just yet . . . had been crafted by these tiny hands he held.

"You knew her," he wheezed. "How wild is that? And *you* designed the wolf's-head chain and the turquoise guitar—"

"Never realizing her Daniel was my bull-rider hero, Danny Diablo. Not a clue," she cut in with a chuckle. "Mariel and I talked a *lot* during our appointments. The man she described was strong and masculine and, yeah, a little younger, but *damn*, her face lit up when she talked about you!"

When Norah shook her head, those blond-streaked waves drifted around her radiant face. "Her man was never a rodeo has-been or someone she took pity on. Never a man she considered beneath her, Danny. You were *it!*" she exclaimed. "I knew she had some kids and that she'd been widowed a while back, but she was mostly focused on putting your . . . maleness and strength into jewelry not just any man could wear."

She chuckled, as amazed about this revelation as he was. "I didn't know it was *you*," she repeated, "but I sure as hell wanted to meet the guy who got her talking that way. *Glowing* that way."

Danny felt a smile warming his face, like a ray of sunshine

beaming between dark storm clouds. "We were good together," he murmured. "Not to say you and I weren't good back at the—"

"This isn't about me, Danny." Norah let out a wistful sigh as she gazed up into his onyx eyes. "I missed seeing Mariel this fall . . . wondered what might have happened to her—or to her Daniel."

Her order alone could've bought back my gold and silver— my entire inventory. Not to mention my pride.

But that wasn't the issue here, either. No sense in wishing for what could never be. Norah swiped at a stray tear. "The tumor must've taken her down pretty fast."

He nodded grimly.

"Better that way," she assured him. "Better for both of you that she didn't suffer long."

Norah wished for a simple way to erase the pain that creased his brow beneath that midnight hair, but no such magic wand existed, did it? And what could she, a flat-assed-broke jewelry designer, give to the man who had everything—even if Danny had nothing that mattered to him right now?

She reached into the big cardboard box, lifting out the foil pan of frosted sugar cookies. A large angel caught her eye: she'd spent way too much time on the details of its gown and wings that sparkled with rainbow stripes of sanding sugar. Yet now this queen of her cookie collection suggested more than just a sugar fix.

"Let's set her on the windowsill where she'll catch the light," Norah suggested. Then she reached into the box again. Pulled out a star that shimmered in yellow sugar. "The star can sit on top of the window, and the angel can watch over you after I've gone back—"

"Don't go."

Danny embraced her, yet she sensed much more than loneliness in the hands that moved up and down her back. "I feel like I'm cheating on her, asking you to—and you probably feel awkward here in her home—but please, Norah. I don't want to spend Christmas Eve alone."

Her arms tightened around him. When her head found his chest, the staccato heartbeat told her he'd forgotten all about Jack Daniel. Maybe, in his pain, any woman could've served as Danny Diablo's angel tonight—but *she* was here. With a heart full of *yes*.

And then she was kissing him, following the lead of those hungry lips that had so thoroughly pleasured her already. His breath escaped in little moans as he devoured her, rekindling her own feverish desires. Danny framed her face in his long callused hands, kissing her with a wild passion that transcended where he'd taken her before.

He broke it off, breathless. Searched her face. "Will you? Please?"

"Here?" She held her breath, watching the hopeful shine in those bottomless black eyes.

"I've been sleeping in the guest suite ever since, well—when Mariel got really sick, we both slept better alone, so—"

Norah laid a finger on his lips. "No need to explain," she breathed. "Just take me there. Anywhere you want me, Danny."

He grabbed her hand and kissed it hard. Then he took off at a rapid stride that forced Norah to double-time it. They passed through the high-ceilinged foyer . . . clattered across the glossy parquet floor . . . scrambled up the carpeted stairway. The hall could've been in a hotel, it was so long.

So elegant, Norah noted, although the deep shades of blue, rust and sand had a masculine feel to them. As fresh as this house looked, Mariel must've redecorated to match the vitality her life had taken on when Danny came here.

He led her into the first room, where the blinds were drawn

and the bed unmade, and shut the door. The passion lighting his dark eyes spurred her own needs. Norah waited for him to make the moves, to set the mood for this flaring of lust.

That's all it could be, right? Hadn't they just talked about his wife dying down the hall?

"Norah," he breathed, stroking the hair that feathered across her forehead. "It's you I want, never doubt that, angel. But—well, I never had to be concerned about . . . protection with Mariel. So if we need to keep things on the safe side—"

"I'll take my chances."

Danny sucked air. Had she really said that?

He stood before her looking as aroused and rampant as the bulls he used to ride: there was no being "safe" with this man, even if he had a whole box of condoms with him.

"I'm on the pill. I've had my tests," she continued in a halting voice. "If you can trust me to—"

"I've already put my life in your hands," he breathed. "So there's no going back, is there, Norah? If you want out of this anytime soon, you better say so now."

She lunged, her lips seeking his. He growled into the kiss, unleashing the tension that had tightened his body as they'd talked about Mariel. This gentle woman, so kind and caring, was about to transport him far higher than any star her angel cookie could fly to. Yet Norah could get down and dirty, and she was a risk taker, too.

High time he started fighting again, taking the chances instead of letting the chances take him.

11

She tasted hot and restless. Her mouth drew out the warrior in him, made the wolf in his heart howl with recognition of a kindred spirit—a soul mate, maybe for life. As they fumbled with buttons, as shirts dropped off and skin met skin, Danny wondered what had possessed him to make love to Norah here, where he'd felt nothing but uncomfortable these past six months.

She's chasing your demons. Challenging the negative energy that's kept you from healing. From living again.

It rang true, didn't it? The fact that Norah had known and respected Mariel—had crafted the special jewelry he'd worn with such joy—brought this incredible situation full circle.

She was an angel—*his* angel. Sent to raise him up and kick his ass into gear again. He'd nearly died six years ago, and Mariel had healed him; Norah was here to resurrect the man his wife had meant him to be—as if both women had worked together, one handing him over into the other's care, as part of some providential plan.

But his spirits weren't the only thing on the rise. Now that she'd said yes to him, was eager to mate with him in the most elemental way, Danny surged. It was a high he hadn't known since before that bull gored him. It felt mighty damn fine to be riding this razor's edge of desire and adrenaline and need again. To be a *man* again.

As Norah watched him tighten from the inside out, she felt a heady sense of power. *She*, dressed in oversize men's clothing, had inspired this need within him—this sense of long-lost freedom. Just as he'd shown her there was a way to rise above her troubles. A way to love again.

Stripped of his black shirt, peeling off his jeans a few steps away, Danny Diablo was a bronzed god with battle scars that excited something deep within her. His black bikini brief bulged with his yearning for her: if she could inspire such heat and lust in a fine male animal like this one, why would she consider anyone less? Norah needed to believe she could put all that ugly reality behind her, now that she'd found a man who appreciated her art and her spirit and her need to share them.

Danny stepped toward her, his arms extended in invitation. His heart beat steadily now. What a wonderful thing, to meet a woman who'd wanted him for years because of who he was and what he excited in her. Mariel's love had been his salvation, but now he loved from a position of power, and it made all the difference. He ran his hands through Norah's blond, exotic hair, grinning.

She wound herself around his corded body, hanging on as he lifted her toward the bed. Danny landed on top of her, bracing his weight on his hands. Yet it was his kiss that pinned her to that rumpled bed: his lips held her in a hot trance that spiraled and sparkled around her. It was like a magic, beaded veil that would protect her from all evil.

Norah raised her mouth to duel with his, pushing away the reality that would rear its face soon enough. For now, she could fly because he'd given her spirit wings.

Danny closed his eyes to experience her more fully. She smelled like sugar cookies and the juniper shampoo from Chico's shower. Her softness invited him to bury himself and never come out, and when he fumbled with her zipper, Norah arched up so he could peel his jeans down her legs. She was all girlie-fresh innocence in his clothing, yet the soft bob of her breasts had reminded him—every moment since they left the cabin—that she wore nothing underneath it.

The idea that her most intimate skin had rubbed in his jeans . . . left her essence in the seam . . . sent his need for her to a dizzying new height. He wanted to thrust hard and deep, to brand her as his own.

But once he'd freed Norah's ankles of the heavy denim, she was on him. She flipped him playfully onto his back.

"You think I'm going to make this easy for you?" she teased. When she straddled him, her wispy blond waves fell around his face like a mysterious curtain. Her eyes shone dark with desire as her lips parted to pant his name.

"Danny . . . Danny Diablo," she rasped, a siren spirit luring him into her lair. "Get ready to be humped within an inch of your life, big boy, 'cause this cowgirl's ready to ride. No ropes, no saddle. Just my hot little pussy suckin' you up and suckin' you dry."

He arched up to touch her with his tip. "Ride on, Queen Norah."

Queen Norah. It had a nice ring to it.

Tossing her hair back over her shoulder, she grabbed his insistent cock. "If you want inside me, you're gonna have to ask real nice," she crooned. "Extra credit for begging."

"A wolf never begs, *mi querida,*" he growled. "Make me howl, and we'll see how high you fly."

Norah mounted him hard and fast. Danny grabbed the halves of her ass to hold her in place, nailing those green eyes with a gaze that brought out the spitfire in her. "Remember who you're dealing with, my queen. I'm used to being the one on top. In control."

"Change is a good thing," she countered. She squeezed him then, reveling in the hot length of him inside her without the latex barrier. A dicey move, but it pushed them past all previous pretenses and the social niceties lovers hid behind. It was male and female now, unfettered and uninhibited. Skin to skin, slick and smooth, hot and hard. Wet and wild and primal.

Danny moved within her, meeting her soft hips with his solid thrusts. So willing she felt, so pliant and soft. He dug his fingers in, and she moaned.

Norah shimmied above him then. She lowered herself to tease his nose with a hardened nipple, and he sucked it between his teeth.

"Oh, you've done it now, mister," she rasped. She made him struggle upward to keep his lips locked on her breast, setting the pace below with steady strokes. Up and down him she moved, indulging herself in his hard, virile heat. Finding all their best hot buttons. He was breathing rapidly now, closing his eyes and clenching his stubbled jaw.

God, he was gorgeous. His raven hair spread like wings away from his forehead. His skin, the color of melting caramel, made such a sweet contrast to her own as those long, dark lashes brushed his high cheekbones.

And she was his. At least in this most elemental way. At least for now.

Norah shook her mane over him, releasing all thoughts of what might or might not happen, come tomorrow. She wanted it to be the best, for both of them. Inside her, he grew more insistent. His slender hips bumped against hers, grinding in an escalating rhythm that made her gasp to keep up with him.

"Say yes, *querida*," he breathed. "Tell me how bad you want it. Tell me when."

Norah's head flew back, and her eyes closed with the intensity of their impending climax. He watched the vein throb in her slender neck . . . such lovely, pale skin, and all that hair drifting above him in wild disarray. Would he ever see her this way again? Would she find a reason . . . maybe that reason she'd been running from . . . to say it was time to go home after this?

"Norah. Norah, I'm begging you," he whispered. "Open yourself to me completely. Mind and body. Heart and soul."

It was what her battered inner angel needed to hear. All she needed to know at this moment. And weren't all relationships, hot or not, a matter of one moment following the next?

"Take it!" she breathed against his ear. She ran her wet tongue around its hard rim, and then wiggled it in the opening. "Take *me*, Danny Diablo!"

Danny lunged upward. "Wicked thing!" he said with a rough chuckle. "You're gonna get it now! You damn well better be ready!"

"Yeah, well, that's pretty tough talk." Norah ground herself against him mercilessly, straining to stay ahead of the spiraling wildfires inside her. In just moments she would belong to him in the most intimate and important of ways, and she wanted to remember it as the highlight of her life. A longtime dream come true at last.

"Look at me, Danny." She braced her arms on either side of his head and gripped him with her knees. "I want to watch you come. I want to see the stars in your eyes when you cut loose inside me, cowboy."

With another growl, Danny locked his gaze into hers. The hairs along his jaw rippled with his concentration. "Get ready."

She nodded, fascinated by his contrasts: the thrashing of his hips and the sweet serenity of his smile; the dark desires he wanted to set loose while he adored her like no other man ever had.

His first low moan was her complete undoing. Norah cried

out, and her hips took over. It required all her effort to focus on those devilish eyes, yet she wouldn't have missed that burst of onyx fire for anything in this world.

He shot into her, and she spasmed. His fingers dug into her flesh, and she demanded more—gave more than she knew she had, to watch the grimace of ecstasy transform his face.

When she collapsed on him, Danny rolled her to one side. He kissed her softly, as though her face were his most precious possession. As though she *mattered* to him.

"Norah, please say we can talk about what comes next, when we have the strength to speak again," he pleaded.

What would he do if she brushed him off? What if she asked him to drive her back to her car, so she could disappear from his life? He held his breath, awaiting her answer.

"I—I want that, too, Danny."

Pure joy filled him. He held her hard, closing his eyes to keep his tears from ruining the moment's sheer sweetness. When he could think straight, he knew what he had to do.

"Stay right here," he whispered. He rolled from the rumpled bed before she could quiz him, before he could question his own motives. The gift he had in mind would've sent any other woman running, but his gut told him Norah would understand it.

Norah lay limp in soft, blue sheets that smelled like Danny Diablo. Her pulse pounded steadily. She'd never felt happier or more complete. The joy on Danny's face had touched her profoundly—and then he left! Whatever he was doing down the hall would be a wonderful surprise. She just knew it!

And when he stepped through the doorway, his vulnerable smile made her breath catch. He held something behind his back, smiling slyly.

"I want you to have this, *mi vida*," he whispered as he sat on the edge of the bed. "It's the one piece I saved because Mariel loved it so . . . because I couldn't bear to part with it when I gave her daughter the rest of her jewelry."

Norah nipped her lip. How did she feel about wearing a dead woman's treasure? Truly, Danny was offering her a keepsake that held deep meaning for him, and Mariel *had* been a dear friend in her own right, yet—

When she saw the glimmer of ivory and pearls in the dimness, the air left her lungs. *Days* she'd spent getting the proportion and details just right on this choker for Mariel Langston, lavishing her love on a piece she herself could never afford, grateful for the chance to work with such fabulous materials. This garland of roses and ivy, fashioned from mother-of-pearl, ivory and dozens of seed pearls, remained her masterpiece even though she'd often worked with costlier gemstones and gold.

"Oh, Danny . . ."

"Will you accept it, knowing how Mariel would've wanted you to have it?" he asked in a tentative whisper. "I—I'll understand if this seems awkward—"

"Thank you. You can't imagine how honored I feel that you saved this piece back . . . and that you want *me* to have it."

Silently she sat up. A fierce bravery overrode the sadness in those onyx eyes as Danny fastened the wide, beaded band around her neck. It was a moment she knew she'd never forget. A binding of his soul to her own.

Then she saw what he'd fetched for himself.

Norah grinned and ran her fingers over the three pewter wolves' heads, again recalling the hours she'd poured into making them perfect. So masculine this piece was; no two links of its heavy chain were alike. The ruby eyes in the larger center face gave it a devilish gleam she'd delighted in as she'd crafted it, wondering what sort of man Mariel intended it for.

"This is so perfect for—so *you*," she murmured with intense satisfaction. She surrendered again as Danny kissed her, sealing something sacred into place between them.

They heard a *whump* outside.

Danny stiffened, listening. Placing a finger on his lips to signal for silence, he rose with the swift grace of a panther. He peered outside from behind the edge of the closed blind.

"Shit. It's Jennifer," he muttered. "Mariel's daughter. The truck's out front, so she knows I'm here. Better go see what she's after this time."

He pulled on his jeans and shirt, his face taut with distaste.

Norah lay absolutely still, sensing nothing good would come of this visit. Could she hole up in Danny's room without giving her presence away? If Jennifer stormed up here, could she find someplace to hide?

She tasted a new strength in Danny when he kissed her hard on the mouth.

"Thank you, angel," he whispered. He fingered the wolves' heads on their heavy chain. "You've given me this talisman, this work of your hands from your heart. Jennifer won't be staying long."

12

<hr>

"Give it up, Danny boy. Can't hide behind Mom's skirts anymore." A harsh voice rose from the entryway. "My brothers and I have requested a court order to get your gigolo ass out of our house."

Norah scowled. The Lincoln Navigator parked behind Danny's truck bespoke a woman of more class than what she was overhearing, and it made her blood boil. Maybe Jennifer needed a talking-to only another woman could give her.

No doubt her appearance would incriminate Danny further, but she dressed quickly in his plaid shirt and rolled jeans anyway. She smoothed her hair and looked in the mirror. She would support her man to the max, after the way he'd pulled her out of much more than a snowy ditch the other night.

"And what's with the scraggly beard?" Jennifer taunted. She was in her thirties, Danny had said, yet her voice had the defiant, edgy whine of a teenager's. "Jesus, you look like a waiter in a really cheap restaurant. Mom would not be impressed."

Out the door Norah stalked, her bare feet sinking into the lush carpet. She had no desire to keep her presence a secret now, since it was so obvious Jennifer had come here on a merciless mission.

Danny's response, weary and irritated, rose up the stairway as Norah started down. "Jennifer, I realize—*believe* me, I realize—how difficult this first Christmas without your mother is. But can't we at least be civil? I've done nothing to—"

"That's right! You've done *nothing!*" came the shrill response. "Nothing except bum off Mom's estate and use her property to your own—and who is *this?*"

Norah stopped three steps from the bottom, fixing her gaze on Jennifer. To keep from lunging at this foul woman, she crossed her arms as though she had every right to be here.

Danny glanced back at her for a long moment. She smiled steadily at him.

"This is Norah Dalton," he said firmly. "She's the designer who created the wonderful jewelry your mother loved, and—"

"And she's your whore! Shacking up with—wearing *your* clothes!" Jennifer howled. "Jesus, Danny, Mom's hardly even cold, and you're already—"

Norah descended a couple more steps, remaining one level above this presumptuous intruder. Amazing, the strength that came from hearing Danny say her full name for the first time . . . like she *mattered*. She looked at the wealthy young woman in her high-dollar clothes and a face that blazed in an unbecoming shade of *spoiled*. Jennifer had her mother's high cheekbones and thick chestnut hair, but Mariel's patient wisdom had obviously skipped this generation.

"I got to know your mom pretty well over the past five years, Jennifer," she said in a low voice. "She'd be appalled at *your* behavior. Your lack of respect for her memory and for the man she loved."

"Oh, don't give me that—" Jennifer stepped toward her then, scowling. "What's that around your neck?"

She glared at Danny then, her color rising. "That's the neck-lace *I* wanted! I asked you for—"

"No, you demanded I hand it over," he corrected, "so I kept it as a remembrance of your mother's love and beauty. Hoping someday you would rise to her level of sophistication."

"Lying bastard!"

Norah stepped to the foyer floor, ready to set this selfish bitch straight—until Jennifer grabbed the choker, *hard*.

Silence echoed in the airless foyer. The tension alone choked her.

Jennifer's grip tightened. "This is mine, and I'm going to—"

"Let me warn you what'll happen if you rip this off me." Norah focused intently on what Mariel's hazel eyes must've looked like twenty years ago. "Any force you apply will pop seed pearls from their threads. Then the other pearls and the ivy will come loose and bounce all over this tile floor." She kept her voice low, as if explaining this to an impulsive child. "And if you yank hard enough, the gold wire holding all these mother-of-pearl roses in place will cut into my neck. You'll ruin this necklace, and I'll have to file charges for assault."

"Ha! My brother Chas is an attorney, so—"

"No secret why your mother had somebody outside the family handle her estate, is it?" Danny asked sadly. "If you take me to court—or injure Norah—she'll be physical evidence of your attack. It'll no longer be my word against yours."

His dark eyes filled with a deep sadness, a regret Norah wished she could wipe away. "Your mother would never have tolerated such crude behavior from the daughter she loved so much, Jennifer," he murmured. "You know that."

Jennifer's lip curled, and the hand she removed from Norah's neck landed on Danny's face with a resounding *smack*.

"Don't think you'll get away with this!" she spat. "When Chas and Phillip hear about—when I tell them you're shacking up with this artsy-fartsy designer—you won't have a pot left to piss in!"

She pivoted on her heel and left with a loud slam of the door.

Danny let out a long, tired sigh. His shoulders sagged. "I'm sorry you had to see that, Norah. Are you all right?"

"I'm sorry if I—maybe I should've stayed in your room," she rasped, "but I could tell your confrontation was going nowhere productive. Why'd she come here, anyway?"

"I have no idea. But we can bet it wasn't to wish me a Merry Christmas."

He took her in his arms then. Ran a gentle finger over the rose choker. "It confirms my original instinct about keeping this piece, hoping Jennifer's bitterness would pass—"

"If you want it back—if it rightfully belongs to—"

"It belongs to *you*, Norah. Because I said so." Danny's black eyes blazed into hers. "I can see now that Mariel's kids won't come to terms with her death until they've gotten me out of the picture. Off this ranch."

Norah wasn't sure how to interpret that, but she sensed he needed to talk it out—with himself, mostly. "Were they close to their mom? She didn't talk about them much, but, then, I was only doing jewelry for her."

Danny shrugged. "Hard to tell, since all three of them despised me from the get-go. It was the one part of our relationship I regretted—that I might have caused a rift between Mariel and her—"

"No, Danny. Her children are adults—responsible for their own bad behavior," she insisted vehemently. "*You* were responsible for Mariel's happiness . . . for the glow on her face. *You* inspired the most incredible pieces I've ever created."

She fingered the three wolves' heads, stirred once again by their power, by the virile force of the man she'd made them for. It was another example of providence, the perfect way the pewter and rubies complemented this rugged man, and vice versa.

"Thanks for saying that." Danny's dark eyes softened. He exhaled sadly. "The past few months have been so full of their verbal attacks, I'd begun to believe them ... to question my own motives about marrying Mariel in the first place. You've clarified things for me, Norah."

"Happy to help," she murmured. "But I'm sure seeing me in your clothes and her mother's jewelry hasn't improved Jennifer's mindset."

A smile curved his lush lips. "But, as you said, it's *her* mindset. And it's *her* problem," he said. "I've done nothing wrong, Norah, and you've reminded me of that. It's a powerful Christmas gift, this freedom."

He closed his eyes and kissed her then, softly yet with a fervor that kindled an inner warmth she'd been missing for months now.

It would be so easy to believe him—so easy to fall for the affection radiating from Danny's handsome face. If they could stay at this fine home—or better yet, hole up in the cabin, just the two of them—forever, wouldn't life be wonderful? She rested her head on his shoulder, letting his warmth seep through her body.

His problems were as annoying as her own, yet they at least sounded like aboveboard, understandable problems. What would Danny think if he ever learned of her situation?

Norah tightened her arms around him. It was Christmas Eve, and they were warm and safe. Better to let the fantasy carry them through the night. Better to succumb to his wondrous lovemaking while she could, because all too soon it would be time for good-bye.

"Norah," he murmured against her ear. "It's too early to say this, but I've learned that life's fragile, so ... I want you to know I'm falling in love with you."

13

That night they made Christmas magic. Although she could easily imagine how glorious Mariel's rustic home would look decked out with a tall tree and greenery garlands, Norah was too wrapped up in Danny's loving to miss the trappings of the season. It was a night of bright stars in her eyes and whispered promises on his lips. A night that sparkled with hope for both of them.

Twice they made love, driven by the desire to give more than they received. Even in the dimness of Danny's room, they glowed together, their bodies alight with desire and the fever they'd kindled in the cabin. He felt strong and confident again, moving inside her and around her, lavishing himself on every inch of her beautiful body, sensing this winter wonderland of a night would end all too soon.

Norah accepted the love light in his dark eyes; reveled in the way they fit together and instinctively pleased each other. It seemed so natural to move from one position into the next, testing and pleasuring, drawing out the joys each had been missing for so long.

They slept entwined, in a bed wrecked from their loving.

Danny awoke first. He watched the dawn peek through the edges of the blinds to light Norah's pretty face. Her hair swept wildly over his pillows, and her scent filled him with the desire to protect her. To love her. Still asleep, she seemed so innocent. Free from the secrets he saw in her green eyes when she didn't know he was watching.

He wondered about those secrets again . . . wanted to wipe away their stress and watch laughter transform her face. Wanted to hear that laughter change this mausoleum into a home again. Wanted her to stay and make a go of this relationship.

Was he in a rebound situation? Looking for a way to end his loneliness and endure the courtroom ordeal Mariel's kids had threatened him with? Danny stroked her wild blond waves, careful not to waken her. He slipped downstairs then, to start their coffee and think about things. More questions than answers ran amok in his mind—which was *not* the way he ran a ranch or lived his life.

How could he be so wrapped up in Norah so soon? Just a couple days ago he'd been awash in grief, yet now, on Christmas morning, all was calm and bright. He felt as sparkly as that sunlit snow out there—like a kid whose belief in Santa had been renewed. The cookies on the window sill made him smile. Norah was like a kid in many ways, too: loving and giving. Shiny-bright like the star.

He swore he heard a tinkling sound. *Angels we have heard on high . . .*

Danny lifted the flap of the big box Norah had carried in, and damned if her cell phone wasn't ringing. Old as it was, the battery should've been shot from leaving it on all night. It was just like Norah to have an angel song for a ring tone, wasn't it?

He stared at the number on the screen. Was it the jerk she'd been running from? Should he answer this call—stand up to Norah's demons like she'd confronted his?

Instinct made him press the TALK button. As he put the phone to his ear, he prayed for the right words—

"Merrrrrr-ry Christmas, Miss Dalton! HA HA HA!" came a gravelly male voice. The guy sounded rude and crude. Too much spike in the eggnog already? "Whatsa matter, Norah? Pussy got your tongue?" he jeered after a moment. "Too busy helping the *homeless* to pay your rent or answer my voice mail? Well, you're gonna loooove what Santa's got planned for—"

Click. Danny silenced that reptilian voice, heat rising in his cheeks. He had no right, but he accessed her voice mail then— zapped that, too, when he saw the same number flash on the screen. That oily sneer had painted a vivid, instant picture in his mind: a snapshot of Norah's life before the storm.

He couldn't imagine her living in such ugliness.

She didn't have to go back. He'd see to that.

Norah tossed her arm across the bed. She'd been vaguely aware of when Danny got up, but she lingered in his sheets, savoring the scent of their sex. What should she do, now that he was so wrapped up in her? From downstairs she heard rapid-fire runs on a guitar—a flashier version of "Angels We Have Heard On High" than he'd played the other day.

The music stunned her with its clarity. Its complexity. Behind his skillful rendering of the song rang a daredevil passion for the music—and his passion for *her.*

What a wonderful, romantic way to awaken on Christmas! What woman wouldn't love such a serenade, even if the man playing it was mentally wrestling with something? She free-wheeled the same way when she created new jewelry, challenging the rules of symmetry and line, following each idea to its finish by sheer instinct. She designed because she *had* to, just as Danny grabbed his guitar to express parts of himself words couldn't touch.

She smelled coffee with a hint of chocolate. Looked around this room with its dark, masculine furnishings, maybe for the last time. As Norah dressed, she wondered how to explain her misgivings . . . things she needed to resolve . . . without making Danny feel she was rejecting him.

No two ways about it: she had to leave before he found out about Leon.

She sighed and got dressed. She loved the ruggedness of Danny's jeans on her legs and the softness of his red flannelette shirt. It spoke volumes that his labels proclaimed Brooks Brothers and Lands' End rather than Wal-Mart, where she always shopped.

Just one more reason you can't fantasize about life with Danny Diablo.

Better to recall that nasty chat with Jennifer and envision Mariel's two high-powered sons joining the crusade to reclaim their mom's estate. Fights like that never ended, even after gavels came down and papers got signed. If she'd inspired Danny to stand up to them, well, she'd left him in better shape than she'd found him, right? Repayment for getting pulled out of his ditch. It didn't satisfy her longings, but at least it evened the score.

At the top of the stairs she fondled the glossy newel post, listening to Danny's improvisation of "Hark, the Herald Angels Sing." His bravado mellowed as he caressed these chords, and the melody sang sweetly to her heart, as though he sensed she was listening.

A man who played angel songs had to have something inside him she could cling to. Too bad his music put an ironic twist on the ring tone of her phone—that reminder of how Leon had taunted her into losing control. Losing herself.

Or are Danny's songs the solution to all my problems?

Better not to see it that way. All her life she'd had a tendency to romanticize, and look where she'd landed.

Norah took the stairs slowly. Danny sat in the front parlor, too wrapped up in his music to notice her. His black hair fell over his eyes, but she could hear their shine in the glorious riff he played. Those calloused fingertips had inspired the same joy in her soul, and she would miss it. Her nipples hardened against the softness of his shirt, and she closed her eyes to images that would haunt her for months to come.

She poured two mugs of coffee, in a kitchen that bespoke Mariel Langston's love of the finer things: the top-line appliances and rich ceramic tile made Norah's heart ache. This lifestyle could never be hers, could it? The best home she could hope for was more like the sugar cutout she took from the foil pan: a small cookie-cutter house decorated on the cheap.

She put their breakfast on a tray and joined Danny in the sunlit front parlor. From the picture window, pastures blanketed in snow dazzled her like a scene from a Hallmark Christmas card. If only such beauty and serenity could be hers forever. . . .

When the music stopped, Danny smiled at her. He set his guitar aside and stood up with a kiss in his eyes.

She set the tray on the nearest table and lost herself in his embrace. One more time she melted against him, reminding herself to disengage somehow without hurting him.

When he took a big bite of a butterscotch brownie, Norah sighed. "We should probably fetch my car this morning, Danny. I—I hate to break the spell, but I need to . . . check on some things."

He nodded, his expression guarded. His eyes held the hot shine of coffee—something he wasn't telling her yet. "I hope you'll call me if you need my help—and even if you don't, *mi querida*. Please tell me that what we've started here won't end."

She buried her face in his twill shirt, blotting sudden tears. "I want to be with you, but I can't make any promises about . . .

well, about anything. It's not *you*, Danny! You've been wonderful, and I so appreciate—"

He pressed a fingertip to her lips, smiling. "Let's enjoy our breakfast, and then we'll go whenever you're ready."

The cabin, wrapped in its winter blanket, looked so much like another Christmas card that Norah wished she could go inside and burrow between the sheets naked with Danny. Instead, she cleared the snow from her car and scraped the windshield while the defroster blasted heat from the inside. Danny shoveled the drifts and cleared a path between the tracks his truck had made.

"You know how to get back to the highway?"

She gazed up the snow-packed road, nodding. "In the daylight, it's no big deal. Won't take me half an hour to get home."

He nodded, tossing the scraper to her back floor. The wind whipped his raven hair around a face that looked worried yet . . . determined. So damned handsome she had to be crazy, leaving when he'd begged her to stay.

"Thank you for understanding," she began in a quavery voice. "I wish I could promise you—"

His kiss made her weak with wanting him. She broke away too soon.

"Here's my number," he insisted, tucking a slip of paper into her jacket pocket. "Call me, Norah. No matter *what*, I want you. I want *us*."

She nodded. Slipped into the driver's seat and turned down the defrost fan, wishing the perfect words would come—wishing she could blurt out how she, too, was falling in love.

"Thanks again, Danny," she wheezed. "You were wonderful."

Before tears could dribble down her cheeks, she put the Grand Prix in gear. She focused on the road ahead, swiping at her eyes. She'd just tasted heaven, and it didn't feel good to be driving away. That angel costume in her backseat, with its lop-sided halo bobbing on top, was a dismal reminder of what she was returning to on a Christmas morning that should've been—could've been—bright with promise.

After carefully maneuvering around snow-piled intersections in open country, it was a relief to find the highway clear and sanded in town. As Norah made all the familiar turns, her body tensed and her pulse pounded into a headache. If she hadn't left all her clothes—if she didn't feel so responsible for unpaid rent—she'd turn the car around right now—

"*Ohhh, you better watch out! You better not cry! You better not pout—*"

She cranked the radio off, even though she realized the song was right. She had to hang tough. Had to face up to Scurtz somehow and get the hell *out* of that situation. She hadn't checked her phone, because it was a no-brainer that he was still pissed at her. Not likely to forgive a month's rent or consider her apologies.

By the time Norah pulled up beside the delapidated house, she was shaking with fear—which then turned to rage. Underneath the window of her apartment, familiar items littered the snow: her clothes had landed in colorful heaps, and Mama's lamp with the stained-glass shade lay broken on top of them. The wicker chest in which she stored her beads had spilled its sparkling contents all over the sidewalk, like a rainbow. The crowning glory of this spectacle was her underwear, which decorated the spruce tree beside the front door: Scurtz had obviously enjoyed hanging her panties and bras in provocative poses. The fact that he'd handled them made her gag.

Norah gripped the steering wheel, wishing she could just drive away. But she couldn't afford to replace her clothes any more than she could pay her rent. She'd made a desperate deal, thinking she'd find work, and she'd lost. She had no idea what she'd say . . . what Leon might try when she went inside.

The flutter of the blind in his downstairs window told her he was watching. Poised to pounce.

14

When she stepped into the dingy entryway, the stench of cooked cabbage turned her stomach. Not only did this ratty old house not smell like Christmas, it was a blatant reminder of what she'd left behind at Danny's. She hadn't reached the second step on the scarred wooden stairway when Leon Scurtz opened his door.

"Whatcha goin' up there for, girlie?" he said with a smirk. "Don't say I didn't warn ya! Don't tell me ya didn't see your stuff outside—and I've changed your lock anyways. It's time we had us a little . . . talk."

Norah gripped the bannister to keep her hold on rational thought—and breakfast. The heat billowing out from his apartment carried more of that sickening cabbage smell. Leon's old undershirt didn't cover his belly, and his faded sweatpants hit him midcalf. He scratched his graying chest hair, watching her. Waiting for her to cry, or blurt out her excuses, or beg for another reprieve.

But what could she say? She had no money, and he knew it. His foxlike expression said he intended to spread her thighs no matter what she said or did. That was the deal she'd made in her eleventh-hour desperation, hoping to sell some more jewelry before Christmas.

"So where'd you get those clothes?" he jeered. "What happened to that angel who went flittin' outta here the other night, promisin' me a go at her beaded—"

"That outfit's right out here in my car. Just let me fetch it!"

Norah bolted, knowing an escape clause when she heard one. Why had she even come inside? Driving far, far away would at least preserve one last scrap of dignity and control. She could go to that homeless shelter she'd been heading for, or—

Scurtz grabbed her hair before she reached the door. Her frightened cry echoed in the entryway and made him laugh.

"Don't think for a minute you're gettin' outta this, Miss Fancy-Pants Designer," he muttered against her ear. His breath reeked of soured beer, and his erection prodded her from behind. "A deal's a deal, and you owe me for—"

"How much?" a voice demanded outside. "Get your filthy hands off her!"

Norah held her breath. Danny Diablo swung open the door, poised to spring at Scurtz. A black Stetson slanted down over his dark glasses, and his leather jacket whispered with a jaguar's power as he stepped inside. He gripped his cell phone like a weapon, looking so much like an updated Lone Ranger she wanted to cheer.

Scurtz snorted. "Close the damn door! It's cold out—"

"Not half as cold as you'll be if you don't turn her loose. I'm calling the cops." Danny thumbed in a few numbers and put his phone to his ear, advancing with each step Scurtz took backward. "Yes, ma'am, I'd like to report a domestic disturbance at fifteen—"

"Get off the fuckin' phone! You've got no right to—"

Norah kicked back at Leon's shin and escaped his grasp.

Her heart was pounding so hard she ducked Danny's open arm to dart outside.

"So, what's she owe you?" the man in black demanded. "Let's just settle up and be done with it."

"If you think you can sashay in here like some—some stud *cowboy* to—those are *your* clothes she's wearin', ain't they?" Scurtz jeered. "Said she was headin' for some charity gig, and here she's been shackin' up with—"

Norah snatched her underwear off the spruce tree, following their conversation. She wanted to grab her stuff and drive off, yet she couldn't leave Danny here to get all the sordid details from Leon's side—and she owed him a huge thank you for tailing her. For sensing she was in trouble and rescuing her in the nick of time.

"How much?" Danny insisted, and then into the phone he continued, "Yes, officer, we're at fifteen twelve—"

"Three months' rent, that's what!" Scurtz jeered. "And at five hundred bucks a—"

"One month, at three-fifty!" Norah hollered into the open doorway. "I've got the rental agreement to prove it—unless you trashed that, too!"

She scooped her boxes of beads and paints back into the broken wicker chest, heedless of the snow that went in with them. She wasn't sure what Danny might do—what her rights were if the police *did* show up—but she was *not* going to let anyone else witness her disgrace.

As she came back from her car to gather another load, Danny stepped outside. His dark shades made his expression unreadable. "Leave it, Norah. Follow me in your car, and we'll—"

"I can't just let you pay my—"

"—get some breakfast uptown. Where we can talk in private."

Norah's tears spilled over. Danny's words were kind and

gentle. The doorway looked bleary, but Scurtz wasn't coming through it to taunt her or grab her again. "What'd you do to—"

"I paid him," Danny replied with a shrug. "I had money, just like you had cookies the other night. We use whatever we have, honey, but the results are the same, right? We're free to move forward."

She swiped at her eyes. Had she heard him right? That smile curved beneath his shades—an expression that made Danny Diablo excruciatingly sexy, even here in this crappy little yard still littered with her things.

"Okay, we'll talk," she murmured, "but I can't let you—"

"We'll see about that. Right now I'm offering you breakfast and a chance to be my angel a little longer."

What did he mean by that? Her heart thudded, but she didn't dare get too hopeful: Danny had not only seen her low-life situation, but now she owed him money. Big-time.

Wasn't that the way Mariel rescued this man years ago? Isn't Danny's plan the best option—the only option—I've got right now?

Norah climbed into her car. Followed him along the busy streets in a daze, to a truck stop on the edge of town. As he held the door for her, they were enveloped in aromas of ham and biscuits and cinnamon. Danny put his hand at the small of her back as though it were the most natural thing—as though he wanted to touch her for who she was, rather than steer her into another dubious situation.

He slid into a booth and removed his shades and Stetson. Then he reached across the table for her hands. "I'd like a carafe of coffee and twenty minutes to talk to this lady uninterrupted," he said to the waitress.

When the coffee arrived, he poured for them. Norah's hand shook within his, and her eyes looked wide enough to jump into. She was so accustomed to men mistreating her—so afraid of what he'd think of her—she couldn't ask him for help. God, what he'd give to wipe away the time she'd spent with a land-lord too disgusting to describe.

"I have a confession," he breathed. He leaned on his elbows, focusing on Norah's huge green eyes. "I hope you won't be mad at me for overstepping."

She sipped her coffee, blinking nervously.

"I answered your phone this morning before you woke up, honey. When I heard what that scumbag was saying, I hung up on him," he whispered fiercely. "I also deleted his earlier voice mail without listening to it, in case you were wondering."

Norah's shoulders fell. Coffee sloshed out of her mug, and once again she wished the floor would open up. "What'd he tell you?"

"He hinted that he had a Christmas surprise for you. Mentioned that you hadn't paid your rent, using language and a tone that pretty much told the tale. It was all I needed to hear."

She clenched her eyes against tears. "So now you know what a slut I—"

"You were in a financial bind. Which happens to a lot of us."

He leaned across the table, imploring her to look into eyes as dark as Dove chocolate. "I copied your address from the label on your cookie box. Got directions on MapQuest, because I had a hunch things would get ugly," he explained earnestly. "It killed me to watch you drive off, Norah, but I knew you had to set things right.

"After you left, I stopped at the ATM for that Christmas present I was wanting to give you—the first of many, I hope." His grin flickered. "Felt good to get my hat and leather jacket from behind the truck seat. To live like I *mean* it again."

How could he be saying these things in that soft, sexy voice? Danny was holding her hand again . . . waiting. His expression told her he had all day with nothing better to do than sit here with her—and that he liked it that way. His eyes glimmered with a sure, feral strength, like the ones she'd chosen for those wolves' heads at his throat.

It was time to come clean.

She set her mug on the table and stared into it. "I . . . I lost my jewelry shop. Unlocked the door a couple months ago to discover my partner, Alex, had cleaned out the inventory and disappeared with my tools, as well," she wheezed. A rodeo bull could've just kicked her in the chest, it hurt so bad, but she had to go on. "Found out the hard way that letting your partner be your lover is a stupid mistake, because he had access to my account numbers. In the blink of an eye, I had . . . absolutely nothing."

Danny nodded, his sexy beard flickering in sympathy.

"I had to find a cheaper apartment. My suppliers wouldn't float me, because Alex ran up some unpaid charges on my cards. I looked for a job in somebody else's shop," she continued forlornly, "but it didn't happen. Had thoughts about loading up my stuff and just staying at that homeless shelter I was headed for, but Scurtz told me he'd follow me if I skipped out on him."

"Which makes going off the road in a snowstorm a better way to end up, really." Danny grinned at her, waiting for her to finish. He was a man with a plan, and it was falling into place very nicely.

Norah sighed over another sip of coffee. "I don't know what else to say, except thank you for showing up when you—"

"That's behind you now, sweetheart," he reminded her. "Even if you decide not to stay with me, I want to set you up with inventory and tools—find you a shop to work from again."

"But I can't expect you to—"

"And if you won't accept those things from me, Norah, consider them Mariel's last gift to you," he finished tenderly.

"It's her money, after all. She would've done this for you in a heartbeat."

Norah blinked. Danny was forgiving her unsavory situation while leaving her options open. And he was right: Mariel Langston had supported major charities, yes, but stories of an anonymous angel playing Santa to families in need pointed to her, as well. Had she been alive, Mariel would've restored her jewelry business and made it look like a selfish indulgence—a way to continue buying high-dollar pieces for the man who'd been the light of her life.

"Thank you, Danny," she rasped.

"You're quite welcome."

His eyes sparkled like black diamonds in a face so radiant, so gorgeous, she wanted to cry. How could he possibly want her now? How could she accept his generosity without—hadn't she already behaved stupidly by giving herself to him, heart and soul, without protection? Surely he believed she had no morals or common sense or—

"When I put the pieces together this morning, after what Scurtz blurted into the phone, it occurred to me that you'd used the last of your cash to bake those cookies—to whip up an angel outfit—so you could bring Christmas to some homeless kids. Honey, that's the neatest story I've ever heard."

Danny squeezed her hands to make her look at him. "Sure, I wanted your body—wanted to paw that bead bikini off you from the get-go," he admitted with a grin. "But now that I've met the *real* you—the designer of beautiful jewelry, a giver of gifts from your heart—well, I'm proud to know you, Norah Dalton. Damn glad you slid off the road and into my life."

Her heart welled up. Even a blind woman could see the love on his handsome face as he gazed at her. He was *proud* of her! She hadn't heard that from anyone since her mother died.

"Ready for breakfast?" He nodded toward the steam table, where biscuits and bacon and wedges of fresh pineapple beckoned to her hungry stomach like Danny Diablo called to her soul.

"I can't believe how hungry I am all of a sudden," she remarked. "Can't believe this is really happening."

Danny smiled and took her hand as they scooted out of the booth. "Get used to it, sweetheart. It's the season for miracles."

15

Ohhhh, tidings of comfort and joy, comfort and joy!

Norah sighed happily as she checked her list twice on the screen of Danny's computer. A couple of phone calls had gotten her into her previous storefront and the good graces of that landlord again. Now, a simple click would have gold, gemstones and new tools on their way from the supplier she'd always dealt with. She gazed at the winter wonderland outside Danny's office window with a wondrous sense of peace and goodwill, toward one man in particular.

"Ready?"

She nodded and let him enter his credit-card number. His lean bronze fingers tapped the keys as deftly as he played his guitar, and then he clicked out of the site.

"Looks like your stuff should start arriving in a couple of days," he said with a sly grin. "Now the only question is . . . how do you want to spend those couple of days?"

His hot-coffee eyes made her hold her breath. "You know where I'd like to go, Danny. But I can't be beholden to you for—"

"You can stay at the cabin as long as you want. No strings," he added pointedly. And when he leaned back in the swivel chair, his . . . point . . . became plainly visible. "But if you prefer your own place, closer to your shop, that's okay, too. You won't be working out your rent—or any other debts—in trade, ever again, Norah. You can repay me as you're able."

Norah closed her eyes. Grasped his outstretched hand. He'd arranged for her to keep track of her donations to that homeless shelter—to tick off those dollars he'd loaned her by helping those less fortunate.

Thanks to him, she was no longer among them.

"I hope Mariel's kids don't give you any grief about my staying—"

"Not to worry." He stood, taking her into his arms. "Danny Diablo used to ride a lot tougher beasts than they are, angel, and that man is back. I've improved Langston property and portfolios in a big way, and it's time to show them what I'm made of."

As she snuggled against him, Norah felt the steady beating of his heart—the pulse that invited hers out to play. "I hope they're ready to fight."

"I hope you're ready for something a lot nicer than fighting," he murmured. "Lets gather up some groceries and head back to the cabin. If we're lucky, it'll snow tonight."

"But where will Chico live? When his vacation's over—"

"He can have the house on the north spread, along with a promotion to ranch manager. I can't think he'll object."

"You're too nice—"

"And you're too naughty, sweetheart!" He brushed his lips against hers, hinting at Christmas gifts yet to come. "I want to see you in that halo and your sparkly underwear again. I want to eat your cookies by the fire and talk about what happens next. Been a long time since I could look forward to anything, Norah. You've given me more than I can possibly repay."

The glow in his dark eyes assured her he was totally sincere: she was free to do as she pleased with the rest of her life because he said so.

No strings. She could say *no* this very moment, and he'd be okay with it.

Well, not okay, but he'd let her go.

And what a waste of a dream that would be. She'd always wanted to be Danny Diablo's woman, hadn't she? And he was making her fondest fantasies come true.

"Let's go," she whispered. "I can't wait."

The clean sheets didn't have a chance to get warm before Danny was rolling her on them. Something about his reassurances had struck the right cord, and Norah entrusted herself fully to this man—just as he'd given himself to her.

"Norah . . . you're so hot in that thong, baby." He removed his jeans and then scooped himself out of his black bikini, loving the way her eyes lit up at the sight of his hard cock. She tugged the fabric down his thighs, needy and impatient.

He was on her then, teasing her slit with his tongue and those faceted beads, making her gasp his name. Relentlessly he stroked her, parting her lower lips to delve into her most sensitive spots.

Norah wiggled, laughing out loud. It was the best Christmas song he'd ever heard, that joyous sound, so he kept licking and lapping at her sweetness.

"Come here, cowboy," she rasped. "Time for a ride—and it better last more than eight seconds!"

He straddled her swiftly. Danny paused to gaze at her wild blond waves fanned over the pillow, framing a face alight with love and happiness. Had he really made her feel this good again? Such a simple gift that had been, to restore her confidence—her ability to delight those who bought her jewelry as well as those homeless kids she'd made cookies for.

"What a woman you are," he murmured. He cupped her breasts, gently pressing the colored beads against her nipples. She was giggling beneath him, holding his hips so she could capture his cock between her legs. Her desire spurred him into a higher gear.

"This what you want?" he teased.

She moaned when he entered her, and as her body convulsed to suck him deeper inside her, Danny began to thrust. He wanted to keep it slow and sweet this time—except that Norah took control by squeezing him. *Hard.*

His eyes closed. He entered that state of incredible bliss in which his body simply moved with hers, giving and taking the love he hoped to be sharing with her long after the New Year dawned.

Danny curled himself around her to kiss her as their bodies sang the sweetest of duets. Now this was music . . . and it was Norah's song he coaxed forth with his steady thrusts.

She started low with that moan, and as their bodies crescendoed toward climax, the little bedroom rang with their cries. They rode the waves out, clutching each other until the last spasms racked them.

He relaxed alongside her then, holding her close. The crackling of the fire out front and the scent of their sex soothed his soul. She was still saying yes to him. Overcoming her fears and trusting him to be her hero.

How awesome was that? He was back in the saddle, in a position of power again. He could stand up to whatever Mariel's kids hurled at him, because he was fighting fair, but he was fighting back! Norah wasn't the only one celebrating a glorious rebirth this Christmas.

They snuggled and talked for a while—words of love and hope. She mixed a can of chili beans into a can of tomato soup for their dinner, and he'd never eaten anything more delicious. When he played Christmas songs on his guitar and sang for her,

Norah chimed in with childlike glee—something Mariel had never shared with him.

At this moment, in a cabin alight with new love, everything felt possible. Like the colorful cookies she'd arranged on a plate, good things were now his for the taking. Life sparkled again, like that beaded Santa hanging from his lamp, catching the light.

Danny slipped out for another armful of firewood. The last rays of sunlight illuminated flakes—*thousands* of flakes, which sparkled like Norah's clear beads as they drifted down through the dusk.

He laughed and ducked inside. "Ohhhh, the weather outside is frightful!"

Norah grinned and glanced outside. "More snow?"

"How many inches are you hoping for, *querida?*"

"How many inches ya got?" She watched his lean, lithe body as he stacked the wood beside the hearth. When that tight ass was pointed at her, the weather was the last thing on her mind.

But what a lovely winter thought, to be snowed in with this man—this hero of all her fantasies—now that they truly understood each other. Now that each felt safe in the other's care.

Norah studied the cookie plate, pondering which flavor she felt like licking off his fine, tight body this time. Gingerbread? Or buttercream? Or maybe the deep, sweet chocolate of that raspberry brownie he was reaching for.

She snatched it before Danny could, laughing. "I feel another spell of cabin fever coming on. How 'bout you?"

Triple Xmas

VALERIE MARTINEZ

Special thanks to Bee and Byron for taking me on the hunt for lumberjacks.

1

December 1st

He was the spitting image of the Brawny Man himself. Deb looked from the packaged paper towels on her workbench and back out the window to the man swinging an ax across the street. He wore a red, flannel shirt, and his thick, reddish brown hair was slightly wavy against his wide forehead. The ax lifted into the air, the blade catching the last glint of the setting sun, and then fiercely swung down to expertly slice the base of a Christmas tree's trunk. Deb ripped the shrink-wrap off the roll of paper towels and tore off a sheet. She was sweaty, despite the cold weather, and she dabbed her brow. It had been a hard day at work, and she had one more sculpture to finish before closing up shop.

Deb picked up her chainsaw and went outside. Everywhere it smelled like Christmas, appropriate in a place called Kristmas-town. During the holiday season the struggling timber town exploded with tourists, mostly from the neighboring counties, who came to buy their trees and check out the town's extravagant Christmas decorations. There was always an inevitable blackout from the surge in electricity to illuminate all the reindeer and Santas that traversed the streetlights of Main Street.

Deb had her own subdued version of Christmas decorations: a single strand of Christmas-tree lights hung from the cedar poles that supported a large tarp sheltering the outdoor woodworking area. The blinking lights gave Deb enough light to work at dusk. Normally Deb wouldn't be working this late, but Christmastime put her business into overdrive. Chainsaw art was a popular gift among holiday shoppers. Deb tried to focus on the half-carved log in front of her—the bear's head was still just a block of wood—but she couldn't help stealing a peek at the Brawny Man across the street. His broad back was to her as he bundled up the Christmas tree for a young couple. Every year a different logger set up in the empty lot across from Deb's business to sell Christmas trees. Usually they were her father's age and retiring from a hard life of falling towering evergreens. This one, though, looked fresh from the woods and fresh in his thirties.

Deb tugged the starter rope of the chainsaw. The saw only sputtered, but the noise caught the attention of the lumberjack across the street. He looked up from the cash in his hand. He had the squarest jaw in a man she had ever seen. She thought she saw it clench when he looked right at her, but she couldn't quite tell from a distance. If his gaze lasted one second longer, she would have been sure that he was checking her out, but he prematurely returned his attention to the couple.

Deb sighed and concentrated back on the bear. The man who had ordered it for his son's Christmas present was going to pick it up in the morning. He wanted the bear to wear a Santa hat. Deb plucked the carpenter's pencil from behind her ear and sketched onto the log with the eye of a Michelangelo. Like the Renaissance master, she too believed that the forms were already inside the wood; Deb would wield her chainsaw with the precision of a surgeon's scalpel to free them. Folks from all over Washington State ordered her sculptures, which were mostly of wildlife: bears and bald eagles. Sometimes, though, she filled the bizarre custom request, like for a life-sized rendering of Kurt Cobain.

This time, when she pulled the starter rope, the chainsaw roared to life, and soon a blizzard of wood chips filled the air. Usually her work brought her a sense of center—calm, even, amidst the din of the saw. This evening, however, she felt her concentration falter. When she almost decapitated the bear, Deb decided prudently to switch off the dangerous machinery. The chainsaw grumbled to a standstill. Deb stripped off her protective goggles and leather gloves to wipe her forehead where beads of sweat had again gathered along her hairline. She couldn't still be hot—it was in the high thirties and dropping outside. Heat suddenly seared her cheeks. He was staring right at her, leaning on the long handle of his ax as if it were a crutch. The Brawny Man's relaxed manner suggested that he had been watching her for a while from his post across the street. He wasn't leering exactly; in fact, his face was impassive. Deb almost wondered if there was something behind her and turned around to check. Her own reflection spooked her in the darkened windows of the woodshop.

She was undeniably attractive, if not handsome. Deb's features were angular and her frame lean with muscles, but her model-like height and high cheekbones forgave her more masculine qualities. A long, low whistle interrupted her vanity.

Deb whirled back around to face the Christmas-tree lot as a dog bounded out of its miniature forest. The man had been whistling for his dog, not at her. The husky had a red bandanna tied around its neck and leaped faithfully at its master. Brawny Man broke his cool to crouch down and affectionately rub the dog. He did not look at Deb again. Trumped by man's best friend, Deb chastised herself that she had let this hulk of a lumberjack—okay, hunk of a lumberjack—distract her from her work. The chainsaw once again cut through the silence of the evening, and Deb fervently went back to work on the bear.

Ranger Rick Rockett paced the floor of the cabin. He knew that Deb came home late often these days, but she was never this late. He had pulled the casserole out of the oven an hour ago and even set the table with the pinecone-shaped candles she liked. The cuckoo clock, an engagement gift from his batty aunt, announced the hour with its lunatic call. It was eight o'clock. Rick leaned over the table and blew out the candles. Wetting his fingers with spit, he dampened the extinguished wicks, just to be on the safe side. He grabbed his Smokey Bear hat, as Deb teasingly called it, and was out the door.

The shop was completely dark when Rick pulled up in his muddy Land Cruiser. He parked next to Deb's truck and got out. No signs of life. The Christmas lights he had helped her string up were unplugged. Rick grabbed his flashlight from his holster, feeling more like a cop at that moment than a forest ranger. He was about to call out Deb's name when he heard the sound of running water. Smiling to himself, he switched off the Maglite and tiptoed around the building. A full moon illuminated the path. Sure enough, out back, steam was rising from the outdoor shower. Rick knew that Deb sometimes used the shower after all her employees went home. She liked how the hot water felt against her body in the crisp, forest air with the stars spread above her. She called it her spa treatment.

Four walls of thick pine planks enclosed the shower from the ground to six feet standing. Only the showerhead cleared the top, and its noisy rain allowed Rick to approach unde-tected. Right as he was about to surprise her, he heard another sound. Like a moan, or a whimper. Stealthily Rick got close enough to peep through a crack between the planks. There was his fiancée, naked and lathered with soap. Her hands slipped all over her wet body as she touched herself pleasurably. The tented crotch of his khakis pressed against the hardwood planks as Rick leaned in for a better viewing of Deb's sleek limbs. The vapors of Dr. Bronner's eucalyptus soap widened his nostrils as he watched her sudsy hand travel to the dark triangle between her legs. In the moonlight, Deb's skin was paler than its usual olive hue, and the patch between her legs appeared black as night. She searched that shadowy place until a tight gasp signaled that she had found what she was looking for.

Silently but with haste, Rick unbuttoned his khaki ranger shirt and unlaced his work boots without removing his eyes from Deb's hand buried deep in her muff. He had never really seen her touch herself before, and his eyes widened in astonishment as she began to finger herself hard. His cock throbbed, feeling painfully left out, and he tore off his pants. As Rick charged into the stall, Deb screamed and covered her small but perky breasts. Recognition crossed her face as Rick pushed her up against the wall, the head of his cock finding her moist crevice primed for entry. Before she could say anything, he penetrated her in one fell swoop. Whatever word had been on the tip of her tongue unfurled into a wet, hot gasp, and her head lolled to the side, where the stream of water slapped her cheek. Rick cupped her face back to him as he thrust up again. Deb's back arched against the pine planks as she took it.

"*Rick.*" She was able to say his name now that the element of surprise was fading and the heat of their lovemaking surging. One of her legs was wrapped around his waist, and he ran his hand along the length of her strong thigh, slippery when wet. He pulsed inside of her with tiny circular movements of his waist. She was looking at him with wonder, her lush mouth parted, and he answered her by tenderly sucking her top lip and then her bottom. She draped her arms around his neck to kiss him, and he lifted her other leg off the ground, effortlessly holding her with her long limbs tangled around him.

"How's your shower?" he asked as he kissed her flushed cheekbones.

"Hot," she murmured into his neck, where she nipped at his tendons. Rick thought of how he had spied her in her solitary state of arousal, selfishly enjoying the slickness of her wet skin. His cock, still pulsating inside her, hardened even more and demanded that he finish the vigorous job she had started on herself. Brashly Rick pushed her back against the smooth wood, his hands encircling her upper rib cage to hold her there. His thumbs propped up her firm tits, which gleamed from the water bouncing off them; he bowed his head to tug on each raspberry nipple with his teeth. Deb cried out, and he plunged up into her with a ferocity that turned her animal. Her wet hair lashed against his face with the sting of a whip, and a wild look in her eyes drove him to pump even faster. Rick's arm muscles rippled to hold Deb in place as she sunk into the center of her pleasure, where he prodded her unremittingly. Deb's eyes glazed over, the telltale sign that she was about to come. Suddenly she grabbed on to Rick's taut biceps and reared her head. Her eyes fluttered open to the stars as the pressure boiling up inside her released like a burst of steam into the night air.

Rick let her collapse against him as he struggled for his own release. It came in a rapid succession of spasms that jerked both their bodies. They stayed connected for some time under the warm rain of the shower, listening to the serene night sounds of the woods. Rick's fingers were still laced between Deb's heaving ribs, and he waited until her breathing calmed before gently letting her go. As Deb slid languidly off his body, she asked her fiancé what he had made for dinner.

Usually the hooting of an owl lulled Deb to sleep, but tonight it only enhanced her insomnia. She should be asleep, she reasoned: she was more than satiated after hot sex followed by a hearty, home-cooked meal. She rolled over to gaze at her sleeping fiancé. His drawn lips naturally turned down at the corners, giving the lower lip a delectable pout; not a sound escaped them to betray his earlier passion. She followed a swath of moonlight across the bridge of his perfectly straight nose, thinned by shadows, to his smooth, illuminated cheek. His pretty, boyish looks that sometimes made her feel like she was engaged to an Eagle Scout were deceiving: he had been all man pressing her against the pine boards of the shower. He had surprised her indeed; the minute she had been getting bored with their sex life and getting cold feet about the wedding, he had literally stepped in and fulfilled her fantasy. Except that her fantasy hadn't been about him exactly . . . but rather it had been about him *and* a third party. Deb rolled back over to her side of the bed and tried to block out the images that had had her so charged up earlier. She was trying to get to sleep, not get excited again. But Brawny Man and his massive shoulders loomed like a mountain in her mind.

After he had driven off in his Dodge truck, Deb hadn't given the burly logger a second thought. She had finished the bear scarcely an hour later but then found herself loitering about the shop: resweeping the floor her apprentice, Sherri, had swept right before she had left, making sure all the tools were in their proper drawers, checking the sharpness of the saw bars. Finally she decided that she couldn't go home without showering—she stunk to high heaven—and she should take advantage of not having any employees around to catch her indecent.

Deb had undressed outside the stall, enjoying the feeling of being exposed to nature. Behind the woodshop, the forest ran up into the foothills. Sometimes Rick would stop by the shop, and the two of them would hike up to a spot that overlooked the Sound. Logs floated in the water by the sawmill like schools of skinny fish. Rick hated the logging industry, but then again, what forest ranger didn't. Sometimes he gave Deb a hard time about her own business, though she was prudent to buy wood from eco-friendly sources. Deb loved trees, and she had faced them—second-growth Douglas fir and western hemlock—as she'd peeled off her overalls and brushed the sawdust from her thermal underwear. She never wore a bra when she wore overalls. Her shivering, erect nipples added another dimension to the waffle texture of her thermal. Swiftly she stripped completely, enlivened by the pinpricks of cold air on her naked skin.

It was only when the shower began to churn her body with warmth that Deb thought of the lumberjack again. First she only wondered—just out of curiosity—what his bare chest looked like. Was it hairy? Did he have muscular pecs? Then her contemplation had traveled south. Next thing she knew, her imagination had carried Brawny Man into the shower with her, and his mighty hands were giving her a rubdown with the same vigor and attention she had witnessed him give to his husky.

In the dark solitude of the woods, it was easy for her fantasy to give way to her deepest, secret erotic wish: a threesome involving a stranger and her fiancé. She had never shared this fantasy with Rick, but lately it had been encroaching more and more on her bedroom thoughts. They were getting married the first of the year, and suddenly, inexplicably Deb felt convinced that she had to have this sexual experience before they tied the knot. Actually she was obsessed with the idea. She found herself carving threes of everything at the woodshop: trios of salmon, owls, raccoons. Two of the animals were always bigger, more masculine than a smaller, more feminine one sandwiched in between. Not that she had any idea how a threesome worked. This evening's stint in the outdoor shower was perhaps the most adventurous sex she'd ever had. Then again, she really had only been with Rick; the two were high school sweethearts and were still together ten years later. Only, now they were making official their unofficial marriage. This evening not withstanding, Rick was such a sweet, if not conventional lover, and she couldn't imagine how to broach the subject of a ménage à trois with him. Before tonight, the third party had been just a face-less body, but now she knew just the face and body she wanted.

Deb rolled back toward Rick. How could he sleep so peace-fully when she was tossing and turning and thinking about bringing another man into their prenuptial bed? It was an im-plausible wish: even if she could convince Rick to be open to something like this, which she had no clue if he would be, who could say whether she would be able to seduce the lumberjack (a complete stranger, she reminded herself) into such a triangle? And then, of course, a logger would be like sleeping with the enemy from the point of view of her environmentalist fiancé. Yet this, Deb decided, was all she wanted for Christmas this year. Now if only it were so easy as whispering in Santa's ear. . . .

2

December 2nd

Deb woke up to the sun streaming in her face. The cheerful chirping of birds had replaced the melancholy hooting of the owl. It was one of those mornings, few and far between, that Deb woke up happy, feeling rested. Deb shot up in bed. She was rested because she had overslept! Jumping out of the toasty cocoon of flannel sheets and down comforters, Deb charged into the main room of the cabin.

"Rockett!" Soon she would be Mrs. Rockett, but for now, Deb used the surname in vain.

Rick was nowhere in sight. She glanced at the cuckoo clock, a gift she had wanted to toss in the firewood pile but that Rick had insisted they hang on their cabin's wall in case his crazy old aunt should decide to drop in one day, something she had never done in their ten years of cohabitation. It was ten o'clock.

"Shit, Rockett," she swore and grabbed the note he had stabbed through a deer antler mounted next to the clock.

Good morning, Deer,

Rick could be a real cheese.

> *You looked so beautiful asleep and didn't wake up to the alarm. I figured you could use the sleep after last night's workout. I'll see you at dinner! Veal?*
> *Just kidding,*
> *R.R.*

Deb didn't have time to be annoyed, although Rick really should have known that this was the busiest time of year for her business. Luckily she had recently trusted Sherri with a set of keys. Hopefully she could trust Sherri not to be late today. Unlike her boss.

Not a big makeup wearer (only when Rick took her to Seattle for a fancy dinner), and certainly not one to spend time on her hair (she cut it short, no fuss, just below her ears), Deb was out the door in five minutes flat.

Sure enough, her teenage apprentice had opened up the shop.

"Sherri, I'm so sorry I'm late." Deb rushed through the door, causing a small whirlwind of sawdust to rise off the floor. It settled at the feet of a pair of heavy boots. What made Deb stare at them, she couldn't have said for sure. They were unremarkable—worn black leather, laced up to the midcalf, muddy—except for their massive size. She heard her apprentice giggling, talking to whoever stood in those titanic boots.

Deb cleared her throat, interrupting Sherri's flirtations. The man turned around. Deb, a tall woman, came up to his chest. He wore another flannel, this one a blue plaid. Brown suspenders were clipped to his dirty, blue jeans. Not only was her lumberjack crush as tall as a Sitka spruce, but his chest was twice as wide as her. Not used to feeling small, Deb shrunk even more under the heavy gaze of his eyes. They were auburn, like the color of redwood.

But she ignored him even though he was occluding her view from everything else. "Sherri, would you mind getting me set up for the McKinley order? I need to finish it by tonight, and I had an, um, emergency this morning."

Sherri peeked around the pillar of manliness that stood between them and opened her mouth to say something, but Deb shot her a get-to-work look. Sherri tossed her glossy curls and left in a huff. Since when did her apprentice get an attitude? Deb reminded herself that the girl was, after all, seventeen.

With her jailbait assistant out of the way, Sherri could address the logger at hand. "I'm Deb, the owner of Deb's Chainsaw Carvings." She realized how redundant that sounded, but Brawny Man was fixated on a key chain of a carved, flying squirrel dangling from his index finger.

Deb continued with her professional air. "Can I help you with something?"

"How much for this?" His voice was somewhat gruff and matched his rugged look. Reddish bristles of a nascent beard carpeted his square jaw. He smelled like camping: smoke and pine needles.

"Um, five dollars." She usually sold it for eight.

"I'll take it." He clenched his hand around the figurine, and the squirrel disappeared into his fist. Deb swallowed hard. His hands up close looked just as powerful as she had imagined them, his knuckles thick like burls. Deb quickly walked over to the cash register to ring him up. Followed by his hulking presence—the man nearly cast a shadow over half the shop—Deb, distracted, accidentally punched $500.00 in the register. She swore under her breath. Not only was she flustered from getting to work late, but now the object of her ultimate erotic fan-

tasy was standing right there in the flesh. Buying a key chain of
an arboreal creature.

"Uh, ma'am."

"Sorry, it'll just be a second here." Instead of the CANCEL
button, she hit CASH, and the drawer shot open, almost punch-
ing her in the gut. This time she cussed a little louder. If only
she could think of something clever to say. *What do you say
after work you, me and my fiancé have a threesome?*

"Uh, ma'm. Sorry, but you have something hanging out
your cuff." Before she had a chance to look herself, he grabbed
a hold and pulled. To her horror, her size A, fuchsia bra hung
between his thumb and forefinger.

It was ridiculous. She didn't even wear a bra when she wore
her overalls, but she had grabbed a shirt off the floor in such a
rush this morning she hadn't notice the bra lodged in its sleeve.
Instinctively she snatched at it, but Brawny Man held fast to
one of its straps. Each held a strap in a lingerie tug of war, and
he smirked in amusement.

"Let go of my bra." Her growl surprised them both. He let
go, and the bra snapped back at her. "Thanks," she muttered,
utterly embarrassed by the situation and the fact that she had
just lashed out at him. She stuffed the bra deep into her pocket,
where she wished she, too, could delve. This was not how she
had wanted them to meet. She was too mortified to look him in
the face as he handed her a five-dollar bill.

"Do you want a bag?" At this point, she just wanted him to
leave.

"No, thank you, Deb." Hearing her name, and in such a cor-
dial tone, Deb braved to meet his eye.

He winked. And just like that, he walked jauntily out of the
shop with the flying squirrel swinging from his pinky finger.
She never got his name.

3

December 9th

"What do you say we buy a Christmas tree this year?"

Deb stopped stirring the pancake batter and looked at Rick with surprise. "What? I thought you were against buying Christmas trees."

They hadn't had a Christmas tree for the whole time they had lived together. It wasn't because Rick lacked holiday spirit—he had even been known to dress up as an elf for the annual charity auction put on by the forest service—Rick just didn't think it was environmentally sound to cut down a living evergreen for decorative purposes.

Rick took the bowl of batter from Deb and started stirring. "Well, I've been reading up, and Christmas-tree farms are actually sustainable. Good for preventing soil erosion, sheltering wildlife and providing oxygen. An acre of a Christmas-tree farm provides the daily oxygen for eighteen people. Plus, the trees are renewable. For every tree harvested, three more are planted by farmers to ensure a steady supply."

"Wow, sounds like you've been doing your research, Rockett." Deb was impressed. She watched her fiancé pour two globs of batter onto the skillet. Sundays were their only day off together, and Rick always whipped up a huge breakfast for the two of them. Sometimes she helped.

"There's a guy across the street from the shop that sells some pretty good-looking ones," Deb attempted to suggest casually. Could trees be good-looking? Well, their vendor certainly was. For a week, she had watched Brawny Man from her stakeout across the street. She had no reason to cross over and was still embarrassed about the bra incident, but she had tried to think of a dozen excuses to do so anyway. Now she had the perfect excuse. Plus, she could see how the two men interacted.

"We could go today." She was eager. Christmas was approaching fast. Soon after, they would wed. Rick wanted to get married on New Year's Day. They had planned a small ceremony—in the woods, of course.

Rick flipped over the two pancakes; they were cooked to golden perfection. Deb was practically salivating to eat and get over to the Christmas-tree lot. She stole the spatula from Rick and scooped the pancakes off the skillet and onto her plate. She plopped down on a stool at the kitchen counter.

"I'm starving!" She doused the pancakes in maple syrup and greedily tore at them with her fork.

"Rawwwrrrr." Rick came up behind her, giving her a playful roar in her ear, and then nuzzled her neck. "Such a voracious appetite my future wife has."

Deb suddenly choked on a spongy piece of pancake. Rick rushed to pat her on the back. She swallowed the piece whole and then gulped down an entire glass of orange juice.

"You okay, honey?" Rick's green eyes were sweet with concern. After all these years, his eyes still killed her. Sometimes they were the color of sea foam; other days, they were almost hazel. When he was aroused, amber rimmed his pupils like tiny eclipsed suns. There was always a clear quality to them, an innocence, which today made it hard for her to bring up her secret Christmas wish.

"I'm fine. Just eating too fast." Facing him, she pushed up the sleeve of his soft, gray thermal to admire his slender forearm, sleekly contoured with muscles. "I'm so happy you want to buy a tree this year. After Christmas we can put it in my wood chipper and turn it into mulch for our garden."

"Good idea. By the way, you haven't told me what you want for Christmas." Last year, Rick had adopted a spotted owl that was being rehabilitated at a conservation center. They had gotten to go to Olympic National Park when it was released back into the old-growth forest. This year, however, her wish wasn't so virtuous.

"Um, actually I've been thinking a lot about what I want." Deb bit her lip. How could she put this? "I want to have a threesome." Well, blurting it out was one way to broach the subject. Rick looked confused.

Deb stuttered to explain. "What I mean is, I want to . . . I mean, we've been together so long—been *only* with each other—and I just thought before we get married—"

"Wait, are you saying you want to have sex with someone else?" Something dark flickered across his eyes, and then they were clear like glass again.

"Well, no. Yes. Well, with you and someone else."

He took a step back. "A man or a woman?"

Deb looked down at the empty space between them. Suddenly she felt guilty, as if she had cheated on him. Maybe fantasizing about another man was cheating. She wasn't sure.

"A man." She stared at Rick's hands, which were folded calmly in front of him. She wanted to grab those sensitive fingers, the nails always clean and trimmed, and pull them to her heart and reason—or plead—with him. This is what she wanted; this is what she desperately needed. And then she would marry him and would never have to wonder "what if," would never have any regrets as they grew old together.

Without a word, Rick walked over to the sink and stared out the window. He had installed it himself so that they could have a view of their garden while washing dishes. Perhaps he was looking at the rows of dormant soil, seeds dreaming of spring or gazing beyond at the purple Olympic Mountains far in the distance; she couldn't tell. After some time of silence, he sighed. Deb thought he was going to say something, but instead he turned on the faucet to start washing their breakfast dishes.

The conversation was over.

Deb took the curves in the hillside road fast. Her Ford truck, which had once belonged to her dad, rattled like its screws were going to fly loose. She hated Rick's silent treatment. He rarely pulled it, but when he did, he was obdurate. Not that Deb had tried to push the conversation further, but she had no idea what he was thinking; he had just shut down. Unable to take Rick's silence, which had stretched into the afternoon hours, Deb had finally stormed out of the cabin to go for a drive.

Her drive took her to the Christmas-tree lot. She parked across the street in front of her closed business. The lumberjack was busy with the last of the Sunday afternoon shoppers. Deb knew from her surveillance that he usually called it a day around four o'clock. It was a quarter 'til.

Deb checked her face in the rearview mirror and frowned. She grabbed her oversize purse, made of buckskin and fringed with turquoise beads, and dug deep for a semblance of a grooming aid. All she could find was a crusty tube of Chap Stick. At least it was cherry flavored.

After rubbing her fruity lips together, Deb felt prepared to face the lumberjack. She emerged confidently from the truck, aware of the tightness of her blue jeans—a far cry from her baggy work overalls—and the low-cut neckline of her wool sweater that had the tendency to slip from her shoulder. Perhaps, when she had "thrown on" clothes to leave the cabin in a huff, she had known exactly where her drive was headed. Her beat-up cowboy boots kicked up bits of gravel as she crossed the street.

Brawny Man's husky bounded into the road to bark at her ardently.

"Shasta!" the lumberjack yelled after his dog, and Deb reflexively grabbed its bandanna collar. She guided the dog safely across the street.

"Thanks." He roughly took hold of the bandanna, and Deb let go. "Shasta gets excited when he sees a pretty lady. I've tried to teach him to keep it cool."

Deb laughed at his good-natured flattery. Today he was wearing a green flannel that complimented his russet-colored hair. He wore red suspenders. Deb thought he looked just like a Christmas present all wrapped up for her.

"Well, it works for me." Deb leaned down to pet her canine admirer, who was rubbing up against her knees. She didn't adjust her sweater when it gaped open from her chest. It's not like he hadn't seen her bra before.

"Oh, I didn't realize you were that easy."

Deb straightened up. "Excuse me?"

"I was joking." His smile was broad like the rest of him and as charming as it was toothy. She could tell it let him get away with things.

"Oh, I'm sorry, I don't understand logger humor." She was being caustic—not like her, but talking to him revved her up. She supposed this was her way of flirting. Deb wasn't sure if she had ever really flirted with a man, since she had been practically engaged to Rick since she was sixteen. She wasn't sure if she was doing it right, or even if it was right to do.

"You're quite the pistol, Deb." Well, *he* was definitely hitting on her.

"What's your name anyway?" She felt the need to put a cap

on the flirtation before things got carried away. She looked down to avoid his eyes, which bore through her like a chainsaw hollowing a soft log. Her eyes fell straight to his crotch. Something about the way his jeans bunched there—the material slightly darker than that of the worn legs—mesmerized her. It wasn't that he had popped a woody (his pants were too loose for her to tell), but something about that sexy bulge of denim made her want to kneel before him right there in the mud.

"Dale. Dale Lix." *Licks*. Deb glanced up and giggled before she could stop herself. What was she, thirteen?

"Can I help you with something?"

Deb, embarrassed, regained her composure. "Actually I'm in the market for a Christmas tree."

Dale cocked his eyebrow. She really hadn't expected him to be so charming. Most lumberjacks she knew were pretty gruff. Dale was definitely rough around the edges, but there was a warmth to him, like a big ole fireplace to cozy up to on a cold winter's day.

"Any kind in mind?" They were all business now.

"Well, I haven't bought one for years. What do you have?"

"I've got mostly firs, a couple of Scotch pines left. I'll show you."

Deb silently followed Dale as he showed his coniferous wares. The lot wasn't big, but once they got to its center, she felt like she was in a labyrinth. She realized there wasn't a soul around, and the road was blocked from her view by the thicket of Christmas trees. All the holiday shoppers were driving back to their neighboring counties to get home in time for dinner.

"What about this one?" Dale emerged from a cluster of Douglas firs with a smaller tree; its tight bundles of needles were bluish gray like frostbitten fingers.

"Where'd you get that?" Deb knew enough about trees to know that blue spruce weren't usually grown in the Pacific Northwest.

"My uncle grows a select few on his farm."

"It's beautiful." Deb reached out to touch the tree, but Dale grabbed her wrist.

"Careful!" He was wearing workman's gloves, and the coarse leather chafed the tender underside of her wrist. His grip was tight like a clamp.

Seeing that he had startled her, he quickly let go. "Sorry, the needles are just really sharp. I didn't want you to hurt yourself."

Deb rubbed her wrist. It felt raw. And hot, like rope burn. Dale hastily took off his gloves, stuffed them in his back pocket, and gently asked, "Did I hurt you? May I see?"

Deb held out her wrist. As Dale cradled it in his encompassing palm, his brow furrowed. She saw a little storm brew between his fiery eyebrows. He seemed angry with himself.

"I'm fine," she insisted. Her pulse beat rapidly against the feeble tendons of her wrist as he closely examined the broken skin. Could he see her veins throbbing? His breath, brushing up against her slight abrasion, both stung and thrilled her. The smell of the Christmas trees was intoxicating.

"Really, I'm fine," she reassured him again.

The flat tip of his thumb slid down the sensitive side of her wrist as he removed his hand. The sensation, almost tickling, made the tiny hairs on her arm stand on end.

Dale looked at her and waited, like he had that first day when she saw him leaning on the handle of his ax with an ease that exuded confidence but that was also unreadable.

"I'll take it." She motioned to the blue spruce that Dale had pitched against a seven-foot fir in his chivalrous move to prevent her from getting pricked. The spruce leaned against the fir as if resting its head on the taller tree's chest.

"I'll bundle it up for you." Dale put his gloves back on to grab hold of the trunk. Deb stepped aside as he carried her tree effortlessly over to a pair of sawhorses.

"Thanks. My truck is parked across the street. I'll pull it over."

He nodded at her and then began to unravel twine from an enormous spool. Deb left him to his work.

"You said you haven't had a Christmas tree for a while. Why's that?"

Dale and Deb sat on a log overlooking Kristmastown and the Sound. It was the same hilltop clearing she and Rick frequented. The sun was setting, swathing everything in pink so that even the evergreen forest looked rosy.

"Well, it's just that . . ." She wasn't sure if she wanted to tell him about Rick and spoil the moment. "My business is always so busy right up until Christmas that I guess I just never had time to get and decorate a tree."

She had told a lie, and she knew it. But Rick and their fight seemed a distant memory. She felt suspended above the earth with the town so far below, and in this other realm she felt strangely at peace, exempt.

The trip up the hill had been Dale's suggestion. After they had loaded her bundled tree into the back of her pickup, he had abruptly asked her if she wanted to "catch" the sunset with him. He made it sound as if it were something to be netted, like a fish. Deb agreed without hesitation. Dale grabbed two beers from the cooler in the back of his truck, and, adequately supplied, they embarked on their ascent.

"You an environmentalist or something?" Dale took a swig from his beer. He sat maybe two feet away from her on the log they shared, a distance that felt both intimate and aloof.

"No, but my—" Deb stopped herself. She sensed Dale looking at her curiously, but she continued to stare straight ahead at the setting sun even though it hurt her eyes. "No, not at all. Actually, my father was a logger."

"Really? Around here?" She felt the log shift as he stretched out his legs. The heels of his heavy boots sunk into the damp earth like anchors.

"Yup, for thirty years. He was a cutter. Competed in a lot of logging shows, too. Mostly in spar-climbing contests."

"What was his name? I used to go to a lot of jubilees in Washington as a kid."

"Dewey. Dewey Collins."

"That was your dad?!" His excitement rocked the log. "I remember him. He was the reigning champ of spar climbing. Undefeated, as I remember, until—" Dale stopped short.

"He died," Deb finished his sentence flatly.

"I'm sorry. I remember when that happened. My uncle went to his funereal even though he didn't know him well."

A tree had killed her father. She was sixteen. An eight-foot-thick cedar—tipped the wrong way by his cutting partner—dropped on him. In this land, trees giveth and trees taketh away.

"Loggers from all over the state came to the service. I didn't recognize many of them." The funeral had been a blur of people except for Rick, who had never left her side. They had just started dating, but she clung to him as her mother, stricken by grief, turned away from her and to the bottle. Deb had been the apple of her father's eye. It was as if the two of them had been carved from the same block of wood. He had taught her everything she needed to know about a chainsaw.

"He was a well-respected cutter. Maybe the best, from what I remember my uncle saying." Tenderness coated his strong voice. Deb suddenly felt vulnerable with emotion. Ten years later, the hole her father's loss had punctured in her heart still oozed. She wanted Dale to wrap his arms around her in the same way his voice had embraced her.

Afraid she might cry, Deb changed the subject. "You a cutter?" Cutters were at the top of the logging pyramid. They were the guys that went into the solitary forest with a twenty-pound chainsaw to fall trees, some well over a hundred feet. It was a dangerous job, as Deb knew all too well, and required great skill and accuracy.

"Was."

Deb turned away from the melting sky to Dale. The slanting rays of the sun, in a final burst of light before disappearing, had set his skin aglow with a golden flush that highlighted his heavy bone structure. His face looked smooth but solid, like sanded cottonwood.

"I was logging up in Canada until I wrenched my knee," he continued, with his eyes fixed on nature's spectacular display before them. "Came back down here to help out my uncle during the holiday season with his Christmas-tree farm. It's easy work while my knee fully heals."

"Are you from Canada?"

Dale shook his head. "No, Oregon."

They sat for some time in comfortable silence. The logger's presence felt familiar and reminded her of her father: the warm whiff of flannel, the low tremble of his throat clearing, his heavy, calloused hands. She felt safe and relaxed in a way she hadn't since before her father died.

Suddenly Dale turned to give her a look that was far from paternal. Deb knew if she didn't look away fast, he would kiss her. But her eyes betrayed her yearning, and he slipped his arm around her waist and pulled her to him with such strength it took her breath away. The split second before his mouth crashed into hers, his head blocked the setting sun, and his face fell into shadow. In this sunless place they joined mouths, and Deb lost herself in a dark, tangled forest of forbidden desire.

His hands supported her neck as he kissed her forcefully. His strong fingers dug into her nape and twisted themselves in her short hair. As if to say stop, she placed her palms flat against his chest, but his expansive chest only swelled against the light pressure she applied. She opened her mouth to take in his tongue, his woodsy smell, his everything. His cheeks and chin were rough against her face, but his lips were soft even as they devoured her. His kissing was relentless, and Deb gasped for air.

"*Stop.*" The sudden realization of what she was doing jerked her away. Dale attempted to bring her face back to his, but she resisted. "I have to go."

Confusion dispersed his lustful expression. It occurred to her that she must look like a crazy person, but she didn't care. She had cheated on Rick, and she had to go.

"Sorry," she whispered and then sprung away from the log.

"Wait," she heard him say as she crashed down the hillside like a startled deer. He didn't chase her.

4

December 15th

Rick and Deb ate their steaks in silence. Saturday night was sloshing all around them as they dined at Up the Creek Grill. Sitting at the polished cedar bar, old loggers reminisced drunkenly about the heyday of the timber industry in the seventies before thousands of acres of old-growth forest were preserved for the spotted owl and before machines replaced men in the mills. Deb couldn't help wondering if her father would have joined their alcoholic ranks. Sometimes one of the down-and-out loggers would snarl at a young waitress, who would continue to bounce on by to serve the families that sat in the booths. A young couple sat at a table with a pile of pull tabs, hoping to strike it rich before the baby came. The broken, losing tabs littered their table like empty peanut shells. The rest of the crowd that sat at the tables between the bar and the booths were rowdy and kept the waitresses, who they knew by their first names, busy by ordering pitchers of beer and buffalo wings. Deb wished she could join them—she knew some of gals from high school—but she and Rick always kept to themselves in the booth the hostess had ready for them every Saturday night.

"Do you want to go out after this?" Deb asked hopefully. Dinner was usually the extent of their Saturday night outing, but sometimes they would go to the Log Cabin Tavern and play pool.

"I got a book out of the library about tree voles that I was looking forward to reading in bed." There it was. Rick would rather to go to bed with tree voles than go out and have some fun with her. His knife scraped the plate as he cut the last bit of meat from the bone. Deb cringed.

"Rick, can we please talk about this?" It had been a week, and although Rick had ostensibly broken his silent treatment, they were still barely speaking.

"About what?" Rick asked, annoyed, as if the question had interrupted the concentration he needed to chew.

"About—" The hostess sashayed over with a water pitcher and refilled their glasses. Deb waited until she left and then lowered her voice. "About my Christmas wish."

Rick swallowed. He looked at her with eyes that shone hard and sharp like brilliant emeralds.

"Why don't you just have an affair with another man and leave me out of it?"

Deb was shocked, slapped in the face without Rick even raising a hand. He had never been so upset with her. And he didn't even know about her woodland kiss with the lumberjack. Struggling with the guilt of cheating, Deb had wanted to tell him all week, but every time she had tried to talk to him, even about trivial household matters—the compost needed to be taken out, there were mice in the pantry—he responded with irritation that bordered on ire.

"Deb! Debbie!"

Only one person called her Debbie, and that was her ditsy apprentice.

"Sherri." Deb turned to greet the teenager, who wore a red miniskirt trimmed with white faux fur and a low-cut top to match. Deb gaped, but it wasn't at Sherri's slutty Mrs. Claus outfit. Sherri's arm was hooked like a candy cane around Dale. A tiny flame flickered in his eyes when he saw Deb but was instantly extinguished when he blinked.

"Hiya, Rick!" Sherri batted her eyelashes, which were fake and silver. It looked as if she had decked her eyes in tinsel.

"Hiya, Sherri." Rick sounded mocking, which was out of character; he was usually quite nice to Sherri. Whenever Deb would complain about Sherri's workmanship, Rick would often remind Deb that the girl was only seventeen and that she should be easy on her.

Only seventeen. And how old was Dale? Early thirties, from what Deb could piece together from his life story. What the hell was he doing with her? Didn't he know Sherri was underage? Deb opened her mouth to say something about this but was cut short by Sherri's needless introduction.

"Deb, this is Dale. You know, he came into the shop one time."

"Yes, I remember." Deb took a deep but imperceptible breath. "Dale, this is my fiancé, Rick. Rick, I got our tree from Dale's lot."

Dale shot his hand across the table to shake Rick's. Deb wondered how that handshake felt. Firm, most likely. Tense.

"Rick Rockett. Nice to meet you." Although still broody, Rick appeared completely unsuspecting. Dale did not look at Deb.

"Oh, you guys are just finishing up. Too bad!" Sherri clung to Dale like a squirrel shimmying up a tree trunk. "It would have been a blast to double date."

So it was a date. Deb ventured a quizzical look at Dale. He was unresponsive except to half grin, half grimace at Sherri when she playfully pinched the cleft in his chin.

Sherri continued her chatter. "We're going to Timber Bowl after dinner. You two should meet us there. We could play teams!" Her entreaties were directed to Rick on this matter.

"Sherri." Deb spoke to her kindly but authoritatively. "I don't think so."

"I thought you were just saying how you wanted to go out," Rick interjected. Deb glared at him, but he smiled coyly. What was he up to?

"Oh, please," Sherri implored Deb, but it was Dale's arm she was twisting. Literally. If she hung on him any harder his limb would break off. "It would be so much fun!"

"Yeah, Deb," Rick unequivocally mocked. "It would be so much fun."

Not one to be a party pooper, even if it meant hanging out with the man she cheated on and the man she cheated with, Deb agreed. "Sure. Why not?" She still harbored the hope that the two men would like each other enough get naked.

"Great!" The hostess signaled to Sherri that a table was ready. "Deb, I'll call your cell when we're done eating."

As Deb watched Sherri drag Dale away by the cuff of his flannel, Deb experienced a twinge of jealousy. She shook it off to smile pleasantly back at her fiancé. Rick looked amused, undoubtedly by Sherri.

Sherri, with her bouncy curls and pert behind, had made Deb's scheme all the more difficult. Deb needed to put a stop to whatever was going on with Dale and her apprentice. Fast. And so she would do something she absolutely hated: go bowling.

"Don't you know she's underage?" Deb hissed in Dale's ear as they leaned over the ball return, waiting for the machine to spit up their bowling balls.

"She turned eighteen last week." This was the first time he had spoken directly to her since they had run into each other at the grill. Apparently Deb had forgotten her employee's birthday. No wonder Sherri had been sulking around work all week.

"Your fiancé seems like a nice guy." His words should have made her optimistic, but his tone was derisive. She deserved it. After all, she hadn't told him she was engaged.

"I'm sorry," was all she could think to say, but the clanking of machinery muffled her words. A hot-pink ball rolled out onto the island between them. Dale picked it up and handed it to Deb. She heard Sherri giggle at something Rick was saying where they sat huddled over the scoring computer. The ball weighed heavily in Deb's hands, like her conscience.

It was Deb's turn. Despite her lithe, athletic build and agility with a chainsaw, she was completely uncoordinated when it came to tossing a ball down an alley of waxed wood. She walked clumsily toward the lane. Her bowling shoes were too big, even though they were supposed to be nines, her size.

"Go, baby!" Rick hollered. He was drunk. So was Sherri. Rick had been ordering pitchers of beer. Even though Sherri was underage—to drink, that is—Rick had been slipping her sips—or gulps, rather—off his pint glass. The two were getting along famously, much to Deb's chagrin. Dale didn't seem to care, though; he would rather glare at Deb than pay attention to his date.

Deb tossed the heavy ball. It actually bounced, not like a basketball but with a thud that sounded as if it would break the floorboards, before it rolled despondently into the gutter. Rick hooted. Sherri giggled. Dale glowered.

Deb swore. Instead of waiting for her ball, she cruised past the ball return and seating area. "Rick, bowl for me," Deb ordered over her shoulder and made a beeline for the bar.

"A shot of Wild Turkey."

The bartender, whose hard-knock wrinkles reminded Deb of her mother, nodded.

"Make that two, ma'am." Deb sensed Dale's hulk behind her and bit her lip that was twitching to smile. She turned around right as Dale extended a fistful of bills to the bartender and was encircled in his reach, trapped between him and the bar.

"Dale!" He had rolled up the sleeves of his shirt to bowl, and his bare forearms bulged with muscles she didn't even know existed in the human anatomy. With one hand on the bar, Dale was positioned as if he were going to perform a one-handed push-up against her.

"Deb." He closed in on her, and she tilted her face up toward the determined, willful line of his lips. "Here's your drink." He had reached behind her to retrieve her shot.

"Oh, thanks." Slightly embarrassed, she took the glass. Dale took a step back.

"Cheers?" she offered. They clinked glasses.

The shot burned down Deb's throat like a forest fire raging through clear-cut slash. She immediately felt tipsy. The bourbon had done the trick that the beers she had been drinking all night had failed to do. Heat flushed her chest, making her heart brave.

"You look good tonight, Dale." She teased the collar of his shirt. He didn't take her hand away, but he did glance over to the seating area. Rick was feeding Sherri cheese fries, trying not to drip the melted Velveeta on the fake fur that trimmed her plunging neckline. She gobbled them up like a fleecy baby bird. Deb frowned. *He's doing this to get back at me.*

"Looks like your fiancé and you are really close." Again with the sardonic tone.

"We're having some troubles right now." Deb dropped her hand, and it ricocheted off his chest like a pebble tumbling down a cliff. Right then, the fluorescent lights of the bowling alley were shut off, and black lights were switched on. Disco bowling. People cheered.

"Anything I could do to help?" Dale's teeth glowed a fluorescent white under the black lights. She was pulled toward their mischievous gleam.

"I can think of a few things." In the relative darkness, Deb pressed closer so that her breasts just skimmed the rise of his pecs. Her nipples pointed like bees aiming to sting, and honey seeped out of the tightness between her legs. Sensing her tense desire, Dale shifted so that his crotch just barely brushed hers. This was enough to ignite a wildfire in that incendiary patch of her sex.

"Dale," her voice strained under the blare of bad music, "I need to see you tonight."

A disco ball lowered from the ceiling, and stars of light ran across Dale's ruminating brow.

"What about him?" Dale jerked his head, and the stars rushed off his forehead like a meteor shower. Deb watched as Rick checked out Sherri's ass as she bent over in her Mrs. Santa Slut miniskirt to bowl granny style.

"He's drunk, and he'll pass out the minute he hits the pillow tonight."

"I mean, what about your engagement?"

Deb knew she was drunk, and recklessly so because she didn't care who saw her proposition this lumberjack. She was like a woman possessed, perhaps by the phosphorescence of his teeth. She had to know what a man that strong, a behemoth who could fall two-hundred-foot trees, could do to her.

"I just think we should talk. About what happened in the woods." Deb wondered if this sounded convincing, and by the penetrating way Dale looked at her, she knew he could see right through it.

"Okay."

"Okay?" He had agreed. Deb took a momentary step back from Dale and her inebriation to consider the naughtiness of her intentions. She wouldn't sleep with him, she told herself. No, she would just give him another taste so she could better lure him into a triangle of domestic bliss.

"Deeeb!" Sherri's squeal was able to travel over the disco mania. She was falling all over herself and Rick. At that moment, Dale and Deb were standing far enough apart to parry suspicion. "Guuuyyyyss, come bowl!"

"Looks like your date needs to be taken home," Deb intimated and gave a cursory wave to her employee, whom she was more than tempted to fire come Monday morning.

"Meet me behind your shop at two," Dale murmured into her ear. His breath was hot and damp on her neck. She resisted turning her head to meet that volcanic mouth that emanated such oppressive heat.

"Make it three. Just to be safe." He nodded and coolly walked, with that jaunty gait of his, back to the lanes. Before returning to her party, Deb ordered another shot of Wild Turkey from the bartender. The woman's crow's-feet bunched up in the corner of her eye as she served Deb the fortifying shot with a wink.

Rick rolled over to fondle Deb in his drunken slumber. Carefully she extricated his hand from her breast and slid out of his reach. She waited another minute and counted the seconds between Rick's snores to keep herself from leaping out of bed in anticipation. He had been asleep for an hour; she was sure of that. Rick was a sound sleeper, and when he had been drinking the way he had, he slept like a log. More like a log getting sawed, by the way he was snoring.

Fifteen minutes later Deb was in her truck, her heart racing around the bends in the road. She was sober now, but the adrenaline pulsing wildly through her veins deluded her to think that she was clearheaded, when really it was her primeval instincts that were driving her into the forest.

Deb parked her truck on the side of a neglected logging road and decided to walk the rest of the way to her shop. Of course, no one in the sleepy town of Kristmastown was awake at three in the morning, but Deb took the extra precaution.

As she approached, the unmistakable sound of a chainsaw rattled her. Hugging the tree line, she ran swiftly toward the noise that buzzed angrily like a hornet's nest. There was no question: it was coming from the clearing behind her shop.

Rounding the building, Deb was met with the most bewitching sight. There stood Dale, bare chested, save for his red suspenders that held up his ragged jeans. Deb thought he must be crazy to be shirtless in the dead of a winter night, even more crazy than her coming to meet him. He was operating a chainsaw over a huge piece of ice, spewing splinters of snow into the air. As Deb stepped forward, she saw that the ice was exquisitely carved into the shape of a stag with a rider. The rider, half formed and straddling the intricately antlered deer, was a woman. Nude. With short hair and small breasts.

"Is that me?" Deb wondered, awestruck. Dale, absorbed in his craftsmanship, didn't notice her immediately. Only when he shut off the saw to trade it for a chisel did he see her. He smiled proudly.

"It—It's beautiful," Deb stammered and drew closer. Dale rested on bended knee before his frozen masterpiece.

"You like it?" She nodded. If anybody could appreciate the artistry wielded by a chainsaw, it was she. Her wood carvings were clumsy compared with the smooth fluidity of the ice. His diaphanous sculpture appeared weightless, like hardened air.

"But how'd you—"

"My uncle. Ice sculpting is one of his hobbies, and he built a walk-in freezer on his property to store the ice blocks."

"But how'd you get it here? It must weigh a ton." She noticed crystals of ice clinging to the dark chest hair that covered his beefy pecs. Every muscle in his torso was thick like hunks of meat.

"Actually it weighs about three hundred pounds. I woke up my uncle, and he helped me load it into my truck. He was pretty disgruntled until I told him it was to impress a lady."

She crouched down close to his ear. "Well, I'm impressed."

"It's not done yet. I can't quite get the woman the way I want her."

"And how do you want her?" Deb asked deliberately, but Dale didn't take the bait. He studied his sculpture intently.

"Well, I think her proportions are all off. Her torso especially." He gestured to the half-carved belly, pregnant with ice. "I need a model." That was more like it.

Dale dropped the chisel and took Deb squarely by the shoulders. He rose and pulled her up with him. She felt strong under the heavy pressure of his hands, rooted. Sternly Dale looked her straight in the eye as he unzipped her parka. In one swift motion, he stripped it off, throwing her off balance. Her hands caught his waist and gripped a belt of hidden muscle. Suddenly she no longer felt sturdy but grasping like a barnacle clinging to an indifferent buoy. His dense flesh was hot to the touch and damp with sweat, which explained why he had been shirtless.

Dale's eyes were like padlocks, closed and fixed on her face with steel resolve as he unbuttoned her cardigan. When he yanked it off, the force of the motion tore her hands from his waist. A jolt speared through her body straight to her sex. Awoken with a start, her clit pulsed rapidly, like a tiny heart, and flooded her veins with warming desire. As the cardigan joined the parka on the ground, Deb felt no cold.

"Lift up your arms." She followed his command, emboldened by her concealed arousal. Dale peeled her snug-fitting camisole up over her head. Immediately she pressed her bare breasts against his wooly chest, but Dale quickly dislodged her.

"I need to see you." He took a step back and picked up his chisel. Now she began to shiver, the frigid air rushing to fill the gap between them. Instinctively Deb folded her arms across her chest.

"Put your arms down." Deb let her arms fall to her side. Dale grunted in approval. "Turn to the side. I need to see your profile." She rotated, and Dale left her field of vision. She faced the dark woods.

Suddenly Deb felt humiliated. Here she was standing naked from waist up, and Dale was refusing to keep her warm with all his excess body heat. Would he rather turn her into an object that would melt by morning than to touch her? Was he punishing her for that adulterous kiss? The freezing air stung her eyes like tears.

But she stood still. The clink of the chisel nicked away at the hard ice methodically, and Deb concentrated on its sound, seeking promise in its patient rhythm. Her nipples were like frozen blueberries, and her fingers went numb with cold. Just as she couldn't take it anymore, the chiseling stopped.

"Done," Dale announced. "Take a look."

Deb turned and saw herself locked in ice. Deb sized up her body in three dimensions. Dale had captured how the soft slope of her belly scooped out just beneath her ribs. He had shaped her breasts with such added detail that a delicate crease smiled underneath their subtle swell. Her face looked serene, and the expression softened the diagonals of her cheekbones and her angular jaw. A slight cleft in the ice parted her thin lips.

"Wow," she exhaled, her breath visible.

"You must be freezing," Dale exclaimed as if he had just found her abandoned out in the cold. "Let's get you inside."

He grabbed her parka from the ground and gently draped it over her shoulders. Deb started trembling uncontrollably, and he wrapped the goose down close to her body, bundling his arms around her like twine. He was like Jekyll and Hyde: frosty one minute, warm the next. Maybe he had spent too much time alone in the woods.

"Which are the keys to your shop?" he asked while unclipping the carabiner that dangled her keys from her belt loop.

"The s—square one unlocks the b—back door," she stuttered between her chattering teeth. He grabbed the rest of her clothes from the ground and picked her up easily, like she weighed no more than a stick of firewood. As Dale dashed to the building with her tight in his arms, Deb experienced a rush of air and stars and exhilaration as if she were cresting a giant roller coaster.

The shop wasn't much warmer inside than outside. Everything smelled of turpentine. Dale stumbled through the resinous darkness haunted by logs standing as still and silent as tombs. Deb directed him to her office.

Dale turned on her desk lamp and set her down on the bearskin rug that carpeted the small area of floor space. Besides the truck, the rug was her sole inheritance from her father, and Deb wouldn't be surprised if one day she found the bear grizzled from age. There was an old wood-burning stove in the corner of her office, and Dale resourcefully set to work building a fire. Dale fed firewood into the cast-iron belly as Deb huddled underneath her parka, still shivering. Dale struck a match, and she watched as the tiny flame reared into a blaze.

"Here, get closer." He pulled her across the brown expanse of fur so that they sat next to each other in front of the hearth. The flames licked up the wood like angry tongues and spit out orange heat. Deb extended her fingers to thaw.

"Here, let me see those." Dale took her hands between his palms and began to rub vigorously. Slowly the layers of cold sloughed off like bark. Sensation returned with a sharp tingling, as if needles were pricking her leaden, pincushion fingers.

"Better?"

"They hurt." Deb was unaccustomed to complaining, but she wanted Dale to make it all better.

"Stick your hands in your armpits."

"Huh?"

"Your armpits are one of the warmest parts of your body." She tucked her hands underneath her parka. Her armpits were clammy but indeed warm.

"Another good thermal zone is your crotch," he added quietly and looked almost embarrassed, like a teenage boy making an awkward, suggestive comment. But Deb didn't let him shy away.

She slowly rose to her knees, forcing his eyes on her as her unzipped parka parted open, barely concealing her breasts. Protractedly Deb ran her hand down the exposed length of torso but stopped short at the waistband of her jeans to enjoy the shiny way Dale's eyes were glued to her hands, his eyelashes swept up in anticipation.

Then she plunged. Her hand dove underneath the front of her pants. Her pussy felt like a hot, sticky summer's night. She let the parka slip from her shoulders and bared her firm, little tits toward Dale's face. He lunged, taking one breast in his hand and the other in his mouth. His teeth edged around her nipple and then swallowed it whole. As he sucked on her breast and squeezed the other, her hand embedded deeper into the matted dampness of her mound. Dale sucked harder, and the mouth of her pussy salivated around her fingers.

From her slight bird's-eye view, Deb admired Dale's freckled shoulders. His muscles were like thick braids of sandy hair. Deb freed her hands from her pants to tear off his suspenders. One of the loose ends of red elastic snapped back at him with the sting of a rubber band. "Shit!" he swore and then latched his lips back onto her other nipple. Deb dove her hand through the waves of his lustrous hair and grasped the thicket at the nape where he wore it long. Still, all her tugging couldn't release the wet suction of his mouth from her breast.

Deb unzipped her pants, and the jagged sound of the zipper sent Dale's hand bolting down her panties like lightning. Suddenly his suckling ceased, and he looked up at her with his lips gleaming and red as if fresh from a kill.

"You're like a little furnace down there." His trigger finger deftly caught the underside of her clit and flicked up on it like he was turning on a light switch. On. On. On. Deb began to convulse as if touched by a live wire.

"Dale, if you keep doing that I'm going to come," Deb gasped. He looked surprised, as though he didn't realize his own prowess.

"Don't you want to come?" His finger, determined, kept up its jerking.

The quickening between her legs tore at her, but she didn't want to blow her fuse so soon. "I want to come with you."

He slowed his hand but left his finger cushioned between her swollen lips. He kissed her. She loved the silty feel of his tongue, grainy but slippery. It whirled around her mouth like a bat trapped in a cave and beat against the walls of her cheeks. She pressed herself fully against him, and he cupped the back of her neck with his free hand like a professional kisser. She fell into him again and again—her mouth, her body—but he bolstered her. Deb had let go, surrendered to Dale's trunklike sturdiness and to wherever he wanted to take her.

He took her down to the bearskin rug.

The musty smell of animal fur and fresher odor of Dale's sweat incensed Deb's feral desire. With heavy strokes of her tongue, she greedily lapped at the coarse hairs that decorated his chest in curlicues. She relished the foreign taste of such a man, seasoned with unfamiliar salts and experience. Her senses were flared by his scent, rich like warm soil; she dove her nose into his armpit, gulping in the fecund smell.

He rolled on top of her, and the weight of his hard-on ground into her. She struggled to pull down her pants. He lifted to help her and stayed in this planklike position over her to undo the button fly of his dirty jeans. She pushed them down for him, past his anvil thighs half encased in a tight pair of black boxer briefs. She cupped the bulk of his straining package. It took two hands. She squeezed; he moaned. This first wordless utterance of his pleasure pushed her past any hesitation. She rolled down his waistband, admiring the vee of muscles that tapered into the concrete base where his cock stood rigid like a steel bar.

Dale took hold of his cock in one hand as if pointing a loaded gun at her. She stared down its barrel, which grew monstrously out of proportion in her singular focus. At gunpoint, she shimmied out of her cotton bikinis and tossed them overhead, where they landed on the bear's head, covering its silent but deadly roar. Now no one would bear witness to their transgression.

Momentarily releasing his cock, Dale raked his hand down the flank of Deb's thigh and then bent her knee back to her chest. Deb felt her quim exposed, the split of her lips stretched, and her wetness exhibited. Self-conscious by how much her parted sex was leaking under Dale's examining gaze, Deb tried to squeeze her legs together. But Dale only pushed her knee farther into her chest and delivered a quick smack to the underside of her ass.

His hand felt like an oak paddle and left her skin stinging with a thousand splinters. But immediately that same hand soothingly stroked her pussy, lightly trailing a finger down the length of her peeking pink furrow. Dale's ambulatory fingers paced the slick divide until they located the nub of her clit. He pressed his calloused thumb to her most sensitive pressure point until it throbbed painfully against the flat of his fingertip.

"I need you to fuck me." These were not words that usually escaped Deb's lips, even in a whisper, but the palpitations of her clit had made her desperate, like the solicitous pleas of a beggar or a hooker.

He took up his cock again, squeezing it tight in his fist. Its head looked fleshy and delectable like a mushroom cap. Dale tipped forward to kiss her mouth, and she sucked on his tongue as if it were his cock. He pulled away just enough to watch himself enter her.

His thickness overwhelmed her, but her supple pussy gave easily to his girth, and the whole length of him slid right in. Dale fucked her with his thumb pressed down on her clit as if to meet the tip of his cock buried inside. Deb's ass scooted up and down the luxurious coat of bear, rocked by Dale's rhythmic thrusts. Her leg was still pinned to her chest, and she found a foothold in his armpit and toed the soft fur of his underarm hair. He seemed to swell even more inside of her.

"You feel so fucking good, Deb," was all he murmured as he scooped up her whole body so that her legs fell loosely about his waist. Their sexes still joined, they faced each other in an erotic embrace. They moved together with the jubilant trajectory of a swing. His hands cradled the winglike juts of her shoulder blades as they slid up and down. She controlled their movement now, and she angled herself so that his cock hit the sweet spot that made her womb roil into her guts. She started to buck ferociously against his lodged sex.

Her vision began to blur, and Dale's face shuddered in the turbulence of her watery eyes. He clasped the back of her neck to keep her sutured to him, but she proved difficult to restrain. Dale took charge and threw her down to the bearskin rug like a wrestler. Without his prompting, her limber legs flew up close to his ears to open herself up to him more completely, more deeply. Her fervor astounded Dale, and he plunged into her like a man fording a torrential river. He struggled to hold his own, thrashing at his own direction, but her pulling currents were too strong and sucked him down to her. His mouth covered hers in what was not quite a kiss but a whirlpool of abandon. Their movement became fluid, their bodies indistinguishable as water on water.

Dale relinquished first, shaking as he came as if afraid of his own might. As he released himself inside her, he issued a booming sound with a voice that could yell *Timber!* loud enough to echo through acres of woodland. His deep but wordless utterance was revealing; it was as if it gave Deb something he had no control over. Amazed, Deb came soon after in a spurting gush that surprised them both.

What can you say after sex like that?

Deb stared up at the ceiling. Dale was also looking up at the rafters where the fire carelessly flung its amorphous shadow. She was confused. Confused, first off, by her anatomy. She had never come like that, in an ejaculatory way. Dale had wiped off the milky-white substance from the thatch of hair beneath his belly button. He had looked pleased.

Secondly she was confused about having slept with another man. She had never really had sex with anybody but Rick. Her loss of virginity to a logging trucker's son was one of those youthful indiscretions that didn't really count, sealed up with your record and annulled when you turned eighteen. The absence of guilt, however, while in Dale's presence was strange. Dale was so different from Rick she felt her own identity rent in two. There was the Deb who had casual sex on the floor of her office at three in the morning, and then there was the Deb who was betrothed to her high school sweetheart. The split in personality deluded her to think that she wasn't cheating at all.

Deb rolled off her back to press the front of her naked body against the length of Dale's side. Dale clumsily stroked her hair, his hand heavy and lethargic. She watched him inhale, the six-pack of his abdomen rising like golden buns baking in an oven.

"We didn't use a condom."

"You're not on the pill?" Dale turned his head toward her. His eyelids, half hooded in a swoon, struggled to rouse.

"No. I mean, yes." She was, but his assumption irked her.

What if she wasn't? Did that even cross his mind before he came inside her?

"Don't worry, I'm clean. I haven't been with a woman for a while and since I was last tested." So he was a responsible woodsman, and less of a stud than she had thought. Perhaps she had had some preconceptions of her own.

"So you and Sherri—no nooky?"

He shook his head and laughed heartily. "Is that what you call what we just did? Nooky?"

Hardly. "Sorry, I guess that's what my dad used to call it." Why was she always mentioning her dad around Dale? She never talked about him, not even to Rick. She changed the subject. "So there's no future Mrs. Lix around?" She mowed her hand through his brambly chest hair.

"Nah." He closed his eyes again, enjoying how her nails combed his pecs. "Monogamy doesn't really interest me."

Had she been single, Deb knew this would be one of those dating red flags signaling that she should hightail it to the hills. But in her case, it sounded promising.

"Have you ever had a threesome?"

Again, Dale chuckled. "Who wants to know?"

He took her hand and guided it down the corrugated musculature of his stomach. Where her hand met the untamed border of his pubes, his cock was again beginning to surge.

"Did you enjoy it?" She plucked up his cock, still somewhat tender and pink, and coaxed it into stiffening with the gentle pull of her hand.

"Mmmm, I'm enjoying *this*."

She left her subject of inquiry alone and allowed his cock, for now, to be the third actor in their most unholy trinity.

5

Rick swore at his Stone Age PC. Connecting to the Internet should not be this difficult in the twenty-first century. He tapped the desk with his pen irritably and looked at the cuckoo clock. Deb wouldn't be home for a while, so he would be able to work uninterrupted. Not that they would say much to each other anyway, but their unspoken tension would disrupt his concentration all the same.

Finally the dial-up connected. Rick had already finished his report on black bears for the forest service but still had to fact-check a couple things. Rick scrolled down the results of his search for bears and came across a curious link. He clicked on it. Immediately Rick was bombarded by pics of hairy-chested, heavily bearded men wearing nothing but leather accoutrements that hardly covered their chubby bellies or, well, their *chubbies*. Shocked but nonetheless riveted, Rick realized he had entered a gay porn site devoted to "bears." Instead of closing the window, Rick took a surreptitious glance around the empty cabin and, watched only by the glassy-eyed taxidermy that hung on the walls, clicked on the PERSONALS button.

Smirking as if to an inside joke, Rick thought it would be amusing to cruise the Internet for these hairy and heavy men. He quickly created a screen name, Cub4yerChub, and began to scan the other profiles. All the men, however, looked the same to him. Most had shaved or balding heads, saggy pecs and full goatees. Rick soon got bored and was just about to return to his work on the animal kingdom's black bear, when he spotted Woofin@U's ad. Woofin had a full head of thick brown hair, and his chiseled face was cleanly shaven. He wore a plaid, flannel shirt with its sleeves ripped off, and it was unbuttoned to flaunt the solid heft of his chest and bulging muscles of his arms. A hand was smugly tucked down the front of his jeans where the pattern of his body hair also seemed directed. Rick forgot his imposter pretense and openly admired Woofin's hypermasculinity. Rather than make Rick insecure, the pic made Rick's own sense of manhood swell as though by appreciating Woofin's manliness, he was appreciating his own. But Rick's anatomical manhood also swelled, and not out of a fraternal sentiment.

Bewildered, Rick glanced down at his crotch. He was only wearing boxers and, sure enough, his dick was stirring against the loose fabric, straining to peek its head out the gaping fly and get its own glimpse of Woofin. Rick clamped his hand down in his lap, which only made his erection rear in anger.

Suddenly the computer screen blinked off. Gone was Woofin, and gone were all the lights. A blackout.

There was enough light from the windows—which dusk had tinted a deep sapphire—for Rick to search the cabin for the emergency stash of candles. He rummaged through kitchen drawers and cabinets until he found them bundled up like dynamite in the hallway closet. Focused on arranging and lighting the candles around the cabin, Rick put all thoughts of Woofin and his hairy breed on the back burner and instead contemplated what to make for dinner, on the gas stove, for when Deb came home.

Due to the blackout, Deb had to close the shop earlier than she had wanted. It wasn't because she was behind on her Christmas orders that Deb had intended to work well past five—they were all shipped out or waiting to be picked up—but because she wanted to avoid going home, avoid Rick, for as long as possible. Driving home through town, Deb silently cursed the holiday decorations, which, unilluminated, looked dismal as if lining the streets for a funeral procession. Their incandescent extravagance was undoubtedly responsible for this latest blackout.

Deb had expected to get caught when she'd snuck back into the cabin at dawn after meeting Dale. She had imagined Rick would be waiting for her with the antique rifle, removed from its station on the mantel, but instead found him sound asleep just as she had left him. Even though she had wanted to shower, stinking of sweat and of sawdust and of another man, she thought that the water might wake him, and so she dutifully slipped under the covers. Rick had rolled over and clasped her to him in his slumber. Her last thought before falling asleep in the already brightening bedroom was that she would confess to Rick in the morning.

But she hadn't.

Deb reached the cabin by flashlight. She opened the front door to a living room twinkling with candlelight. The smell of a roast in the oven welcomed her along with the inviting warmth of a fire. Rick was nowhere in sight, and Deb, exhausted from the past few days of guilt-induced insomnia, sprawled on the couch in front of the fireplace and kicked off her work boots. She stripped off her fleece pullover, under which she wore only a flesh-colored camisole, and closed her eyes, succumbing to the ambience of the candles. The mouth-watering aromas emanating from the kitchen made her stomach growl.

"Grrrr." She opened her eyes to a bearlike echo. Rick stood above her holding two steaming mugs and offered one to her. "Hot toddy?"

Deb accepted and took a sip. It was sweetened with honey just enough to mask the strong taste of whiskey. The lemony elixir warmed her to her toes, and Deb felt the chilliness between them begin to thaw.

"Mmmm, Rick that's *delish.*"

"Thought you might like it. You've been looking weary lately. I'm fixing us a nice dinner. Figured since we have this mood lighting, courtesy of a Kristmastown blackout and all."

Deb smiled. Why was Rick being such a sweetheart after nearly two weeks of churlishness since she had told him her Christmas wish?

"May I join you on the couch?"

"Of course." She swung her feet off to make room, but Rick took them into his lap as he sat. Between sips of his toddy, he massaged her toes through her damp wool socks. His fingers squeezed with deep, slow pressure but eased up when they came too close to the bone.

Deb sighed languidly. She had to give it to Rick: he always took care of her, starting with the day her father had died. This was why she knew she would marry him despite their recent troubles and her lapse in fidelity, granted that he never found out.

Deb promised herself it wouldn't happen again. She had told Dale so when she pried herself out of his arms after they had fucked for a second time on the bearskin rug. Admittedly it was hard to leave his arms; their erotic exertions had been taxing. He had only nodded when she told him this was the first and last time, but then he'd pulled her back into his impossibly strong arms. She had lain against the shag of his chest for a few more minutes before slipping out of his embrace for good.

For good, Deb repeated to herself and closed her eyes as if to seal her oath. For the past three business days, she and Dale had kept to their respective sides of the street. Deb had furtively watched the deforestation of his lot as Christmas rapidly approached. Each day he arrived later and later as the demand for Christmas trees dwindled. The only time he so much looked in the direction of her shop was to call out to Shasta when the dog ran too close to the road. Sherri, on the other hand, openly gawked across the street. When she started complaining to Deb about how Dale hadn't called, Deb immediately reprimanded her for drinking underage in public and launched into a harangue about how she represented Deb's Chainsaw Carvings and so on. Sherri hadn't complained about Dale's lack of attention again.

Deb opened her eyes back to her fiancé. Rick was staring into the fire, looking pensive but at ease. His attuned fingers continued to rub her feet.

"You put up our stockings," Deb said, noticing for the first time. They had been a gift from Rick's cuckoo aunt years ago, and she had embroidered the couple's names in loopy cursive onto the felt cuffs. Deb had forgotten to hang them when she trimmed the blue spruce tree, which she did all by herself because Rick had been too pissed off the evening she had brought it home from Dale's lot. Apparently his holiday cheer had returned.

"Don't want Santa to pass us over." He grinned boyishly at her. In the firelight his youthful skin radiated the soft yellows and pinks of a peach. "Deb." He turned to her. "I'm so sorry I've been such a jerk."

"Rick, no. It's okay," Deb burst out. She couldn't stand for him to apologize when it was she who had cheated. But he silenced her with two gentle fingers to her lips.

"No, I'm sorry. I'm sorry that I shut down after you revealed your fantasy to me. I guess I just wasn't secure enough to handle it."

"Rick, really. Forget about it. It was stupid." She had all but given up on her wish coming true.

"It's not stupid. I want to be able to satisfy you as my wife, and if that means bringing somebody else into the picture, then I'm willing to experiment."

Deb couldn't believe her ears. Was she drunk? Was *Rick* drunk? Seeing that she was speechless, he continued. "If you can find someone before our wedding who we can both agree on, I'm game."

"Rick, I don't know what to say. . . . Are you sure?" Baffled, Deb wondered at his change of heart. Rick took her hand and fingered her engagement ring. The diamond was small, almost a fleck, but he was now offering her the engagement present of a lifetime.

"Did you have anybody in mind?" She could tell Rick was swallowing his pride to ask her this. In a surge of guilt about Dale—if only she had waited for Rick's permission, his participation—she answered no.

Rick looked relieved. Although pleased by this unexpected turn of events, Deb also felt in turmoil. She had already blown off Dale, and she worried that if she solicited him for a threesome with Rick, he would tell her fiancé about their recent history. Secondly she had no idea if Dale was the kind of man who would be open to another man. Judging by his macho demeanor, she ventured not. Even though Dale had implicitly admitted to having a threesome, Deb imagined it had involved two forest nymphs. She pictured them frolicking around his manhood as if it were a maypole.

"Well, if you find anybody, let me know." Rick was gently kneading her thigh. She smiled gratefully. As she leaned forward for a kiss, her hand skimmed an arresting protuberance in his lap.

"Why, Mr. Rick Rockett! You've got a rocket in your pocket," she teased him with an old schoolyard taunt. Rick grinned sheepishly and then bit his fleshy lower lip as she squeezed his hardon through his pants.

"All this talk about threesomes making you randy, Rick?" she ventured, baiting him playfully. She squeezed harder, commanding an answer.

"A little bit," he gasped reluctantly. Rick's head lolled back against the couch as she felt up the solid length of his rod. His eyelids half shuttered his irises like window shades hastily drawn in foreplay.

"And what exactly about you, me and another man excites you?" His rocket, impatiently docked, twitched against the fabric of his pants, but he didn't answer. Maintaining her crotch hold, Deb shimmied up his body to his lips. She tried to draw out an answer with her mouth, sucking on his sulky lower lip first and then moving to the refined line of his top one. He tasted like cinnamon and cloves.

"Maybe," she suggested seductively, "you want him to watch us fuck."

She watched him closely for a reaction, but he only reached to jiggle her tit. His head remained tossed back like an indolent prince.

"Or maybe . . ." She started to unzip him. Rick moaned in anticipation; he was about to bust out of his britches. "Maybe you want to watch me suck him."

She reached into his boxers and released his cock. Although it lacked Dale's girth, Rick's dick was one lean, long fucking machine.

"Like this," she added and lowered her mouth onto the sweet angle of his erection. She rolled her tongue around the perfectly shaped tip, pushing her lips over the cock head and then dragging them back over the delicate ridge.

"Do you want me to do that to him?" She looked up at Rick with her mouth wet and vacant, waiting for his response.

He nodded and confessed hoarsely, "I want you to take him in all the way while I watch."

Deb's pussy wept with joy, and she eagerly throated his cock. Rick arched his lower back in pleasure, giving her even more to swallow, and her mouth ravenously worked the full length of his shaft.

Rick's teeth clenched. In a low, gravelly voice, he continued the fantasy Deb had started. "While you're sucking him off, on your knees, I'd kneel down behind you and play with your clit. You'd be all wet and swollen but couldn't ask for anything because you'd have a big dick in your mouth."

Deb murmured a yes with Rick lodged in her mouth and her own clit pounding for attention.

"You'd feel my boner press up against your ass, and maybe I'd slip a finger or two in your tight little asshole while you took his load."

Deb gasped for air. "*Rick, I need you to take me.*"

Rick's proud member glistened between them, all lubed up from her mouth and harder than ever. In the luciferous candlelight, Rick's smile was wicked; shadows haunted his face.

"Strip."

Deb's pussy flustered at his charge. She had to rise off the couch to remove her jeans, swiftly followed by the damp twist of her panties. Before she had a chance to take off her camisole, Rick had her pressed against the arm of the couch. With his pants and underwear around his ankles like shackles, he took her standing. Deb's toes still touched the ground as he penetrated her.

In the reflection of the mirror hung over the mantel, she watched Rick's buttocks clench and release, clench and release.

Rick knew his length could be too much for Deb to take up to the hilt right away, and so he prodded Deb slowly, gradually working himself up into her. His thrusts deepened, and Deb cried out when he sheathed himself all the way. He gyrated inside her, massaging the stretched walls until her inflamed pussy calmed into undulations of pleasure. With Deb's center molded to his shaft, Rick picked her up and carried her to the bedroom.

Stout candles slumped on the vanity, dripping hot wax onto the maple finish. A molten puddle of wax scalded Deb's bare ass as Rick set her down. She yelped, and Rick slipped out as he quickly moved her off the dresser.

"Let me see that." He turned her around, and she stuck out her behind for him to examine the singe mark reddening like a hickey. He kissed it tenderly. "All better."

She straightened back up, facing the mirror. Taking his time, Rick peeled off her camisole and then his own T-shirt. His hairless chest was remarkably smooth and solid like a bar of soap. She leaned back against him; his stimulated nipples tickled the elbows of her shoulder blades.

They watched each other in the mirror as Rick reached around and parted her downy cleft to reveal the pearlescence of her clit. He stroked her with finesse until her arousal pooled and drenched his fingers. Her breathing quickened with the throbbing of her splayed sex.

He withdrew his hand to taste her silky juices.

"Mmmm, Deb, you taste *delish*," he whispered hotly into her ear. His exquisite fingers wrapped around her hip bones, and he bent her forward from the hinge of her waist. Her hands grasped the ledge of the dresser to brace herself as his stiff dick blindly knocked around her back door. Rick redirected its target by sinking his hand into the curve of her lower back so that her quim dawned between her thighs. This time, Rick tossed aside niceties and penetrated her with the full length of his pointed sex.

"I've missed being inside you," Rick panted damply into her ear as he banged her from behind. His long strokes, though readily encompassed by her cunt, pushed tears from her eyes. In the heightened awareness of passion, Deb realized that she, too, had missed him.

The juncture of their sexes was seamless, and they moved with the synchronicity of having discovered the secrets of each other's bodies long ago.

Rick tweezed Deb's nipple between his slender fingers as his climax built from behind his slightly bent knees. As Rick began to pump without regard for rhythm or precision, Deb's molten core surged with him, hotly, madly.

"*Oh, fuck me, fuck me, Dale!*" The words were ripped right out of her crazed womb and escaped in the same breath as her orgasm. Rick, midcoming, let out a tremendous noise. The sound was a confusion of ecstasy and horror.

6
_____

December 21st

Deb was in the doghouse. Literally. She was on hands and knees trying to coax Shasta out of the long-forgotten doghouse behind her shop. The previous owners of the woodshop had had a dog, and its former dwelling, splintered and peeling paint, was almost enveloped by the blackberry bushes that bordered the clearing. Deb had happened to look out the window of her office at the exact moment Shasta had made a mad dash across the road with an indeterminate species of fresh roadkill flopping from his jowls. He had darted into the doghouse with his prize.

"Shasta!" Deb scolded. "Get out of there!" Really she wanted to get him over to his side of the street before Dale got back from wherever he had driven off to in his truck. So she was on her hands and knees, trying to cajole the dog out.

"Whatcha got there, Shasta? I've got a treat for you outside." Deb had no such thing, and Shasta only took a brief, wary glance up from his feast of carrion.

"I didn't realize you liked it doggy style."

Fuck. Dale.

Deb rose off the ground and wiped herself off. The mud had stained the knees of her jeans.

"Hello, Dale." They hadn't spoken since the night on the bearskin rug, and she didn't want to speak to him now. Also she didn't appreciate his smart-ass remark; he had no idea what trouble he had caused her. She had slept the last two nights in the shop because of him, somehow managing to evade the notice of her employees.

"You holding my dog hostage?" He stepped toward her.

Much to her vexation, she noticed he was wearing his Brawny Man, red flannel. The same one he had worn the first day when he had caught her eye. She was reminded of the inviting broadness of his chest.

"Seems like he got a hold of some dinner," she explained.

Dale called his dog with commanding ease. Shasta immediately emerged from his shelter. "Drop it." Shasta dropped the mangled carcass at Deb's feet. It was part raccoon. She felt a wave of revulsion and breathed through her mouth.

"Sorry about that," Dale apologized. "Where are all your elves?" Dale looked around the empty clearing. They were alone in the charmed circle.

" 'Scuse me?"

"Your workers."

"I sent them home early. It's the start of their Christmas vacation."

"And what about yours? Why are you still here?"

"Why are you?" she echoed flippantly.

He grinned, unscathed. It was hard not to be charmed by his smile and that slight wave of thick hair against his forehead, but Deb resisted.

"I won't keep you." He motioned to Shasta, and the dog

trotted obediently to Dale's heel. "I'm sure you have to get home for dinner."

An internal twinge surfaced on her face, perhaps only in a slight tightening of her temples or in a minute quiver of her lips, but Dale noticed it all the same.

"Or you're not going home for dinner?"

Deb shook her head and looked past him at her open office door. She could just make out the blue of her sleeping bag on the couch.

"What happened, Deb?" Dale placed his hand on her shoulder gently. She tried to ignore how his touch assuaged the past couple days of distress.

"I told Rick."

He looked shocked. "Told Rick . . . about us?" He sounded like he didn't want to believe it, like it gave too much weight to their sexual encounter. A weight that was emotional, perhaps invested with meaning, rather than purely physical. Deb felt the need to assure him this was not the case.

"I didn't intend on telling him. It just sort of came out." No need to go into details there. "This has nothing to do with you."

With her last cutting remark, she noticed the petrified hardness of his amber eyes soften a little, like sap. He looked almost bruised. This confused her. Had it been more than sex?

"Sorry, I just haven't been sleeping well." She motioned to the office. "I'm on the couch."

Dale nodded as though he understood completely. "Hopefully you two will make up by Christmas."

"I'm not so sure." Deb thought back to the moment when Rick had swiped all the candles off the dresser. She had never seen the man raise his hand to anything, and his fury had terrified her. Fortunately the candles had snuffed themselves out on the hardwood floor, and the only things damaged were her nerves. And possibly her heart.

Rick had known right away what her exclamation had meant. *"Did you fuck that logger?" Rick asked her bluntly in the mirror. He still stood behind her, naked and heaving. She couldn't lie, rendered susceptible from their lovemaking.*

Deb nodded yes and then cried. Rick started shouting immediately and knocking over the candles. He became convinced that she had wanted a threesome to cuckold him in front of her lover and to legitimize the affair that, he was also convinced, she had been having for some time. She pleaded to the contrary, but Rick's rage shamed her before she could even form a semblance of a coherent explanation or apology. Then he kicked her out.

"Deb. *Deb.*" The weight of Dale's hand returned to her shoulder.

"I'm sorry, I just need to be alone right now." She looked away from him. He slowly withdrew his hand.

"Let me know if there's anything I can do."

Deb had to restrain herself from looking back at him appreciatively. Appreciation could so easily transmute into attraction.

"C'mon, Shasta." She watched them cross the road. Dale, for once, wasn't wearing suspenders, and his jeans hung with just the perfect looseness from his hips. Watching him walk away, Deb found the gallant breadth of his shoulders even more alluring; she felt the urge to run after him. But she didn't.

Dale got into his truck with Shasta. The Dodge spit up gravel and then sped away. Deb was left all alone in the clearing with the dead raccoon.

7

December 23rd

Two days until Christmas. This was the first thought that occurred to Deb when she woke up. She squeezed her eyes shut
to make it untrue, but a chirping bird outside her office window mocked her misery, and she was unable to slip back to
sleep.

Deb clambered out of her sleeping bag and stretched. For
the fourth morning in a row she had awoken with a crick in her
neck from sleeping on the ratty couch. She told herself she
would use her holiday revenue to buy a new one.

Tomorrow is Christmas Eve. The thought was so depressing
Deb sat back on the couch and planted her face in her hands.
She couldn't imagine a Christmas apart from Rick or, for that
matter, a life without him. With each solitary day spent in her
shop with only animals carved of wood to keep her company,
the reality sank in that she might have destroyed her life as she
knew it in Kristmastown. And for what? For a paper-towel-
icon look-alike?

She had to try calling Rick again. He hadn't taken any of her calls, but she had to keep trying. She dialed. To her surprise, Rick picked up.

"Rick!" He didn't say anything. "It's Deb. I just . . . I just," she stuttered but then regained her composure. "I just want to explain everything and tell you how deeply sorry I am."

He sighed but didn't say anything. But he didn't hang up either.

"Rick? Will you talk to me? Please!" She began to choke up. "I made a huge mistake. I love you, and I can't live without you." The waterworks were now flowing freely. "You have to forgive me!"

"I'm not ready to talk yet, Deb." She could tell that Rick was choosing his words carefully so as to betray nothing.

"What about Christmas?" she sniffled.

"I'm going to my mother's. Deb, I'm going to get off the phone now." He sounded almost regretful, but he hung up before Deb could wedge open any emotion. For a few moments afterward, Deb sat paralyzed and listened to the dial tone for signs of life.

She put down the phone and slowly rose to open the back door of her office to let in some fresh air and sunlight. A deer was nibbling at the blackberries at the edge of the clearing. It darted into the bushes when it saw Deb. Deb exhaled the stale air from her lungs into the crisp but sunny morning. She tripped as she took a step outside.

On her doorstep sat a basket with a note tucked into its handle. Deb read the note.

D.
So you don't starve to death in there.—D.

Deb lifted the checkered fabric covering the basket to reveal a loaf of fresh-baked gingerbread slathered with white frosting.

She had no idea if Dale had made it himself, but, as she tore off a piece, it tasted as though it were baked with loving care. There was a postscript on the note, which Deb read as she chewed: *Nobody should spend Christmas alone.* He included his phone number.

Deb sat down on the step and chewed thoughtfully in the sun. Dale must have dropped it off that morning while she was still asleep. She had hardly eaten in the last few days, but after a few bites of the moist, still-warm-from-the-oven gingerbread, her hunger returned. Her whetted appetite, however, was not for food alone.

Dale showed up at the back door that afternoon with a Christmas tree.

"Making door-to-door sales?" Deb quipped. Deb had called to thank him for the muffins but, unable to stop herself, ended up inviting him over to the shop for afternoon "cocktails." She might as well have left out the "tails" part of it—she knew what she was getting herself into.

"More like making a special delivery." Dale grinned his fetching grin. Deb had spruced herself up for him—running to town to buy a new outfit since all her clothes were at the cabin—and the snug sweater dress made a visible impression on him. It gave her curves she didn't quite have.

"Is that tree for me?" He nodded, beaming. "Oh, Dale, you shouldn't have!" She gave him a quick peck on the cheek. It was freshly shaven, and she caught a whiff of his aftershave: Old Spice, no doubt. He had cleaned up for her, too; his flannel shirt looked new and his jeans washed. He wore his red suspenders. She let him through the door.

Dale set down the tree, a small noble fir. "That's not all," he announced and disappeared back outside. He returned with two grocery bags.

"What's in there?"

"It's depressing in here," Dale observed not unkindly. "Thought I'd help you deck the halls."

He set the bags on her desk and pulled out a wreath of holly, some garlands of pine, a store-bought box of ornaments, a string of Christmas-tree lights and an old-fashioned milk bottle full of—

"Fresh eggnog," Dale explained. "You have cups?"

Deb pulled two coffee mugs from a cabinet along with a bottle of bourbon she had bought for the occasion. "Will this do?"

"Perfect. You pour." He handed her the bottle of frothy nog and then started to untangle the strand of lights. Deb had the radio on, and a Sinatra type crooned Christmas songs.

She handed Dale his cup of eggnog. "Cheers." She made eyes with him over the rim of her raised mug.

"Oh, I almost forgot." Dale reached back into the grocery bag and retrieved a spray of mistletoe. He dangled it over the crown of her head. She wasn't sure if he seriously meant for them to kiss, but he was looking at her with such unnerving earnestness that Deb giggled. He smirked and waited, confident and unhurried, for her to kiss him.

Deb had to stand on her tippy toes to reach his mouth. Their kiss was simple; their mouths were closed. It felt safe and filled Deb with a warm feeling of security. The kiss didn't last more than a few seconds.

"Cheers." Dale clinked her mug. He took a swig and almost choked. "Damn! How much bourbon did you put in here? Trying to get me drunk, lady?" But he took another gulp.

Deb shrugged impishly and then burst out laughing when she saw Dale's milk—that is, *nog*—mustache. As she wiped it for him, he threaded his arm around her waist. He pressed her slender body against his with his hand moored on the ledge of her rump. This time, they kissed ardently.

Deb pulled away first. There was something strangely sobering about kissing Dale with the afternoon daylight streaking through her grimy office window. It made her nervous. Now that she was, however temporarily, separated from Rick, she was unsure of her footing with Dale. Even though they were standing on the same bearskin rug on which their illicit tryst had transpired, Deb felt herself entering unfamiliar terrain.

Stepping off the fur, Deb busied herself with hanging the garlands around the office. She took creamy chugs of eggnog and poured herself another cup. Dale whistled along to a Christmas tune as he strung the lights around the tree. Every so often, she would catch him checking out the way her sweater dress clung to her ass with static electricity.

By the time the office was entirely decorated, Deb was tipsy. She was now working on her third mug of eggnog, which was indeed mostly bourbon with just a creamer of nog. For the final touch, Dale plugged in the Christmas-tree lights. The office was no longer a dreary place housing Deb's misery but rather sparkled brightly like a celebration. Dale sat down on the couch to admire the work they had done. His legs yawned open cockily. The top couple buttons of his shirt had come undone. Deb slinked over to him and sat on his knee to flirt with his open collar.

His leg beneath her ass was tense with muscle. She perched in such a way that her crotch ground subtly against his thigh's tautness. Dale sensed her shifting and ran his hand underneath the short hem of her dress. His fingers worked the small knobs of her lower vertebrae, as if digging pearls out of oysters, and then shoveled down the back of her tights. His hands were cold as he squeezed her bare butt cheeks. She squirmed, which he seemed to enjoy.

"Tell Santa: have you been a good little girl this year?" It was naughty and made Deb's panties wet. Her Santa pinched her nipples, erect like giant goose bumps, through the stretchy wool of her dress.

Deb nodded as he squeezed her ass harder. "Are you sure you've been good?" Deb shook her head. She had been bad. Very, very bad.

Dale responded deftly by bending her over his other leg. He yanked down her schoolgirl tights and landed a giant smack on her exposed ass. Her whole pussy jumped.

"Have you been a bad girl?"

"Yes!" She cried for more. His hand dropped back on her bare behind. The stinging *whams* resounded up her cunt. Deb wanted more, wriggling her ass for it, and he gave it to her in a quick succession of spanks.

Only when he seemed tired of spanking did he stop to announce: "Now I need the front of you."

He stood her up. She swayed, the blood seemed to rush straight from her head to her inflamed buttocks, but Dale propped her upright between his legs. He helped her the rest of the way out of her tights, which had jammed around her knees.

"Show me your pussy," he commanded evenly.

Deb shimmied her dress up to her waist to ingenuously display her sex. The gleam trapped between her pussy lips was starting to show. Dale reached to thumb her clit but appeared to change his mind.

"That's only for good girls, and you're naughty for enjoying that spanking."

Deb dropped her dress with a pout. "So what do naughty girls get?"

His eyes simmered but didn't spill an answer. Without fanfare, Dale grabbed Deb and threw her over his shoulder like a sackful of presents. He carried her out the back door.

He took her deep into the woods. The disappearing daylight

flashed between the leaves like cymbals. Dale hummed as he tromped along with his human bounty; his boots crunching twigs and weak roots seemed louder than his tune. Finally Dale set Deb down at the base of a sizable Douglas fir.

"You know, Deb." His voice was gravely and made her long for the gritty feel of his tongue. "Every time I see you I want to press you up against something." Dale crushed her against the trunk, throwing the full weight of his body behind his tunneling hard-on. Their mouths met in open passion.

Dale pawed his way up her dress until it flew off her and landed on a low-hanging bough. Now that she was naked, Dale unstrapped his suspenders. It wasn't, however, the prelude to his own disrobing.

"Put your arms back around the tree."

"What?" Deb's heart began to beat like that of a hummingbird, too fast for its tiny chest cavity.

"I'm going to tie you up." She had certainly entered unknown territory with Dale. Looking around, she didn't even recognize this part of the woods.

"Nobody's here to see," he reassured but then quickly barked, "Hands back *now*."

Deb wrapped her arms behind the trunk, which was just the right circumference for her wrists to cross in back. She realized that Dale had picked his way through the woods in search of a tree with just the right girth. As Dale bound her hands with his suspenders, Deb's chest thrust open to the forest. The cold air perked up her nipples.

Everything felt raw: the bark scraping up her back, the elastic rubbing her wrists, the primal state of the woods that mirrored her own nakedness.

Dale looped back around the tree to spread her legs. He was crouched before her, positioning her feet apart and onto gnarled roots, when he noticed her pussy leaking down her inner thighs. He began to lick up the sleekness captured in the tender hollows where leg meets pelvis. The lavish strokes of his tongue neared her swell but eschewed actual contact. Deb began to fidget in an attempt to trick his tongue into plunging deep into her swollen folds, but Dale only clamped his hands around her ankles to still her.

"Dale, *please*," she begged. Apparently that was all it took for Dale to give her the tongue thrashing she so desperately needed.

He buried his whole head in the fissure of her sex: his tongue, his nose, his lips—all ate at her. Then his tongue took over the brunt of the work and lapped, lapped her up. In a final flourish, he stung her clit with jabs of his tongue until it began to spasm on its accord.

But he didn't let her come. He cinched her waist and kissed his way up her navel line. Their eyes met somewhere around her sternum.

"Take out your cock." She may be trussed to a tree, but Deb was going to get what she wanted. Never, she believed, had she desired something as much as she desired Dale at that moment. Her lust made her the furthest thing from herself and the closest thing to her sex; she spoke with the voracious mouth of her pussy. "I need you to stick it in me."

Dale rose all the way, loosened his belt, and released his stout, ruddy cock. She opened herself as wide as she could without having her hands to assist her. Dale pressed her thighs even further apart, more than she thought she could ever spread. He stuck two fingers in her, jiggling them around as if to loosen her up. The second they pulled out, Dale's swift, hard cock replaced them.

He pounded her against the tree. Neither needed much to come. Deb couldn't hold on to anything, couldn't do anything but be fucked, and so she surrendered completely. Her sex responded without her. It trembled and quaked. It became a canon in which her fetal orgasm was curled up like a ball, rumbling and waiting in the dark to be ejected. Light burst behind Deb's eyelids as she came with an explosion that shook the treetops overhead.

"Ouch, Dale, that hurts!" Deb lay on her stomach on the bearskin rug. Dale straddled over her on his knees.

"Sorry." He tried to apply the aloe vera more gently to her abrasions, but they still stung.

"That's the last time I let you tie me to a tree!" But Deb smiled to herself. Her backside may have some scratches, but the rough ride had been well worth it. She was sure she had never come so hard in her life. She was not so sure, however, what she was doing with the lumberjack.

Dale blew gingerly on her skin to extinguish the tiny flames that seemed to bedevil her back. She rested her cheek on the soft fur of the rug. The sound of the crackling fire began to soothe her, along with the salve.

"Better?" Dale asked sweetly. She nodded. Dale reached for a carton of takeout.

"More Mongolian beef?" He extended a tasty morsel between a pair of chopsticks.

Deb shook her head. "I think I've had my fill."

They had stuffed themselves on Chinese food after returning from their romp in the woods. As soon as the deliveryman drove away, they had taken off their clothes and feasted naked. Their blood was still hot from their lovemaking, and the fire in the stove only magnified their afterglow. Dale fed her bite after bite of the greasy cuisine, sometimes sneaking a kiss in between. There was a moment when Deb worried about someone spying them in their postcoital binge—a Peeping Tom or an employee who had forgotten something in the shop—but then she remembered, with that sinking feeling all over again, that the only person she was concerned about knowing already knew.

Dale lowered himself down next to her on the rug and cuddled her the best he could without irritating her back. Deb tried to get comfortable but kept fidgeting on her stomach.

"What's wrong, babe?" Dale shifted his arm, which rested affectionately under the tuck of her buttocks.

"Just thinking about Christmas." She turned her head toward him. His face was only a few inches from hers. She admired the durable quality of his square features, their unbreakable masculinity. She noticed light brown freckles on his nose.

"Sorry I won't be around."

"Oh?" She was confused.

"My uncle and I go camping every Christmas Eve. Neither of us is too big on the Christmas thing." Now Deb was really confused. Didn't he just deck out her office in Christmas paraphernalia? Didn't he write *Nobody should spend Christmas alone* on the note attached to freshly baked holiday fare?

"Oh." Deb felt embarrassed. Had she expected him to spend Christmas with her? She should have known; he was a lumberjack. They always disappeared into the woods, especially when you needed them most. This was a complaint she had often heard growing up from the women around town.

Still their intimacy confused her. He had called her "babe." He had come to her rescue in her moment of abject despair and succored her loneliness with sex and Chinese food. Then again, what more did she want?

"That sounds nice." If her voice betrayed her feeling of abandonment, Dale didn't seem to notice, or he ignored it.

"When are you leaving?"

"Tomorrow after lunchtime."

There was really no more to be said. Deb would be alone on Christmas. Resigned, she decided to try to get some sleep. Between Dale's nuclear body heat and the robust fire, she wouldn't need a blanket to keep her warm. She settled into the luxurious feel of the fur against her full belly. Soon the uncomfortable silence between them drifted into a natural, drowsy lull. Deb fell asleep to the trickle of Dale's fingers tracing the backs of her thighs.

8

December 24th

Deb sat in a booth at the Pine Tree Diner and immediately regretted making the forty-five-minute drive north to have breakfast. In order to avoid running into anybody she knew in Kristmastown, Deb had agreed to have brunch with Dale in the town where his uncle lived. Then he could leave straightaway after eating to go camping. But the drive, following Dale's Dodge around the endless switchbacks, had only made Deb's hangover worse. She promised herself if she made it to the diner without puking, she would never drink alcohol again.

Deb stared at the greasy plate of food in front of her and tried not to think of eggnog.

"Do you want my bacon?" Deb pushed her untouched plate toward Dale, noticing that his "lumberjack special" had come without the staple foodstuff.

"I don't eat meat," Dale replied between shoveled mouthfuls.

"What are you talking about?" In her hangover haze, Deb struggled to wrap her mind around this one.

"I'm a vegetarian."

"But what about the Mongolian beef last night?"

"I didn't touch it."

Apparently she had been too absorbed in her own gluttony to notice. The thought of the slimy meat twisted its way up her esophagus, and Deb swallowed hard.

"So you're a vegetarian?" Deb was incredulous. The man *was* solid meat—how could he maintain his bulk without it?

Dale nodded.

"I would have thought you ate spotted owl for dessert."

Dale grinned. "You going to eat those?" He pointed his fork at her hash browns.

"Go for it. I'm feeling a bit queasy this morning."

Dale wielded his fork like a bulldozer and scooped mounds of hash browns into his mouth. Deb's stomach turned, and she looked away. She gazed out the window at the overcast day. The street was practically empty, and Deb and Dale were the only diners in the restaurant. Perhaps for the first time in her life, Deb wondered what life outside these depressed mill towns would be like.

Deb felt gloomy. After Christmas, Dale would be returning to Canada. What would she do? Continue living in her office? Move in, god forbid, with her mother and run into Rick at the grocery store? The thought of this was too much to bear, and Deb groaned.

"What's wrong?"

"Nothing, I'm just really hungover. I'm gonna go outside to get some air."

The air smelled like rain. The gray sky felt oppressive. Deb paced outside the storefront and tried to figure out a plan from the cracks in the sidewalk.

"*Deb?*"

Her head shot up.

"Rick!" Panic superseded her shock. The look on his face, however, remained firmly fixed in surprise. "What are you doing here?"

"Thought I'd stop in for some food on my way back from the park." He gestured to the Pine Tree Diner but fortunately didn't notice Dale inside.

Of course! The town was on his drive home from his job in the national park. He was wearing his uniform khakis and Smokey Bear hat.

"Working on Christmas Eve?" Deb nervously tried to keep the conversation going to delay Rick from entering the diner.

He shrugged. "Trying to keep busy." There was a dispirited slump to his shoulders that made him look worn. Usually he looked so strapping, so vigorous in his crisp ranger uniform, and Deb felt the urge to hug him. Instead she took a baby step forward.

"What are you doing here?" His turn to ask.

"Oh, just having some brunch," she offered vaguely.

"Alone?" Rick tightened his jaw as if to brace himself.

Deb felt herself go hollow, like a tree rotting from the inside. As Rick stormed past her, she felt she might tip unpredictably like a dead conifer.

"Rick, don't!" But Rick was already inside. She reached the glass door of the diner right as Dale and Rick scuffled out of it.

There wasn't much Deb could do as the two men faced each other on the sidewalk, trying to psyche each other out with fancy footwork as if competing in a log-rolling contest. She yelled at them to stop.

Rick threw a punch, missed, and Dale struck back with an uppercut to Rick's gut.

"Rick!" Deb screamed, seeing him clutch his stomach in pain. But Rick shook it off and landed an impressive blow to

Dale's cheek. Dale touched his cheek, stunned by the forest ranger's might, and Rick took advantage of his bewilderment to hit him again.

"Rick!" Now Deb hollered at him to stop hitting Dale. Neither, though, paid any attention to her. Townspeople emerged out of the woodwork, and a small crowd formed around the fighting men. Deb tried to get between the two, but someone held her back. Their punches were wild, savage, and blood flowed from Dale's nose. Two townsmen tried to break them apart, but the foes were too tightly engaged; they literally held each other in a vicious embrace.

Deb heard the sound of approaching sirens. The proprietor of the Pine Tree must have called the police. Dale and Rick were impervious to the telltale sound of the law and continued to slug each other. As the sirens reached their piercing apex, Deb turned only to see the vehicles speed on by in a fury of green. They weren't police; they were wildland fire engines. Deb recognized the transport vehicle of a fire crew. Strange, she didn't smell smoke.

People in the crowd began to look at each other quizzically and up at the darkening sky. Two more green engines screeched by, and the two men fighting were no longer the main attraction. A pickup tailing the emergency vehicles slowed down enough to shout out the window, "Forest fire heading south toward Mason County!"

Kristmastown! This time nobody blocked Deb from entering the already forgotten fray.

"Rick! Dale!" Deb managed to get between them and extended her arms in opposite directions against the heaving and rival chests. "Fire! Approaching Kristmastown!"

It took a moment for the two men to register, through their seething eye combat, what she was saying. Dale looked up at the sky just as a helicopter flew right over them and headed south with the wind. "Deb, you got a chainsaw in your truck?"

Rick yelled over the chopper noise. She nodded. Rick took off in the direction of her truck. Dale sprinted to his. Deb ran after the both of them.

When she caught up with Rick, he was hauling a twenty-five-pound chainsaw out of the back of her Ford.

Dale called out to Rick through the passenger's-side window of his truck, the engine already running. "Do you know the logging roads well around here?"

Rick was already heading to his own truck with Deb's chainsaw but stopped to answer. "Yup."

"Better come with me then." Deb was unsure what silent communication passed between them, but Rick quickly lifted the chainsaw into the back of Dale's truck and jumped in the front.

Deb ran up to the window of Dale's idling Dodge.

"What are you guys doing?" She tried to choke down her hysteria, but it was swirling all around her: truck doors slamming, yelling, people racing away on foot or on wheels.

"We're going to follow the fire crew. Help with the firebreak." Rick spoke with levelheaded calm.

"Rick! That's crazy! You don't have any gear. You guys are going to get yourselves killed." She tried to appeal to Dale, but his eyes were already rushing ahead on the road toward Kristmastown. Deb grabbed Rick's hand through the open window.

"I will not be a widow like my mother!" Her words were hysterical, unlike her, but she had caught a whiff of smoke that conjured up an image of fire indiscriminately consuming trees, wildlife, humans.

Dale stepped in, impatiently. "Deb, we've got to go."

"Stay here. You'll be safe," Rick added. He pried her hand off his and gave her fingers a squeeze before dropping them out the window. Dale immediately gunned the engine, and the Dodge sped away, chasing the sirens.

Pissed, Deb swore and kicked the sidewalk with the steel toe of her cowboy boots. Fuck both of them for being macho ass-holes, she cursed. One minute, they're fighting each other like alpha males; the next, they're ditching her to go recklessly prove their manhood. Deb kicked the sidewalk again.

Well, she certainly wasn't going to sit tight and let Kristmas-town burn. She could handle a chainsaw and knew the forest just as well as the two of them.

Deb jumped in her car and drove toward the smoke.

All the roads into Mason County were blocked off, but Deb turned off onto a logging road that circuitously looped around to Kristmastown. She still hadn't seen the fire, only the smoke that grew thicker and darker as she approached. Judging by the plume, the fire was just northwest of Kristmastown, around where the national forest met the urban interface. Ash fell from the sky like rain, and Deb switched on her windshield wipers.

As she navigated through her soot-smeared windshield, Deb listened to the radio, which reported that the fire had originally started as a controlled burn of logging slash. With an unex-pected wind shift, it had jumped across control lines. Deb imagined Rick would be fuming at this news; he objected to the often reckless, and environmentally unsustainable, way the tim-ber industry burned their clearcut debris. For a moment, Deb wondered how he and the logger were getting along.

A deer crashed out of the woods in front of Deb. She slammed on the brakes just in time. Swarms of birds were cawing in the air, confused in the smoke that had turned daylight to dusk. Deb wasn't sure whether it was better to roll up her windows or keep them down; she was coughing all the same. She shifted the truck into park and got out in the middle of the empty dirt road. She clambered onto the truck's hood and stood un-steadily. There, straight ahead, on a not so distant hill, a blazing strip of orange carved through the forest like a roadway. Deb watched in horror as the canopy of old growth exploded into flame with an audible crackle like the sound of breaking bones. Jumping off the hood, Deb hurried back into her truck and threw it in reverse. It would be too dangerous for her to continue ahead—the wildfire could easily jump the logging road and sandwich her in flames. She decided to take another back road that led to town.

As she approached Kristmastown, which was now in view and unharmed under an ominous cloud cover of smoke, a roadblock slowed her to a stop. Deb recognized the deputy sheriff and called to him from the line of idling cars.

"Yes, Ms. Rockett?" Most people in town already referred to her by Rick's surname.

"You not letting anybody through, Chuck?"

"No, ma'am. We've evacuated town. Fire seems to be heading this-a-way."

"You gotta let me through. I've got my business to protect."

Chuck shook his head. "Too dangerous. All these people are trying to get back in to protect their property." He motioned up the line of impatiently honking cars.

Deb wouldn't take no for an answer. "Well, at least let me help with the firebreak. I've got chainsaws at the shop."

Chuck scratched his grizzled beard. He had been a friend of her father's. "Can you operate a bulldozer?"

"Yes, sir, I can." Deb could operate all sorts of heavy machinery. She waited anxiously as Chuck watched a chopper drag a giant orange bucket full of water across the sky.

"All right," he conceded reluctantly. "But head straight to the mill. The emergency crew there will set you up with a bulldozer."

"Thanks, Chuck."

"Be careful, Deb." He called out to a deputy at the blockade, who waved Deb through.

* * *

Deb bulldozed logs, vegetation, trash—anything in the plow's path that was combustible. Someone at the mill had given her a bandanna, and she had tied it tightly around her nose and mouth. The cotton was soaked with her perspiration and black with soot. Fire crews worked all around her with shovels, Pulaskis and chainsaws to construct a firebreak around the north end of Kristmastown. The wildfire had spread to the surrounding foothills, and its radiant heat began to blister the yellow paint of the Caterpillar she was driving. Deb's sweat ran black down her bare arms. Only once or twice did she look up from her hard labor to the terrifying height of the flames, engulfing hundred-foot-tall trees like a tidal wave. She knew that if she stopped to listen to its roar, she would fear for her life and that of her two lovers, and so she kept on plowing.

Someone at the mill had told her he thought he had seen Rick hitch a ride with the hotshot crew, the elite group of firefighters who battle the hottest part of a forest fire. Deb prayed that Dale had gone with him so that the two men could watch out for each other.

Deb cleared everything that came into her path. Hours passed, but there was no way to tell time by the smoke-choked sky. Deb had become like the bulldozer she operated: mechanical and never tiring. Only when someone yelled at her to get out of the way did Deb reenter her human body just in time to dodge a falling, burning tree. Sparks leaped at her—the tree had landed at the tires of the Caterpillar—and she tumbled out of the bulldozer. The crew surrounded the tree and immediately extinguished the blaze, successfully keeping the fire from leaping the control line they had been working so hard to clear. Someone handed Deb a bottle of water, and she drenched her head before climbing back into the seat of the Caterpillar.

It was the noticeable change in temperature that signaled to Deb that it was nightfall and that the wildfire had lost its ferocity. The wind that blew cool air across the nape of Deb's neck had pushed the fire back, away from Kristmastown. Some of the fire crew was gathering around a radio, and Deb dismounted to join them. The radio confirmed that the forest fire was indeed under control. Everyone cheered and hugged. Deb began chugging water, suddenly hit with an acute thirst. She rinsed out her filthy bandanna and wiped her parched body parts with its refreshing dampness. She coughed to clear the smoke from her lungs.

The radio reported two casualties, and everyone fell silent. Deb looked out at the hills, where flames still licked up skeletal trees. She could now make out arches of water from high-powered hoses and the fluorescent-green dots of the men and women operating them. Dread flooded her. What if . . . She tossed her short hair as she removed her hard hat: no, she wouldn't think about any what-ifs. She would not lose another man, or men, in her life to the forest she had just fought so hard to save.

Deb collapsed onto the couch in her office. Even though she was covered in more soot than a chimney sweep and smelled worse than she looked, Deb was too exhausted to even think about bathing. The only effort she was able to muster she used to plug in the Christmas-tree lights. It was Christmas Eve, after all. *Some Christmas.* Deb sighed but immediately started coughing.

The phone rang. Deb leaped for it and answered, wheezing.

"Hello?!"

"Deb."

"Oh, Rick, thank god! Are you all right?"

"I'm fine. You?"

"I'm, I'm—" She burst into tears of relief, triggering another round of coughing. It took her a moment to catch her breath. "I'm okay. Thank god you're all right. Where are you?" She thought to ask about Dale but decided against it.

"I'm at home." Rick sounded exhausted and paused. "Come home, Deb."

Deb choked back more tears. "Okay, Rick. I'll be right over."

Without grabbing a jacket, Deb sprang out the door of her office with a burst of energy that came not from her depleted body but from her heart.

The night air of Kristmastown still smelled of smoke, but patches of sky had cleared to reveal stars twinkling undisturbed above. Deb rushed up the path to the cabin and threw open the door.

Rick was standing in the middle of the main room, waiting for her. Deb ran straight into his embrace. He held her tight and only let go to get a better look at her.

"Deb, you looked absolutely charred." Rick didn't fare much better. His face was black as a coalminer's, and his teeth were a shock of white when he smiled.

"I wasn't about to sit around and let my town burn down." She held on to his blackened hands and kept squeezing them to make sure he was all in one piece.

"I went back to the Pine Tree to try to find you." Rick's green eyes grew misty. "The owner told me he had seen you take off in your truck toward Mason County."

"Chuck let me into town. I helped with the firebreak." She attempted to rub some of the black off his face, but her fingers only smudged it deeper into his pores. "Someone at the mill told me you joined the hotshot crew."

Soot had settled into the creases around Rick's mouth and exaggerated his proud smile.

"Rick, you could have gotten yourself killed! You're not trained for the frontline of fire suppression."

"Correction." A voice came from the bathroom. "*We* could have gotten ourselves killed." Dale stepped into the room. He, too, was coated black in ash. Somewhat taller than Rick, he stood behind him like a shadow.

"Dale!" Deb looked to Rick, perplexed, and then back to Dale.

"You okay, Deb?" Dale asked with a concern that didn't seem to bother Rick.

"I'm fine," she stammered. "Just a little burned out."

The three of them busted up. They laughed hard and long until they were winded and wheezing from smoke-damaged lungs. Deb started coughing again.

"Let's get you cleaned up." Rick took Deb's arm and led her to the bathroom. He closed the door only partway before helping her undress. As Rick pulled off her filthy tank, she glanced past him and through the gap in the door. Dale stood a few yards away in the other room and watched them. His eyes glowed like embers from his charcoal face.

Rick's back remained to the doorway as he started the shower, testing the water's temperature with his hand. Deb stripped off the rest of her clothes under Dale's smoldering regard. His eyes shifted all over her naked body while his feet remained rooted to the hardwood floor, even when Rick turned to assist Deb into the tub. If Rick saw Dale, he acknowledged the voyeur only as a shadow on the wall. Deb stepped into the warm stream of water.

Rick unhooked the detachable showerhead and started to rinse her down. He hadn't closed the shower curtain, and water sprayed everywhere. As he reached for a mesh sponge attached to a hook dangling from the curtain rod, the showerhead began to slip from his fingers. He struggled for balance.

"Dale," Rick called over his shoulder. "Can you help me with this?" Rick winked at Deb and whispered, "Merry Christmas, honey."

The lumberjack hovered in the doorway and, before entering, located the dimmer switch and turned down the lights.

Under the romantic lighting and rain of water, Deb stood flabbergasted, not to mention completely naked. With his free hand, Rick handed Dale the sponge and then some shower gel. Dale got to work lathering up the mesh, releasing the lavender aromatherapy of the soap. Deb wasn't sure what kind of camaraderie the two had established in fighting the wildfire, but they were now employing a sort of teamwork to bathe her.

Rick shifted to one side, directing the water to Deb's front, so that Dale could scrub her back. She felt the rough mesh scour her neck, where the soot had stained her like a farmer's tan, and her nipples hardened. Rick then rotated her to wash off her soapy back. Murky water ran into the drain. Dale was gentler in washing her front. After he removed all the grime from her neckline, he squirted more soap onto the sponge and circled her breasts with the foamy lather, touching her nipples ever so slightly so that suds clung to their points. Rick kept spraying her back in even strokes as Dale soaped her stomach.

Is this really happening? The sponge delved between her legs. *Yes, it is.*

Deb gasped as Dale washed her privates. Rick quickly handed over control of the showerhead to Dale. Rick stripped off his clothes and climbed, buck naked, into the tub with Deb. Dale was now applying the nozzle directly to her pussy, and Rick pressed up behind her to keep her from squirming away from the intense hydraulic pressure on her clit. At first, the spray assaulted her most sensitive flesh like a thousand splinters, but then, as Dale adjusted the nozzle's setting, a pulsating flow massaged her clit. Rick firmly cupped her ass as Dale doused her. Deb made little startled animal noises as the water churned her sex.

In an almost a choreographed way, Rick reached around and took the showerhead from Dale. Dale, who had been crouched at the level of Deb's crotch, rose to his full height and ripped off his shirt with such violence that a button sprang into the nearby sink. Rick was more aggressive with manipulating the shower-head, practically smashing the nozzle against her clit. She felt his cock homing in toward her sex, and she tilted forward to provide access. Dale tore down his pants, and his hard-on leaped out at her. Deb grabbed a hold of it, more for balance than for anything else, as Rick pushed up inside her. Dale's stiff cock flexed in her clutches.

Rick fucked her from behind with easy, deliberate strokes as he continued to flood her clit with pressurized water. Her grip on Dale's cock loosened as the double stimulation, inside and out, overwhelmed her. Dale quickly clamped his hand down over hers and guided it up and down his shaft. Once she picked up the pace, pumping him as Rick pumped inside her, Dale's hand fell away with a groan. He was still standing outside the tub, and Deb steered him in closer with a tug on his sturdy member. She rubbed her nipples against his scratchy chest hair, and Dale kissed her with eyes wide open. Deb felt Rick's thrusts slow as she and Dale made out. When Rick pulled out, Deb worried that she had crossed a line in this already boundary-busting experience.

But Rick made room for Dale to climb into the tub with them. The showerhead had fallen to the tub's floor and was flinging around like a wild snake. Rick captured it and began to rinse Dale off. Black water sluiced off him. Deb located the mesh sponge and shower gel. As Rick rinsed, she scrubbed Dale's arms and face until his skin appeared rosy and invigo-rated. Once clean, Dale started kissing her again with luscious, wet lips. Rick slipped the showerhead back into its base over the crown of Deb and Dale's heads, and they kissed as if under a waterfall. Rick pressed up against Deb's backside and, still hard, began sucking on the back of her neck. Deb found herself sandwiched between two iron cocks prodding her like red-hot pokers.

Stalwart hands ran all over Deb's slick body. A hand snuck

between her legs where her pussy was still swollen from Rick's ministrations. She was kissing Rick now. As she moved down to kiss his smooth chest, flicking his nipples with her tongue, she sensed Dale hovering above her head. She glanced up just in time to catch the underside of Dale's chin as his lips smacked hard against Rick's. Deb kneeled out of the way and took Rick into her mouth while watching—in reverence—the two men wrestle a kiss. Dale squarely grasped Rick by the back of his neck to plunge his tongue deeper into Rick's mouth. Deb sucked Rick the best she could while watching the hot-and-heavy man-on-man action above her. Dale's boner thudded against the back of her head as she rocked up and down Rick's shaft.

A tugging need began to pull at Deb. The need only a cock could relieve, and it didn't matter whose. She released Rick from her mouth. He immediately broke his own lip-lock to help her up. This time it was Dale who took her. He mounted her from behind like a stallion. Dale's potent flesh was thick inside her, giving her her fill. He curled his powerful upper body around her, crossing his arms over her chest to keep her from buckling under his weight. She felt his balls slap against her quim with his hard, fast thrusts.

Facing Deb, Rick grabbed his hard-on in one hand and the bottle of shower gel in the other. He lubricated the length of his cock with the liquid soap. Rick stroked himself as he watched Dale saw in and out of Deb.

"I wanna make you come, Deb," Dale growled into her ear.

"You are," she purred. He slammed into her G-spot, sending her pussy reeling. She was still rippling with aftershocks when he slammed her again with another direct hit. "I'm going to come," Deb panted directly into Rick's eyes. A heavy black smudge marked Rick's cheekbone like war paint. Looking at her long and hard, he started to jerk off faster as though to urge her on. Behind her, Dale grunted with each laboring thrust, inducing contractions of the deepest pleasure between Deb's thighs.

Rick came first, spurting all over his hand. With the sight of her lover's juices dripping from his still clenched fist, Deb's orgasm came fitfully. Hunkered over Deb's slackening body, Dale was the last to come.

9

Christmas

The faint scent of cinders lingered in Rick's hair. Deb breathed in the nape of his neck where his hair was still slightly damp from the night before. With his eyes still closed, Rick rolled over and pulled Deb close to him. Their sheets had the morning-after smell of a dying campfire. Keeping in Rick's embrace, Deb managed to prop herself up on an elbow to scan the bed for their third party. All that Dale had left behind was his shadow, an ashy imprint on the bedcover.

Deb snuggled back into Rick's arms.

"Good morning," Rick murmured with a sleepy kiss. His lips tasted like morning dew, fresh and cool.

"Merry Christmas, Rockett."

His brilliant green eyes opened, dazzling her. "Merry Christmas." He smiled, having just remembered. He turned his head awkwardly over his shoulder. No Dale.

"He must have snuck out in the middle of the night," Deb surmised.

"Must have," Rick repeated thoughtfully.

After the shower, the three of them had clambered into the king-size bed like a bunch of kids at a slumber party. Deb had dropped off to sleep immediately, curled up like a kitten between the two men. She had no idea when Dale left.

"Rick?"

"Yes, dear?" He clutched her tightly, like a child having received a long-coveted present.

"What happened in the forest between you two?"

"What do you mean?"

"I mean, you guys were pummeling each other outside the Pine Tree. Then you two came back from the forest fire all hot to trot."

"Well." Rick considered for a moment. "We were with the hotshot crew up in the foothills trying to build a firebreak."

Deb nodded—she already knew this part. Rick continued. "We really shouldn't have been that close to the fire, but we were on the other side of a road and assumed the fire wouldn't jump that *and* our break. I couldn't hear anything over the chainsaw and the roar of the flames, so I didn't hear the fir crashing down."

Deb winced. She thought of her own father's death.

"But Dale saw it. He was holding his saw but dropped it to push me out of the way. Somehow he managed to tackle me without either of us landing on my saw's bar. The tree landed only a couple yards away." Rick sighed as if dismissing his brush with death. "So, you could say Dale saved my life."

"But that still doesn't explain how you got him to agree to, er . . ."

"Have a threesome?" Rick laughed. Deb still couldn't believe what a willing participant Rick had been.

"Yeah. How did you ever bring that up?"

"I didn't."

"You didn't?" Deb didn't understand.

"Nope. It just happened."

"You mean you didn't mention it to him *at all?*"

"Nope," Rick repeated innocently. Deb wasn't sure if she believed him. His sincerity, however, was nothing but genuine when he asked, "Did you enjoy yourself?"

Deb thought of the steamy shower with all hands on her. "I did." Then she admitted truthfully, "But I'm glad to have just you now."

Rick looked at her lovingly in a way that she had feared, during their separation, he never would again. When he kissed her, his lips sealed hers like a wedding vow. Then their entwined bodies rolled over and filled the depression in the bedding the woodsman had left behind.

EPILOGUE

"Deb! Deb!" Sherri's call sounded like that of a starling.

"I'm coming!" Deb shouted back, fixing the wreath of wild-flowers to the crown of her head.

"Deb, you don't want to be late for your wedding!" Sherri was now squawking through the screen door of the cabin. From her bedroom, Deb could see that Sherri was holding her bridesmaid's dress off the muddy front step.

"Just a minute!" Deb slid in one last bobby pin. "Perfect," she commented admiringly to herself. She checked her makeup, which Sherri had expertly applied, and smoothed the front of her simple silk sheath. She took a deep breath: time to get married.

"Coming!" she called again and headed to the sound of an impatiently running motor. She was about to push through the screen door when she noticed that the mail had come. Hastily she picked it off the floor and leafed through it. A postcard with unfamiliar handwriting grabbed her eye.

To Deb and Rick,
Congratulations on your wedding.
Sincerely,
Dale

Deb flipped it over. The word CANADA emblazoned on the postcard placed the majestic background. In the foreground, three bears meandered in a clearing.

Deb smiled. Dale had disappeared without a trace after that night. She had assumed he had returned to the woods.

The car outside started honking. Deb quickly tucked the postcard behind the cuckoo clock, hiding it from view. Someday she would find it when her memory had begun to fail and she had forgotten about that one scalding night when her Christmas wish had come true. Someday in the long future she had ahead of her.

Deb pushed through the screen door.